BEYOND

the

FIELDS

AYSHA BAQIR

Marshall Cavendish
Editions

Published by Marshall Cavendish Editions
An imprint of Marshall Cavendish International

A member of the
Times Publishing Group

Other Marshall Cavendish Offices:
Marshall Cavendish Corporation. 99 White Plains Road, Tarrytown NY 10591-9001,
USA • Marshall Cavendish International (Thailand) Co Ltd. 253 Asoke,
12th Flr, Sukhumvit 21 Road, Klongtoey Nua, Wattana, Bangkok 10110, Thailand
• Marshall Cavendish (Malaysia) Sdn Bhd, Times Subang, Lot 46, Subang Hi-Tech
Industrial Park, Batu Tiga, 40000 Shah Alam, Selangor Darul Ehsan, Malaysia

Marshall Cavendish is a registered trademark of Times Publishing Limited

National Library Board, Singapore Cataloguing-in-Publication Data

Name(s): Aysha Baqir.
Title: Beyond the fields / Aysha Baqir.
Description: Singapore : Marshall Cavendish Editions, [2019]
Identifier(s): OCN 1080591148 | ISBN 978-981-48-4118-4 (paperback)
Subject(s): LCSH: Sisters--Pakistan--Fiction. | Rape victims--Pakistan--Fiction. | Rural
families--Pakistan--Fiction. | Justice--Fiction.
Classification: DDC 828.99549103--dc23

Printed in Singapore

For my parents, Freeha and Baqir,
who gave me so much strength
and taught me to persevere

For Ali, Faiz, and Shariq
Thank you for your love and patience

And for the village women of Pakistan

Book One

JOURNEY

1

Two hundred and seven days since the rape. Two hundred and five days since my twin had been taken away. And miles of muck in between.

I sank into my seat and shut my eyes. Laugher burst out. Chatter hummed. Hawker boys screeched deals for sticky sweetmeats and icy colas. I inhaled and tasted dry grit. The horn bleated like a fidgety goat. Closing my eyes, I counted seconds, then went faster than seconds. When the engine growled, and the hollow metal body shuddered, I crouched on the seat. A dust cloud had swallowed my village.

"Down, jaahil!" roared the bus driver.

Flushing, I lowered myself into my seat. I wasn't a jaahil, ignorant. I could prove it. But I wasn't free yet. I was caged from the tip of my head to the soles of my slippers. Abba said I didn't have a choice. Amma said the burka gave me freedom. I could see others without being seen. But I wanted to be seen and heard. Like other girls. Like girls who went to school. Like girls who chased their dreams.

Without warning, the bus lurched to a stop. Dhum. Dhum. A feverish drumbeat led a wedding procession across the road. Starched like a puppet, the groom straddled a white horse, surrounded by a crowd of men whirling pink scarves. Behind him, the bride, swaddled in folds of tinselled red and gold, huddled on a mule, trying to inch forward within the pack of dark, veiled women and a troop of soulful pipers. The horn blared again, and childlike eyes looked up from the folds of cloth.

I shivered. In a dark flicker, I became that bride, bound to a new family. Amma had declared I was old enough. I was fifteen or sixteen; she wasn't sure. She had no records or pictures of our birth, but claimed we had been born the year after the River Sutlej had flooded our village. She had shown me off to aunties wanting 'good girls' for their nephews and to wrinkled men seeking second wives. But they said I wasn't white enough. I made poor tea. And I didn't have much of a dowry.

I smoked a hookah too. But they didn't know that. They didn't know me.

I was caught in a tug of war. How many times had I played that game with my twin, using coils of jute from the charpais on which we slept? I was that twine now, being torn apart. Amma and Abba wanted me married. "The sooner the better," they said. But Tara's scent wrapped around me, and her warmth clung. Split from one cell, we had the same tiger-gold eyes. Her nose. My nose. And the same full mouth. They had forgotten her, but I hadn't. They were okay with the lies; I wasn't. Not anymore.

A tiny lie can push you down a slippery slope.

I jolted up upon hearing my grandmother's words, but Nani was nowhere near. How could she be? Abba had forbidden her from visiting us. The voice was in my head. Despite Nani's warning, I had slipped down the slippery slope and tumbled into a muck of lies. Alone. Without Tara. I cut off my thoughts. I wasn't going there. Not today.

The bus hurtled down the thin blade of a road that sliced through the boundless fields. Rows of cotton saplings swelled like armies of caterpillars on either side. I watched the wheels swallow the grey track. It was time. Holding my breath, I pulled back my veil and flinched. But no one lashed out or scolded. The steady whirr of

the engine soothed the clanking in my head. This was my journey.
I hunted the truth. I studied warriors. Now, I had to become one.

When fields gave way to a broken line of rickety shacks and
sheds, I turned back and met the unblinking stare of my fellow
passenger, the only other woman on the bus. She was a narrow-
jawed woman with kohl-lined eyes and crimson lips. We sat
jammed together on the tiny seats in the women's section at the
front of the bus. There was no other way to sit. The woman's thigh
pressed against mine, and her elbow pinched my ribs.

"First time on the bus?" she probed. Without waiting for me to
answer, she began to talk. Her lips swelled and narrowed like the
mouth of a river fish. She was a professor and her husband was an
engineer. They lived in different hostels and in different countries.
He worked for a company in Saudi Arabia. There were no jobs for
engineers in our country, she said. They were saving to be together.
He had left her the day after their wedding, promising to return
soon. When? She didn't know. But he would return. He had to.
She had left everything to be with him. "What's your name, girl?"

"Zara," I answered after a missed beat. Amma had warned
us against such women. Third class, she called them. Like they
were bogies on a train. In Amma's world, there were three types
of girls. First class girls married whom their parents chose, second
class girls never married and third class girls married against their
parents' wishes. I had believed Amma once. But I didn't believe her
anymore. I didn't know what to believe.

"Travelling alone?" pressed the professor.

Her question exploded like a tomato in my head. Truth had
a rotten core. No one could take too much of it. Seeing the flash
of curiosity in the professor's kohl-lined eyes, I spun a half-truth.
Floods had ruined our crop and Abba had fallen ill. The landlord was
demanding his debt be settled, and as the eldest of five daughters, I

had to help. My uncle had found me a job as a housemaid in the city. Making a clucking sound, the professor lowered her hand to my fist.

I stared at the silver coins. It wasn't *all* lies. My brother, Omer, sat in the men's section of the bus because Abba had forbidden us to sit together. It wasn't safe anymore. Once we reached Lahore, Omer was going to start boarding school and I was going to start work as a maid. "Is the city safe now? Have the riots ended?" I asked, wanting news.

"Shush, they are everywhere." The professor's gaze flitted to the back.

"Who?"

"The wardi wallas. They're everywhere, spying."

"Spying on who?"

"Everyone and anyone who dares to protest. But how would you know?"

"I know enough."

"Enough to know of rape and loot?"

Shivering, I pushed back into the hard metal of the seat. What did she know about rape? The rattle of the engine faded. I heard a door crack and my brother's shouts.

"Are you all right?" The professor's hand skimmed over my arm. Starting to shake my head, I nodded quickly. "What do you teach?"

"History."

"I know so little," I began. I knew my history textbook inside out but I had to keep her talking.

"You just said you knew enough." The professor narrowed her eyes.

I lowered my gaze and the silence stretched between us.

The professor shook her head. "You're too young and outspoken. How can your parents risk sending you to work in the city?" Seeing me protest, she held up her hand, "Fine, if what you say is true, then you better know something about the city before you get there."

Before I could say anything, she leaned forward. "I'll tell you what I tell my students. It will help you." She straightened up with her eyes still on me. "Lahore is a nymph with the soul of a dove and the temper of a tigress, caught between those who want her chained to the clergy and those who want to sell her to the highest bidder."

Her voice deepened, unfolding the city's history, from the rule of the Turks and Mongols to the intrigues of the Mughal emperors. Every conqueror had left his mark; Lahore was a city of forts, tombs, parks and palaces. The walls of these treasures were chipped and smudged with dirt and grime, but the foundations were strong and pure.

The Lahore Fort offered visitors a hallucinogenic view of the city, and the cries of tortured prisoners, long dead, still haunted the stone courtyard, across from which the muezzin's voice soared from the spiralling minarets of the red stone mosque, calling the believers to prayer. The Palace of Mirrors had been stripped of its jewels that now sparkled in foreign lands, much like the politicians. But lush rolling gardens soothed the eyes of pavement dwellers, pale alabaster water fountains calmed heated tempers, and ancient trees swooped down to shelter the common man without prejudice on sweltering summer days. In the maze of narrow lanes lined with grubby stalls, men, women and donkey carts jostled for space. Haggling over Chinese plastics and fried foods, veiled women swatted off the flocks of child beggars.

The professor murmured that after the night prayers, the narrow streets of the old city pulsed with the beat of drums and the tinkle of anklets. Dancing girls swayed and strutted on balconies, enticing beggars and businessmen. Drug dealers scurried through the backstreets of the fort like rats, sniffing out addicts. Others roamed the lanes hunting for more prey. I was to stay away from the old city after dark.

The professor shared stories of family inbreeding and of generations cursed with abnormalities as the bus rattled over the gravel road. She whispered of intoxicating street drinks made up of milk and cannabis paste. Gradually her voice hardened and her eyes glimmered, or was it the changing light?

Modern Lahore was a playground for the rich. They built marble mansions with gilded turrets. They played with long sleek cars, sailing ships and private planes. Their factories ran on the blood and sweat of the workers. Their parties took off after midnight and crashed past sunrise: the nonstop parties, where the wealthy drank more than they ate, frolicked like chimps in the Lahore zoo and abandoned bottle-fed babies to foreign maids. But it was changing. The coup had struck, and it had strangled the city. Raids and strikes jammed the houses and roads. The dark paint on the professor's lips faded and cracked, and her voice sharpened. Finally, she paused, glanced outside and tightened her headscarf. "We've reached," she announced.

I couldn't tear my eyes away from the professor. Words stuck in my throat like grit. "Thank you," I whispered. What did I have to do to be like her?

Digging into her bag, she looked up. "You should be in school, my child. I will worry about you. But here, if you ever need a friend, look me up at the hostel." She pressed her hand on mine, turned away and pulled out a string of beads to pray.

I looked down and curled my fingers around the card. I could never be like her. I hadn't prayed in a long time. The sun had dimmed and dipped into the murky horizon. Dark stone buildings loomed on either side of the double lanes. Had Tara crossed these roads? Horns boomed and blared. Trucks, buses, cars, tongas, rickshaws and motorcycles fought for space. Oncoming headlights reminded me of nocturnal beasts in search of prey.

The city wasn't my friend, but I wasn't here to make friends. I was here to take back.

2

"Float like a butterfly, sting like a bee. His hands can't hit what his eyes can't see," whispered Omer, quoting the famous words of the boxing champion Muhammad Ali.

Omer swung open the iron-barred gate and stepped through it. My eyes blurred, watching my brother disappear into a red-brick dome. We had never been apart. A year or two older, he had taught me to read and write, to wrestle and to play cricket with a broom. My eyes stung, but I couldn't cry, not now. I was in the ring. The whistle had gone off. And I had journeyed too far to back down. And why would I cry? It was my plan. I had schemed to put it together. Reach Lahore and meet Master Saab, our village schoolteacher, and Shafique, his nephew who worked for the employment agency, at the bus station. Drop Omer to school. Start work as a maid. Master Saab would return to the village to tell Abba that we were safe. Were we safe?

I had tricked Master Saab in order to get to Lahore. I had confided in Omer last night. He hadn't been pleased, but he had understood and promised to help. No one else would.

The engine sputtered, the motorbike sprang forward and the school was left behind. Sitting side-saddle behind Shafique, I gripped the burning steel. This city was hotter than my village. Bigger. Dirtier. And louder. Honks and toots ripped the air and spurts of black fumes stung my eyes. We turned onto a boulevard crowded with more cars, tongas, trucks and cycles. A dusty mob hurried past the gnarled beggars sprawled on the sidewalk. Straw-haired girls in tattered dresses zigzagged through the main road, banging their tiny fists on car windows that remained shut. Fear, cold and thick like ghee in winter, hardened in my windpipe. I gripped the red-hot metal. They could beat me. Starve me. Or worse. They had the right. There was no law to protect maids.

"They're rich," Shafique had told Master Saab last night. "It's a powerful family with army connections. I know the head maid, Gloria, well. She's a Filipina and has been with them since their time in the East. She keeps her word. My business has boomed because of her network back home. Foreign maids fetch some value, unlike local ones." He had eyed me like I was a gnat he wanted to swat.

"What do you mean?" Master Saab had asked.

"Landlords own acres of land and with it the soul of every man, woman and child who works on it. Each season, they return to their villages to pluck village children like fruit. Their parents watch helplessly. Some are relieved, in the hope that their children will be fed and clothed. Girls are whisked into maids and boys churned into cooks, guards, or if lucky, drivers. There are always more back home to take their place. It keeps going on year after year. And it's worsened now. No laws. No questions."

The bike shot through a red light and swerved into a side lane. Old trees with swollen roots and thick, arching canopies shaded the roads. It was quieter and cleaner here. Long, sleek cars zipped past. Sunflowers bobbed on trimmed green islands. I took a deep breath and loosened my grip. Was this where the rich lived? Was this where their children, wearing starched white uniforms and buckled black boots, went to school? I had dreamt of going to school once. I had dreamt of becoming a scientist once.

A blaring honk snapped me back to reality. We were in front of a towering wall of pink and purple bougainvillea. The black iron gates moved back slowly. I caught a glimpse of a curving driveway and a rolling hill of green before the motorcycle purred inside.

⁊

If I ever told anyone from my village about where I worked, they would call me jhooti. A liar.

"Now remember, one mistake, and I'll pack you back to the village," Shafique had warned. After parking the bike, he strolled towards a small room next to the garage, where a stocky man squeezed into a dark blue uniform signalled towards an empty chair, spoke into the receiver, and picked up the newspaper again. We waited outside under the fiery sun. And just as I thought I would melt into a puddle, the front door opened.

I stared at the lithe woman with long dark hair. She glided forward in a loose black top and tight black pants. Her arms and legs moved fast, like a spider. Gloria.

At Shafique's nod, I followed her inside the house. And shrivelled like a slug, caught. Despite the sunlight spilling through the wide windows onto the milky white marble floor, a chill grazed my limbs. Rows of dark-eyed and jewelled Mughal emperors stared down at me from life-size tapestries. Hundreds of crystals hung from the tall ceiling and shimmered with fire. I was lost and out of place. The house was big and boundless, and all white and gold. There was no dust or dirt anywhere. Except on me.

"What are you staring at?" I swung towards Gloria in surprise. Had it only been moments since I had stepped inside? It felt longer. She had spoken in English. I spoke English too, but in a different way, not the way she spoke. Was she testing me?

"I wasn't expecting you today," muttered Gloria. "Look at me when I speak to you. Yes, that's good. Now, where can I leave you? Not with the other maids. They'll chew you up like betel leaf and spit you out in seconds. I guess the nursery is the safest for now." Flicking her wrist, Gloria swept ahead. I followed her down a hallway. My heart beat like a war drum in my ears. Gloria signalled to me to wait outside. The door closed with a thud. Hearing voices rise inside, I put my ear against the door.

"Come in," Gloria flung the door open. "But take your slippers off."

Too late to check if my feet were clean. I stepped inside and stared, dazed. A sea-blue wall gleamed with coral and fish. I could walk into it. I took another step, and curled my toes into the soft threads.

My eyes ran over the blue and green shelves crammed with toys and books. I had never seen so many books all together.

"Are you listening? I said look at me when I speak," Gloria's voice broke into my thoughts. "Stay here until I come to get you. Understood? I've told Nanny to supervise you while I'm away."

I followed Gloria's gaze and caught steel glinting behind wire-rimmed spectacles on a bony face. White hair. Withered face. Grey uniform. Nanny. Sitting on the sofa across the room, she stared at me silently.

I nodded.

"Good," chipped in Gloria, and threw Nanny a cool stare. "If there's any problem, you let me know." And she was gone.

"Who does she think she is, telling me what to do?" muttered Nanny, once the door had closed. "Put your shoes in the cupboard over there. Have you had anything to eat?"

I nodded and turned towards the cupboard.

"Woof!"

"Quiet, Scotty," cautioned a boy's voice.

A small ball of white fur with a pink tongue sprawled on the bed beside a young boy in blue dungarees, looking down at the half-open book in his hands. Books. And a dog. It was going to be okay. Feeling the boy's eyes on me, I looked down quickly. Shafique had warned me to keep my eyes and head down in front of my employers.

"Nanny, I'm done," chimed in the boy, yanking Nanny's arm.

"Not yet, Babur Saab," stated Nanny, pulling away. "Read for another ten minutes or I'll cancel the play date." She turned to me. "And you, go on and sit for a bit, but be ready to move. Don't think you can fool me. I might be old, but my eyes are sharper than a hawk's. You understand? You'll have to earn your place with me, and it's not going to happen if you suck up to that poker-faced foreigner. You hear me? Go on, sit."

I edged towards the chair in the furthest corner.

"And don't think you'll get any sympathy from me," continued Nanny. "I wasn't even six when I was sent to look after Babur Saab's mother. I spent my youth raising her and then was packed off along with her dowry. Now I'm raising her son. I should be in charge of this house instead of that foreign woman. Uh, what are you doing, girl? Stop! Have you lost your mind?" She towered over me.

"What?" I shot to my feet.

"I said, have you lost your mind?" hissed Nanny. "You think the sofas and chairs are for you? You sit where you belong. On the floor."

What did she mean, where I belonged? Flames singed my throat. The dog was sitting on the bed.

Catching the steel in Nanny's eyes, I dropped to my knees and crouched. She had won this round, but the fight wasn't over. I bet Babur Saab's bed had more bounce than the stack of hay on my mud roof back home.

3

Three boys in cream ruffled shirts, navy shorts, cream socks and navy buckled boots trooped inside, followed by three Filipina maids in bright shirts and denim jeans. Yells. Shouts. Barks. Minutes later Scotty was shooed out. Boys were devils, said Amma. But these were city boys with clean faces, neatly combed hair and pearly white teeth.

Under Nanny's supervision, I began to bring out the toys. The boys pounced. One cried for the set of racing cars, the other yelled for the train set, and two screamed that they wanted the toy aeroplanes and Lego sets. They grabbed the toys, rattled them, and tossed them away in minutes, wanting more.

My fingers curled. Empty. A fist squeezed my breath. I missed the smooth white river stones Tara and I played with for hours. We had called them our magic stones. We had kept them under our blanket until last autumn. Until they had lost their magic. Like everything else.

A maid rolled in a trolley heaped with snacks and drinks. I inhaled the whiff of fried potatoes and swallowed. Still chatting, the Filipinas popped open bottles of fizzy drinks and set them to one side for the boys. Then, heaping food onto their plates, they began to munch, occasionally slipping a bite or two into the boys' mouths. From Nanny's stony expression, I understood I wouldn't be eating with them.

The maids gossiped and swapped stories about their Madams' and Saabs' fights, their shopping sprees and the childrens' play dates and birthday parties. I stole a quick look at the boys, who weren't playing together anymore. Two fights had already broken out. They weren't too different from the pack of boys that hunted in our village lanes. It had been years, but I still shuddered, thinking about that day.

I had run out to race. Omer and Tara had followed, shouting after me, but I hadn't stopped, wanting to be first. Sprinting around a corner, I hadn't seen them. Leaping out from a side alley, they had trapped me. Two boys with dirt and snot-caked faces. They had laughed wildly, called me filthy sounding names, and grabbed my chador. I had screamed, "Pigs!" back at them. Hearing Omer yell, they had disappeared. But then Tara started crying that I was going to die, and Omer had dragged me inside, telling me to wash up. Hot and sticky, I had rushed inside the room, flung my chador off and halted, feeling warm dampness between my thighs. I pulled up my shirt slowly. Streaks of crimson. Blood, mine. Ice-cold from inside, I had broken into a sweat.

Before I could stop her, Tara had screamed for Amma. Gripping me by the shoulders, Amma had shaken me and said that I had to stop running out to play. She pushed two bundles of thick cloth into my hands. I had to use one, wash it and use it again. Each month. Every month. The same cloth bundles. The blood would come out. I had stared at her, not understanding what she meant. Was I sick? Had I caught a disease?

"Come on, hurry," Gloria's voice snapped me back to the present. I glanced up from where I had been stacking toys on a shelf. The boys had just left. "Now," commanded Gloria tapping her boots. "We don't have all day. Sehr Madam wants to meet you now."

"She can help me clear up first," said Nanny, and nodded to me to continue.

"She can, if she wants to lose her job!" said Gloria as she strode out.

Without looking back at Nanny, I hurried out and followed Gloria through a maze of corridors and into a hall filled with lights. Draped in silver lace, Sehr Madam perched on a maroon divan heaped with silk pillows. Dark eyes. Pale skin. Long black hair that tumbled to her waist. Like a fairy from another land. Her eyes were on me. I lowered my head, remembering Shafique's words. One narrow foot, strapped in a silver sandal, tapped a beat in the air. Spotting the ruby-red nail polish on ten perfect fingers and toes, I curled my fingers. The room smelt sweet, like fields of flowers after a rainfall. I knew I didn't.

Sehr Madam picked up a patterned teacup, lifted it to her lips, and set it down. There was no sound. Was it that bad? At home, we drank tea with zest; the better the tea, the more noise we made, slurping it.

Sehr Madam told Gloria to leave. Had she heard? My gaze strayed towards the long black legs. In a slightly shriller voice, Sehr Madam again ordered Gloria to leave. But Gloria didn't move. Staring straight, she stood still. Ready to sting.

Hairs crackled on my neck and arms. Did Gloria answer to anyone? Sehr Madam's lips tightened. Shifting slightly, she nodded to me. Taking the cue, I narrated the story Shafique had instructed me to tell. I was getting better at telling stories. But before I had finished, Sehr Madam sighed and leaned back to rest her head on the cushion. "You're a poor little thing, but too young."

"We grow up fast in the villages," I answered, and reddened, hearing Gloria snort.

"Too young, but what can one do?" murmured Sehr Madam and turned towards the turquoise sheen of the oval pool outside. I followed her gaze. What did she mean? She could do whatever what she wanted.

"Follow me," commanded Gloria. With one last glance at Sehr Madam, I trailed after Gloria. We turned into a dim passageway that narrowed as we reached the back of the house and climbed a rickety staircase. Washing lines, drooping with damp clothes, were strung from one end of the balcony to the other. I followed Gloria into a small room with a musty smell.

"You'll be sharing this quarter with Bushra, Sehr Madam's maid," said Gloria.

I looked over the tiny, windowless space with two charpais and a narrow chest of drawers. I could be back home.

"You have half an hour to rest up," began Gloria, her black eyes fixed on my face. "But before I leave you alone, I need to know, are you clean? Or have you been with a man, done it?"

Heat flooded my face and my cheeks flamed. It? No one ever talked about *it*. My cousin, Saima Appi, had told us it happened on your wedding night. Took a few minutes. You had to shut your eyes. I shook my head. "I haven't," I whispered.

"Good. Stay clear of the male servants and always take the chador over your head if you know what's good for you. Now clean up. I'll be back for you."

Resisting the urge to curl up and sleep, I sat up. What had Gloria meant? Why did she want to know? Abba had threatened to chop me up into mince if I shamed the family name.

An hour later I was trying to keep up with Gloria as she glided through the mansion, her clipped voice detailing my chores. She stopped to count the antiques, crystal and silver and I kept count with her, wondering how she knew where and when Sehr Madam had purchased them, and their value. But her message was clear. I was responsible if anything broke or went missing.

It was dusk when I returned to my quarters. A tall, hefty woman stood in front of a cracked mirror propped on the chest. I murmured a greeting and the woman turned, her eyes narrowing as she ran the comb down the length of her hair.

"So you're here." She set her comb down. "I heard about you from Nanny. You know who I am?"

"Yes." She had to be Bushra, Sehr Madam's maid.

"Good. Do as I tell you, then we won't have a problem. Understood?" I nodded. Bushra frowned. "You look dead beat. Skip dinner and get some sleep, but keep to your side. That's your charpai," she pointed to the far one. "We'll talk more tomorrow." Deftly knotting her hair into a braid, she slipped out of the room.

Hours later, I was still awake. Shadows stirred. Silence howled. I had schemed, pulled Omer into my search for Tara, and convinced him to help me. But was I risking his life? When would I see him again? And where was Tara? Was I too late? I hunted the truth, but did I have the courage to face it? And what was I going do with it? Thoughts jabbed and pecked my head like a chicken's beak after scattered grain: I had to find Tara. I had to earn money for my dowry. My parents wanted me married. I wanted to study.

The night was darker and quieter than in my village. I missed the hum of the crickets and whispering leaves. Was I alone? Did the night eyes watch me? Should I have told Sehr Madam I had studied once, and that I still wanted to go to school? Would it have made any difference?

I woke up with a jolt. The room stank of sweat and waste. The door to the bathroom was open. Bushra snored from across the room. Pale light seeped in from under the door. I rolled over and grabbed my chador. Tiptoeing across the room, I opened the door and stepped out. A pink glow flamed the dim horizon. Drawn to the open windows, I stared at the stone-grey driveway winding towards the black gates. I stood alone, miles away from my home and light years away from the girl I had been, the girl who had longed to eat kairis, and dreamt of going to school.

Book Two

BAHAWALPUR

Fifteen Months Earlier

4

Kairis made me forget. They spun my senses and hurled me to the skies. They pushed everything out of my mind except the jolt of the tangy fruit exploding in my mouth. And then for a few heartbeats, the universe pulsed. Pure. Perfect. Joy.

My cousin Nazia had whispered that boys did that too, made girls forget everything. I wasn't sure about that.

I inhaled, and imagined thousands of tangy green orbs dotting the mango orchards. My mouth watered. I had wolfed down half a chapatti with a mug of chai at dawn. Nothing since then. Now, the sun was full, and my belly was as hollow as our empty water drum. But I had chores left – rice to sift, clothes to wash and a room to dust.

Another whiff. My belly growled. One more day and it might be too late. The landlord's thugs would be all over the orchards. I had to get out today. Now. Omer had already run out and Amma still napped inside.

I straightened up. The chores weren't going away anywhere. Amma had told me to strain the uncooked rice twice before soaking it. But who was going to tell her? Wavering for a second, I dumped the grains into a pan of water. Signalling to Tara, I slipped out, hoping she would follow. For the past few months, she'd been acting saintlier than our Pir. She did everything Amma wanted, even before Amma wanted it done. Waving to Omer to catch us, I swung towards the grove. Amma's hearing was sharper and better than Abba's. These days she hovered close, listening.

I raced through the fields. Shackles broke. A roaring sound filled my ears, and my skin flamed, hot and damp. In minutes, I had crawled under the barbed wire. Marking out my tree, I leapt, grabbed a twisting branch and locked my ankles around it. The world flipped; I hung upside down, weightless and free. Counting to five, I swung up and balanced on my belly, feeling the warm pulse of the tree. A breeze tickled the sweat on my face and neck. Nani would be proud. Dreams were like fireflies, she said. They lit the dark. We had to grasp them, catch them. Otherwise, they would fly away. And it would be dark again.

"Jump up," I urged, spotting Tara. "Omer will be here any second."

"Your idea, you get them!" retorted Tara. She shrugged off her chador and spread it under the tree.

"Coward," I muttered, scanning the fields for the landlord's thugs. The grounds were clear, except for a trail of farmers who combed the fields for pests. The grass rustled and insects whirred. Fixing my eyes on a cluster of plump kairis, I snaked forward.

"Where's Zara?" Hearing Omer's shout, I gripped a clump of leaves and began to heave it back and forth.

"Where do you think?" answered Tara.

"Grab the loot," I called, as a burst of green fruit hit the ground. Hearing the distant rumble, I frowned.

"Let's go," called Omer. "We've got them."

"Once more." Pushing loose strands of hair behind my ears, I reached out again. "Phitteh muh," I cursed as dust stung my eyes. Summer storms were fast and dark, like Amma's temper.

"Hurry," urged Omer.

The ground tilted, and leaves flashed past me. Landing on my hands and knees, I sprang up and cursed again. My sleeve was caught on a bush. I yanked at it, and winced at the ripping sound. Another tear to mend before Amma notices. I raced after Tara and Omer and crawled under the wire fence.

"You're hurt." Tara darted over.

"What happened?" Omer leaned over me.

I flicked my tongue over the crimson graze and shook my head. "Nothing. I'm good. Do we have time?" I tugged at the knot in Tara's chador.

"If we hurry," said Tara.

"I thought we were going fishing," murmured Omer. "This was risky." He pulled out a folded paper from his side pocket and unfolded it.

I inhaled the tang of the spicy blend for dipping the kairi in. "We only took what's ours," I muttered. 'Daku' blood filled our veins, but we weren't the thieves.

"Shush, you two," warned Tara.

"Why? Afraid of the jinns?" Omer rolled his eyes and began to pass out the kairis.

"It's not the jinns we need to be afraid of …" I began, and flinched at the memory of a dark morning, years ago.

A rumour that our landlord had won a bid to export kairis had hit our village like lightning. The orchards had always belonged to the village's farmers. After a quick meeting, the farmers had hurried to the shrine with sacks of wheat as an offering. Accepting the grain, the Pir, our landlord's younger brother, had assured the farmers that they had nothing to worry about and that he would talk to his brother.

Yet we had woken to an army of thugs swathed in black bandanas breaking open our door. They hauled Abba into the street and shackled him, along with other farmers. Standing on the hood of his jeep with his young son, our landlord had accused us of treachery. His father had ruled over our fathers, and he ruled over us. He had the right to take our land as and when he pleased. He was going to give us one last chance to set it right. We could hand over the orchards to him willingly or else. But Abba and the other farmers had stayed silent.

Hearing the crack of whips, I had grabbed Raja, my month-old mutt, in my arms. Shrieks and shouts rent the air. Flesh split open and streaks of blood darkened the earth. But no one moved to help Abba or any other farmer. We watched, still and silent. It was the law. In our village the land gave life and the land took life.

With the look of a wild bull in his eyes, the landlord had shouted at his guards to be 'men'. Dropping the bamboo sticks, the thugs had come after us and caught my aunt. Hearing her scream, I had wet my pants. Amma had grabbed my shoulder to pull me back, and Raja had dropped out of my arms. In a heartbeat, the landlord's son had nabbed him. I struggled to break free of Amma, but she had held me in an iron grip. I had yelled until I lost my voice, but Amma didn't let go of me until the farmers had surrendered and our landlord and his men had sped off. I never saw my pup again.

But it wasn't over. My uncle had come after my aunt with a stick. Silently, we watched another beating. Finally, the men shuffled away, leaving the women to comfort my aunt and scurry back inside the walls.

Omer's laugh snapped me back to the present. I opened my eyes and blocked the past. I dipped the kairi into the spice blend and bit into it. The flavours swelled and danced. Sour. Tangy. Spicy. My tongue pulsed like it was the centre of my being. But the flavours were gone too soon. I pushed back and licked my fingers.

It had been months since we had run out into the fields or gone fishing. I missed the scent of shrubs and soil. I missed the feel of the damp earth and the springy grass under my feet. As young children, we had spent long afternoons playing pithu gol garam with stones, hopscotch with sticks and even chhupan chhupaee or hide and seek. But those days were gone. Now, Amma said that running out was haram. Playing in the streets was haram. Everything was haram after the bleeding started.

Hearing the sky rumble, I looked up. Jagged cracks split the sky, and the ground lit up silver. Branches swayed and leaves flapped. Omer began to pack up the spices. "We should go. It might worsen."

I nodded. "Last one back cleans the chicken coop for a week." I shot out, turned to run and caught a glint of gold in Tara's eyes. My eyes.

A year ago, she wouldn't have let me win. She would have challenged me or called me a fool. We had spent hours imagining our adventures. We had planned to discover the world together on rafts, ships, trains and even airplanes. But now she stood knotting the chador under her chin.

5

I raced past the sea of swaying stalks that ended before the line of uneven huts. I felt the early evening gust, free to drift where it wanted, brush my cheeks and shivered as it chilled the sweat on my face. Skidding to the door, I took a deep breath. Inside, our rooms were dark and windowless.

Pulling my chador over my head, I nudged the door open, hoping to slip into the shadows.

"Zara?" called Amma in a strained voice.

"Coming!" I stepped inside.

"You went out?" Amma's voice tightened with anger. "Haven't I told you and Tara a thousand times not to? What if someone sees you? Do you want to ruin our family name? And where is Tara?" Amma's dark eyes flashed.

"We're here. Sorry Amma," called Omer, bounding in. Tara followed.

"Where were you?" demanded Amma.

"We went fishing," I began.

"Went fishing, and came back stinking of kairis. Don't lie." I yelped as Amma pinched my chin. "You're becoming more 'tez' day by day, you understand?"

I looked down. "Tez" was Amma's favourite word for me. Smart. Sharp. Sassy. Was it so bad?

"Amma," began Omer, slinging his arm around Amma's

shoulders. "Zara's right. We were going to go fishing. Weren't you saying the other day that you wanted to cook fish for dinner? We were near the river when we heard thunder and hurried back."

"Stories," retorted Amma. "Now hurry and stack the firewood before your father gets back." She pushed Omer away and turned to us. She pinched my chin again, and then Tara's. "You two should know better. Go on now, finish the chores. It's late. And look at the filth on your hands. Wash them right now." She looked at Tara. "Did you sweep the courtyard?"

"Yes," answered Tara.

"Sort and soak the rice?" Amma's eyes were on me.

"Yes," I nodded, praying Amma would not spot the heap of unwashed clothes under the charpais.

"It's ready to boil," added Tara.

"Peel the potatoes and onions?" continued Amma.

"Yes," we said together.

"Good." Amma turned to me. "Finish dusting and take out the bedding." She turned towards Tara. "Throw some scraps out for the poor kittens, they've been meowing away, and then come join me. I'll teach you how to knead the dough for chapattis and fry the potatoes."

"Can I work with Zara instead? We'll work faster," said Tara.

"We'll dust, take out the bedding and then knead the dough together," I added. I always worked better with Tara.

"Not today. Go on now." Amma's voice was firm.

"Phitteh muh," I murmured.

"Did you say something?" Amma snapped, glaring.

Shaking my head, I dragged my feet into the sitting room and squatted beside the sofa and the pair of matching chairs. Feeling the musty shadows and walls close in, I grabbed the dust cloth.

The sofa set was part of the dowry Amma had brought to

Abba's house. I remembered Amma's words. "Your grandfather spent more than half of his savings on my dowry. He travelled to Chiniot to place the order for the furniture." I shifted back, careful not to move the cushions, and yelped as a hand grasped my elbow.

"Shush, it's me," said Tara.

"Why didn't you say something? Scaring me like that!" I whispered.

"I thought a little light might help," said Tara, setting the lamp on the table. A soft glow flooded the room. She paused. "Zara, tell Amma."

"I can't." A trace of kairis stung my throat.

"Tell her before she finds out. Say we both did it."

"You didn't."

"But she doesn't know that," said Tara.

"It's ruined."

"It can be fixed. It'll be worse if Amma discovers it before you tell her. And it wasn't your fault."

"But will she believe me?" I whispered. Bari Masi, one of the village elders, had barged into our house yesterday. Before I could say that Amma was not home, Bari Masi had frowned. "Where is your mother? Has she left you alone? Why isn't your chador on your head? Cover your devil's tails for shame." Grabbing my braids, Bari Masi had pulled me inside.

"Sit," Bari Masi had hissed, pinning us with her pale eyes. "You flit like butterflies now, but one slip is all it takes, and you'll be strangled by a thousand snakes and burn in the fires of hell. Even at night you're not safe. The night eyes – they're everywhere, all around you. You think you can escape, but the night eyes watch you, they will always watch you." Her lips had disappeared into her leathery face.

What did she mean by 'night eyes'? My fingers had tangled into the jute weave of the seat and tugged, listening to Bari Masi's raspy voice warning us that all girls were born stinking of shame. It was up to us to cover ourselves and protect ourselves from temptation, or we would burn in hell forever. Finally, when Bari Masi had gotten up to leave, the wicker strands had curled around my hand. I had stared at the gaping hole in horror.

"Tell Amma what she said," urged Tara.

I shook my head. "What's Amma going to do? Ask her to pay for repairs?"

"She might or might not, but you might try listening to me for once." Tara moved to stand but stopped. "Oops, our bracelets are entangled." She pulled at my wrist.

I unclasped my silver birth bracelet and it fell to the floor, freeing Tara. Since I could remember, I had always known what Tara was going to say before she said it. And when I spoke, she finished my sentences. Now, at times I wasn't sure what she thought or meant, even when she said it.

"Go before Amma catches us," I urged. My back still hurt from the thrashing Amma had given me last week when she had caught me tossing the broken broom over the wall. On a whim, I had tried to practice my batting with a broom when Omer had left to play a game of cricket with his friends. It hadn't been one of my better ideas.

Watching Tara leave, I re-fastened the silver birth bracelet around my wrist. It was the only present I owned. Nani had gifted it to us on our birth. We had been born in the month of Assu, the month of the monsoon rains. Nani said the dai had not yet finished mourning the birth of one baby girl darker than a cooked crab when Amma had shrieked. Muttering and mumbling, the dai had squatted between Amma's thighs and pulled out another jaundiced bundle. "Another girl," she had mourned. Begging Amma to seek their Pir's forgiveness, the dai had disappeared into the night. Nani had washed us and handed us to Amma, who had tucked us, one at each breast. But we had hollered, inconsolable until Amma had cradled us together under one arm. We had turned to each other, two halves of a whole. The next day, Amma put us out in the sun. In days, Tara's yellowness had faded to a creamy peach colour. My redness had cleared too, but the sunbeams had done their work, leaving me dark as a berry. I knew I was darker than Tara and much darker than Amma.

As soon as we learnt to walk, Amma set us on chores. She woke us at dawn and in the time we took to clean our teeth with a sheesham twig, wash our faces and plait our hip-length hair, she had our work lined up. We cooked breakfast, dusted the rooms, swept the floor, sorted grains, fed and washed the livestock. But in the afternoon when Amma went inside to nap, leaving us with more chores, we created adventures. Washing clothes, we pretended to fight monsters crawling up the riverbank; soaking rice and lentils, we stirred the brews to poison the witch who had captured many of the villagers; dusting, we searched for hidden treasures, pretending to be sailors from Treasure Island. We grew up imagining new adventures and creating characters out of the stories our Nani told us, or the books I read.

But then Nani left, taking the stories and adventures with her, and Amma began to pull us apart. She told Tara to cook and me to clean. She told Tara to sweep and me to wash clothes. She told me to bring water and Tara to mend clothes. And she compared us, clicking her tongue and jabbing her thumb on her pinky, going on about who did better. Tara did. Always.

I stepped back to study the sofa. The wood gleamed. Or was it the light? Setting the oil lamp to one side, I shook out the frayed crochet cover over the wooden table, to hide the chipped corners.

I dusted the plastic mats filled with pictures of wild birds and beasts that haunted my dreams. I arranged the set of pink-flowered plastic plates and cups on the two mud shelves. I wiped the poster of the fair, golden-haired baby boy. He sat on his bottom smiling away. He had every reason to smile. He had golden hair and fair skin. And he was a boy. In our village, it made all the difference. Sometimes, I caught Amma staring at the poster when she thought no one was looking.

Plucking a bunch of plastic daisies from the clay vase, I brushed off the dust. Nothing matched, but Amma still crammed this room with her most valued possessions. No one visited anymore, but Amma insisted we sweep and dust daily. I stuffed the flowers back into the vase and hurried to the next room.

Two creaking charpais set against opposite walls took up most of the space. Amma and Abba slept on the slightly larger one while Tara and I slept on the other. I spread the ragged blankets over the charpais and rolled out Omer's bedding, a thin straw mat, between them. I sorted the heap of washed clothes and hung them behind the door. Catching my reflection, a narrow, tanned face with a smattering of freckles, in the cracked mirror, I swung away.

Amma had forbidden us to look in the mirror. She said it was haram. The devil lurked behind the glass, waiting to catch young girls who peered inside. Only Abba used the mirror to clip his moustache. I straightened my chador over my head, and turning away, banged my shin against the tin chest filled with old clothes. In the last year, my arms and legs had shot out, making me stumble when I moved too fast.

I stepped out and stopped. Had the mud walls moved in closer? Why did I suddenly feel trapped? Even the air was still. I shut my eyes and took a deep breath.

We lived at the end of the village, in a small hut tucked between a dirt track and the fields. Our courtyard was crowded with two charpais, one for Abba and the other for our guests. Amma only sat on the charpai while Abba was out. When he was home, she hovered around him or squatted by the cooking pit.

I had a place in the courtyard too. Amma had set Abba's old tool crate in the furthest corner of the courtyard, keeping silent when Abba occasionally and absentmindedly asked why she hadn't thrown the old crate away. Amma made me sit on it for a few days each month. Amma read prayers, blew them into water and sprinkled the water over me or told me to drink it. It didn't help. Nothing helped. Rage. Hatred. Anger. They sucked on me like dark leeches right before the bleeding each month.

Amma said the spirit of Mai Phatto, a crazed barren wretch who was stoned to death for abducting young village girls, was trying to possess my spirit. I had to stop her. The trick was not to feel. I would pretend to be a stone, a pebble, unmoving and lifeless. If I didn't feel, maybe Mai Phatto would leave me alone. But it never worked. I would try to fight back, try not to feel, but Mai Phatto's spirit was clever, it would lie low until I thought I was okay, and then suddenly surge up like a crocodile. I would scream and lash back at Amma and be sent to sit on the crate. I had to sit on it until I had calmed down and was ready to get on with my chores. I wasn't allowed to talk to anyone while I sat on the crate. And no one could speak to me. Tara tried, but Amma kept her away.

I stepped into the courtyard, and catching sight of my sewing basket, swiftly kicked it under the charpai. Amma had told Abba to purchase our sewing baskets from the market last season, saying it was time we started sewing our bridal linen. Tara had already traced out a pattern on her pillowcase and begun embroidering vines and roses with pink and green threads. Lagging weeks behind her, I was in no hurry to catch up.

Tara and Amma squatted near the two shallow pits for cooking and washing dishes. Tara hummed softly as she flipped the chapattis. Amma had forbidden her from singing aloud, saying it would entice the jinns.

"Come help me," called Omer, stacking the firewood.

"Amma, can I?" I asked.

"Hmm, yes," said Amma without looking back, "But after you've rubbed the tonic on your face and hands. It's been ready since the morning. I've told you three times already."

"Do I have to?" I protested.

"Yes, now," said Amma. "And Nasreen Masi was asking me about the potion. Why did you have to mention it to her daughter? There's no need to tell others, you hear that? Now hurry."

Gripped by a surge to rebel, I hesitated. But catching Tara's pleading look, I spun towards the cooking pit.

Amma's obsession with medicinal herbs had begun after Omer had caught typhoid. There was no doctor in our village and she had begged Abba to take Omer to the herbal doctor in Khalid Chacha's village. After their return, she had begun to grow vines and prepare herbal brews for Omer. He had recovered in a few weeks. But Amma hadn't stopped experimenting. She brewed potions to make us taller, to cleanse our stomach of worms, to clear the spots on our faces. Every few weeks she plucked, dried and ground the plants into powder for various remedies and stored these in jars. For the past few months, she had been on a rampage to lighten my complexion. Lifting the dish, I gagged at the stench of the foul-smelling, colourless blend, pinched my nose and dipped my fingers into the slimy goo. I slapped it on my face and arms, and spat out the bitter residue.

"Zara, hold the stack while I tie it up," called Omer.

I skipped over, passing the chickens roosting in crates, waiting for nightfall. Stopping to stroke the kittens, I suddenly wished that Amma would talk to us in the voice she used for the kittens. She crooned and murmured to them, held them gently, and even let them up on the charpai when Abba was out.

What was wrong with me? Shaking my head, I walked and gripped the stack of firewood. An aroma wafted up and my mouth watered at the smell of warm chapattis with spicy potatoes.

"Done. Now come, let's practice," Omer urged, straightening up. He bent his knees, arched his feet and raised his fists. I shook my head. Amma could turn around any moment. "Come on," urged Omer. "Remember: float like a butterfly, sting like a bee."

My arms tingled as if brushed by spiky grass, and a rush of heat swelled my cheeks, remembering Muhammad Ali's fight chant. He was a warrior in the boxing ring, the 1960 Olympic gold medallist and the world's heavyweight boxing champion three times. Our village had burst into celebrations after his last win.

But Muhammad Ali hadn't been born Muhammad Ali. He had been born Cassius Clay, Jr. He had been born poor and black. He had risen to become the world-famous boxing champion.

"Scared?" mocked Omer and swung out one fist after the other. Tightening my fists, I bounced forward, aligned my toes and heels until they were shoulder width apart, and shuffled them to a 45-degree angle. But before we had exchanged a few rounds, a banging shook the door.

"Open the door!" boomed Abba.

6

We jumped back.

"Move," roared Abba, as Omer yanked open the door.

I sprang to one side. Did Abba mean the buffalo or me? What a devilish beast. And it wasn't budging. Omer shoved the door back as far as it would go. "Move," repeated Abba. He slackened his grip and then yanked harder. The horned monster lumbered forward.

"Salam, Abba," I murmured. What was he doing with a buffalo? Amjad Chacha sent over a pan of milk for the morning and afternoon tea in exchange for the fodder that we collected each evening. My eyes flew over the ink-black glistening body, the white markings on the muzzle, the sharp ears and the set of curly horns. My pulse quickened. It was the Nili-Ravi breed, the black gold, the best breed for business. Was Abba planning to sell milk? We could do with the money. I remembered Abba telling Amma we would move into a bigger place with tall pukka walls, a solid wooden door and a cobbled courtyard. But we hadn't moved. Our hut's walls were still low and made of mud. The narrow front door was cracked and faded. The roof leaked when it rained.

"Zara, get your sister!" said Abba knotting the rope around an iron hook.

"Salam, Abba," said Tara, standing behind me.

"Come closer, you two," said Abba. He grasped our hands. "She's yours. Take good care of her."

"For us?" Stumbling, I dropped the rope. Unmarried girls didn't own land or property in our village. Sons inherited all of it. They carried the family name. Abba's land would go to Omer. Our dowry was for our in-laws. There was nothing for us. I knew that. I had been told that.

"Oh good, very good. I was hoping," said Amma. Her voice trailed off and her face flushed.

"Hoping for what?" I searched her face.

Amma shook her head, slapped the leathery skin and sighed. "Tomorrow I'll teach you girls how to care for it and …"

"Yes," interrupted Abba. "You do that, but remember the first stream of milk goes to mother earth."

"But that's just a village superstition."

"You heard me, so do what I tell you. Tell me, do you recognise its breed?" Abba jerked the knot.

Amma shook her head. I looked at her. Why did Amma pretend? She had grown up looking after buffaloes. I had heard her tell her friends.

"I thought you wouldn't," said Abba. "It's the best, the Nili-Ravi. I rushed over as soon as Khalid Bhai told me about the auction. I had to purchase it in instalments. Now if only we get a good season." Rolling back his sleeves, Abba started to walk over to the charpai.

Amma hurried after him. "Set the food out," she called to us, pouring water over Abba's hands and arms. Abba scooped the water in his palms, ran it from his fingers to his elbows and shook his hands dry. Tara had turned towards the cooking pit, but I swerved to look at the beast again. "Zara!" Hearing the warning in Amma's voice, I hurried.

Abba took his place at the head of the mat and sat cross-legged. Amma tossed the remaining water in the washing pit and settled on Abba's left. Omer came and sat next to Amma. After arranging food and plates in front of our parents, Tara and I sat opposite Amma and Omer.

I smelt the spicy potatoes and pushed all thoughts away. This was when it all came together: food, family and stories. Abba farmed wheat and cotton on a plot leased from the landlord. When we had been younger, there were days when Abba would wake up and declare he wasn't going to the fields. He would haul us up on his shoulders and walk to the river, telling us about his childhood days. He would feed us pickles and aloo-parathas that Amma had packed in the tin lunch box. He would hold our hands while we giggled and squealed and dipped our feet into the icy water that tickled our feet. But nowadays, he left after an early breakfast and didn't return until after we were asleep. He rarely joined us for dinner, but when he did, the food tasted better.

"How was the meeting?" asked Amma, scooping food onto Abba's plate.

"A waste," Abba frowned and shook his head, "Our landlord accuses the department of corruption, and they say he's a fraud. They lured us into this 'double the yield' scheme and now have us by our throats. They control the prices and the markets. We can't do much." He tore the chapatti and scooped up the potatoes with it.

"The neighbour of the river is neither hungry nor thirsty," murmured Amma. "They won't get away with it, they …"

"Omer," interrupted Abba. "Did you clean the farming tools as I told you to?"

Omer swallowed. "I was going to when I came back from school, but …"

"School or no school. When I tell you to do something, you do it." Hearing the iron in Abba's voice, I looked up.

"Yes Abba, but …" started Omer.

"No buts. And we'll have to see about school. I'll need your help in the fields and maybe even …" Abba broke off and frowned. "Keep your focus on the land, son, that's your future." He pushed his plate away and started to get up.

I threw Omer a quick look. Famous for his storytelling, Abba had promised to tell us tonight how he had journeyed from Jalandhar, India, to Pakistan during the Partition of the subcontinent. I needed to know his story for the project Master Saab had assigned.

"Sorry, Abba," mumbled Omer. "I'll clean the tools after dinner. And I'll give the fields as much time as you want me to." Seeing Abba nod, Omer pushed ahead. "Will you tell us the tale of how you came to Pakistan? You promised."

Abba gazed at Omer for a few seconds and then nodded again. "You remember, then. Yes, I did promise." He sat down and unfolded his legs, tipping the stack of steel cups over. Tin clanked and water spilled. Bending forward, Amma began to apologise and Tara and I leapt to help her.

Why was Amma sorry? She hadn't done anything wrong. I smothered the sparks in my chest. I had other battles to fight. I was named Zara after Abba's younger sister, whom he had left behind. Nani said Zara meant the top, and the best at everything.

7

Stacking the dishes in my arms, I followed Tara to the washing pit. A storm rumbled inside my head. According to Abba, my grandfather had been one of the most famous dacoits in India. He had looted the rich, puppets of the British Raj, to feed the poor villagers. He had put my father under the tutelage of a wrestling champion, and Abba was being trained for a wrestling competition when the flames of Partition had exploded and torn their village apart. When a mob, armed with daggers and burning batons had attacked, my grandfather had forced Abba to flee to the nearest refugee camp. Abba had been the only son. He had the responsibility to carry on the family name. At the age of thirteen, Abba had hiked through miles and miles of jungle in the rain and sludge to reach the nearest refugee camp. He had never seen his sister or parents again. He had survived the journey to Pakistan alone and camp officers had helped him to locate his relatives. Turning to farming, he fed people and helped build a new country. He had lost his family, but we had gained a nation. More importantly, he had kept his promise to his father and kept the family name alive.

But why had Abba given up on his dream of becoming a wrestling champion? Was it because of his promise to my grandfather? I too longed for my journey and purpose. Amma and Abba didn't know. Nobody knew.

"Girls, have you finished?" Amma's voice broke into my thoughts. From the corner of my eye, I saw her get up.

"Nearly," answered Tara, wiping the clean dishes.

"Good, finish up and get to bed," said Amma, walking over. "You have to start helping your father in the fields from tomorrow. The harvest is on our heads and ..." her voice trailed off.

I nodded, seeing Tara do the same. We had helped Abba in the past when he couldn't afford to hire labour. I enjoyed working in the fields under the open sky. Glancing up, I froze. Amma was almost on top of us. Tiny hairs crackled on the back of my neck and arms.

"You'll have to stop your lessons," said Amma in a low voice, her dark beetle eyes fixed on me. "You'll have no time between helping your father in the fields, and the chores. Anyway, it's time you put your mind to other things."

I turned to stare at her.

"But you promised. You said I could finish my studies," I began, hating how my voice wobbled. Heat stung my eyes.

"Nonsense." Amma tightened her lips. "You'll forget all about them in a few weeks. I've made up my mind."

8

My breath squeezed as if a python coiled around my windpipe. Why did I have to work on the land? It wasn't mine. My dreams were mine. No one was going to snatch them away. Not even Amma.

I clenched my fingers around the stones and counted them silently. They were magic; they could work magic. I pushed up and took a deep breath.

"What do you think Bari Masi meant by night eyes?" whispered Tara. I tensed, feeling her hand curve around my shoulder. "Zara?"

I shifted away. Hadn't she heard Amma? Didn't it matter to her? I tightened my hand into a fist.

"Stop talking, or Amma will barge inside," said Omer. He flipped a page and lowered his head over his books again.

"Nothing, night eyes are nothing. She was trying to scare us," I whispered. I rose on my elbows, took another deep breath and edged towards the side. I had to talk to Omer. I wouldn't make it through the night. Sleep was impossible. "What are you studying?" I probed. Omer shook his head and didn't look up.

"Have you told him?" asked Tara.

"Not yet," I whispered.

"You should."

"Stop talking." Omer thumped the book and straightened up. "I can't study like this. I already lost time cleaning the tools and I can't fall behind."

"Did Amma say anything to you about Zara's lessons?" interrupted Tara.

Omer sighed and slid his books under the charpai. "Yes, she did, right after she spoke to you. I was going to talk to you about it in the morning, but since you're not going to let me study, let's talk now." He met my eyes. "I told Amma it wasn't fair."

"It's not," I shot out.

"And that you wouldn't give up," continued Omer. "But she insisted you wouldn't have the time and it's true. Abba wants us on the fields right after school." Seeing my face, he held up his hand. "But wait, before you say anything I have an idea. How about I tutor you before I go to school? Before Amma and Abba wake up? It's early, but no one's up and there's no other time."

"Yes," I breathed out and lay back, feeling a molten warmth flood my limbs. I reached out to Omer, but then wavered. We hadn't hugged in a long time. Not after Amma had said it wasn't right anymore. I pushed the river stones to the corner of our charpai.

"Good, it's done. Go to sleep or you'll have Amma inside." Watching me for a moment, Omer pinched the flame and slid the lamp under the charpai.

"Thank him," whispered Tara.

I shook my head. It was too late. I wanted to hug Omer, I wanted to turn around to whisper and giggle with Tara like old times, but the python was back, squeezing tighter and spewing thick venom. Last year, when Omer had passed his exams, Amma had spent hours preparing his favourite dessert, the milky kheer. This year, when I had cleared with higher marks, Amma had muttered I needed to learn to make softer chapattis.

I wasn't going to be pushed back. Not this time.

Three years ago, Master Saab, as he later became fondly known, had stumbled across our village by chance, en route to his ancestral home after retiring from the post of principal of a government school in Multan. We had been in the fields, helping Abba with the harvest, when his tonga had broken down outside our village. Spotting the unmoving tonga, we had crowded around it, steered it to the guesthouse and helped Master Saab to unload a small zipper bag, a large blackboard and a massive metal trunk large enough to hold a small buffalo. Overcome by our welcome or for some other reason, Master Saab had decided to stay on.

In a few days, Zubaida Masi, Amma's friend, had dropped by to share the gossip. Troubled by the sight of half-naked children loitering in the village lanes, Master Saab had decided to set up an 'English' school in our village. "An idle mind is the devil's workshop," he had quoted to the village grocer. In response, our Moulvi Saab, who led prayers at the mosque each Friday, had announced that he would start a religious school for children. In the following weeks, our village elders debated the risks and rewards of each system over countless cups of tea and gurgling hookahs, but the discussions broke into scuffles and fights. Following the advice of his friend Amjad Chacha, Abba decided to send Omer to the religious school. But Amma begged him to reconsider, saying the lands belonged to their landlords, and Omer should have the chance to make something of his life. She had pleaded with Abba to seek his cousin, Khalid Chacha's, opinion. A week after Khalid Chacha's visit, Abba had enrolled Omer in the 'Angrezi' school.

A few months later, I had gone inside our room to hang the freshly washed clothes and tripped over Omer's books. Bending to pick up his copy book, I had gaped at the number of crosses and slashes in red ink. Why hadn't he told us how badly he was doing?

Curious, I flipped the pages to the end and buckled, feeling like there was a fist ramming into my belly, unable to tear my eyes away from the gold stars gleaming on pages of smooth writing towards the end. I shut the copy book, but it was too late. Claws ripped my gut. How much had Omer learnt? What had I learnt during these months? Nothing. Fumbling and unable to stop myself, I opened another book. Girls in blue and grey uniforms and shiny black shoes, with hair in neat braids and ponytails, smiled back. Who were they? Did they study and play with the boys in the same school? Why didn't I go to school? What could I be if I went to school?

For months, stealing any opportunity to escape from Amma's sharp eyes, and without saying a word to anyone, I browsed through Omer's copy books. I couldn't read a word, yet they whisked me off to another world. The boys and girls went to school and on holidays. They celebrated their birthdays, shopped with their parents and picnicked in parks.

One afternoon, Omer caught me with his books and warned me of what Amma would do if she ever found out. When I had confided that I wanted to study, Omer hadn't understood. "Why? What is the need?" – I would be married soon. I didn't have to support a family. We had started arguing when Amma walked in. Ignoring Tara's warning look to back down, I announced that I wanted to go to school and flung open the books to show Amma that girls did go to school. In a flash, Amma seized me by my shoulders and began shaking me like a dust cloth. Had I lost my mind? Had I forgotten who I was and where I lived? Girls in our village didn't go to school. She would marry me off in days if I ever talked about going to school. She had loosened her grip only after I promised I wouldn't talk about it again.

But then Omer had bowled a googly and vowed he was going to start tutoring me at home. If Amma didn't allow it, he would stop going to school as well. Our Nani had told him that our grandfather, an English teacher in a government school, had taught Amma until her marriage. If Amma had been home-schooled, why couldn't I be?

Stumped, Amma only agreed after Omer promised no one would find out and I would finish my chores before or after my lessons. When I urged Tara to join us, she refused, saying she didn't have the time.

Within a few days, Omer had borrowed the books and supplies from Master Saab who, thrilled that I could be a model for the rest of the girls in the village, had to be reminded that they had to keep my lessons a secret. He had agreed, but reluctantly. Where he came from, both girls and boys went to school.

Each afternoon I waited for Omer to return from school. Master Saab set me on a target of one book a week. I was behind for my age and had to catch up. He had a trunk full of books, mostly in English, and encouraged the boys to read as much as possible. He wanted all his students to learn English; it would get them jobs in the city, he said.

Within a few months, I was reading stories about Jane and Peter. They visited the seaside, went for picnics and baked cakes with their mummies. I had never been to the seaside. I had never been on a picnic or tasted cake. Their world was far away from mine. I zipped through stories of Rapunzel, Sleeping Beauty and Cinderella. They bored me. There was no place for fairy tales and magical kingdoms in my world. And I didn't want to be a princess.

But the next lot of books that Master Saab sent over, *Treasure Island, Robinson Crusoe, Tarzan* and *The Jungle Book*, tossed me into adventures and hurled me into undiscovered lands. I was hooked. Persuading Tara to join me, I invented our escapades. Depending on what I read, my wooden crate became a boat, an island, a tree, or a rock, and Amma became Long John Silver, the leader of the cannibals, Clayton the hunter, or even Shere Khan, the tiger.

Little House on the Prairie gave me a place in its world. Laura Ingalls Wilder lived in one room with her family and so did I; I had to sew and mend my clothes and so did she; her life was filled with chores, and so was mine. But that's where it ended. She went to school. She rode on ponies, made candy and played in the snow. Having the freedom to roam and explore the American frontier, she experienced the thrill of discovery. She survived storms, famines and disease. She was free to decide how she wanted to live. I knew I wasn't free. My parents weren't free either.

In *Little Women*, I admired Jo, wanting to be like her. No, I wanted to be her. We were different, yet similar from inside. I knew I wasn't alone. Girls across the world were trying to find their way and cross hurdles. It wasn't my struggle alone. But we lived oceans apart, in different worlds. When Jo rebelled, she gained her family's approval; it wasn't the same for me. My obedience was a yardstick of my parents' standing in our village. If I rebelled, I dishonoured them and my family name.

Master Saab sent other books for me. I read about the Mughals, the European Empire and the world wars. I read about the great scientists, poets, painters and inventors. Many stories found a home within me. The books and lessons sparked ideas and questions. Busy learning, I forgot where I came from or where I belonged.

Sometimes Omer was able to answer my questions, and sometimes not. I squeezed out the knowledge I could, but the sun shifted, shadows shortened and time always ran out. There were days I felt like a goldfish in a plastic bag. Circling round and round, I watched and learned about other realms, trapped in a world that was becoming too small for me.

9

The charpai creaked. I dropped my books into the sewing basket and bolted to the cooking pit. Abba and Amma were up. After tutoring me for over an hour, Omer had gone inside to get ready for school. Abba and Omer would want tea before heading out.

For the last few weeks, from dawn to dusk, Tara and I had been on the fields. The rippling crop was all cut and stacked, ready for the landlord's men to carry it off. I was proud of my work. But sweltering under the thick chadors Amma had forced us to wear, I had fumed. The men got away without wearing their shirts, but we had to take our chadors on top of our other clothes. I couldn't wait until Abba handed over the crop to our landlord, stored his share of the wheat bundles on our roof, and planted cotton. Then I could finally get back to my lessons.

"Zara," Omer's voice broke into my reverie. "Master Saab checked our assignments."

"He did? Already?" My belly flipped like a fish out of water, the way it always did before Omer told me my marks. My grip tightened on the saucepan handle. "Do you know what I got?"

"Eighty-eight percent!" Omer beamed. "It's one of the best scores. Master Saab is thrilled. He's insisting that you try for school."

"School?" I echoed, feeling hundreds of tiny wings flutter and flap inside my chest. "It's too late," I muttered. Amma would never allow it.

Omer crouched down and gripped my arm. "It's not too late. You have a chance. Master Saab said so."

I shook my head. "Where will I go? There's no girls' school in our village." I had dreamt of studying in a classroom with proper desks, chairs and a blackboard. But it was a dangerous dream, an impossible dream.

"Master Saab said there's one in Khalid Chacha's village. But you have to score a minimum of eighty-five percent on the admission test. Master Saab says you can do it. I know you can too. We're all above-age, but can catch up if we work hard. And Master Saab is so proud of your results. I'm proud of you. How can you not try?"

"Zara," Amma's voice made us jump apart. "Have you made the tea? No, then why are you talking to Omer? And why are you flushed?" She felt my forehead. "No. You don't have a fever. What's wrong then? Are you hiding something? Tell me right now."

"It's nothing," I murmured.

Amma shook her head. "If it's nothing then get to work. Tara's already cleaned the rooms. Now, what are you staring at? Finish making the tea and then get on with sweeping the floor. Oh, and use the new broom that Abba bought, it's by the door."

After pouring the tea into tin cups, I hurried to pick up the broom. Omer was proud of me. So was Master Saab. Had Amma heard?

Balanced on my haunches, I swept the floor from one end to the other. From the corner of my eyes, I saw Amma straighten Omer's school uniform and comb his hair while he ate his breakfast. Ignoring Amma's warnings of what happened to girls who peered out, I scooted after Omer and squinted through the crack. Like on every school day, Omer and his friends hurried off with school bags hitched on their backs, mimicking Master Saab's voice and goading each other to mastermind pranks.

After sweeping and rinsing the clothes, I began to wash the buffalo. I had decided to name it Kullo. I was in awe of the horned beast. It stood its ground, did what it wanted, whenever it wanted. It chewed grass, swatted flies and squirted streams of warm frothy milk better than the squeaky water pump in our village. My experiment of adding green fodder to the feed had doubled the milk production. The day before, I had asked Omer to find out if the local tea stall needed another milk vendor.

I had sat down with Tara to begin peeling peas when the door rattled. "Open up," cried a sharp voice.

"Majjo Behen," said Amma, lowering her feet from the charpai. "What is she doing here? Tara, open the door and Zara, make some tea."

Majjo or Mahjabeen was Khalid Chacha's younger and unmarried cousin. With hair that wriggled like a coil of worms and skin that glistened like cream, she laughed a lot and loudly, and when she did, the rolls of her chins jiggled. Over the years, the nickname, 'Majjo', had stuck.

Preparing the tea tray with care, I wondered again if Majjo Phuppi was happy being unmarried. She lived with her brother, since she wasn't allowed to live alone. Amma kept warning her everything would change the minute her brother got married and she should think of her future, but Majjo Phuppi declared that she didn't need a husband when there was food and politics. And she ran a poultry farm.

Walking in, I stopped. Majjo Phuppi was beating herself with a roll of paper. "Hai, hai, hai," she wailed.

"Salam, Majjo Phuppi," I murmured, setting the tray down. Before I could straighten up, Majjo Phuppi had grasped my shoulder.

"We're all doomed. Have you heard the news?" she shrieked. I shook my head and tried to step back, but Majjo Phuppi tightened her grip. "The rat of a shopkeeper sold this leaflet to me for the price of gold," she wailed. "And now your Amma's claiming she's forgotten how to read. What good is this paper to me if no one can read it?" She turned to Amma beseechingly and cupped her hands.

"Majjo, please, it is city news for the city people. It has nothing to do with us," soothed Amma.

About to turn away, I halted, seeing tears roll down my aunt's cheeks. Recalling the countless times she had smuggled treats for us, I reached out and wrapped my arms around her. I had never seen her cry. For a moment, Majjo Phuppi sagged against me, but then pushed back.

"Don't read it then," she burst out. "I'll ask a stranger on the street. I can, you know." She shook her fists and then shrieked as the paper fell to the floor. Without thinking, I picked up the leaflet and stared.

"Baton charge," I began, my eyes straying to the black and white picture. Batons. Rifles. The words stuck in my throat. What was going on? What was the police doing to the women? I gasped as Tara snatched the paper from my hand.

"Yes, but why, what's happening?" demanded Majjo Phuppi, her eyes fixed on my face. "But wait!" She shook her head slowly and then her gaze swung from me to Amma. "Is Zara learning to read? Are you teaching her?" She gripped Amma's arm.

My head filled with dark, gushing water. It rose higher and higher, swallowing my voice and thoughts. I couldn't think or breathe. I had promised Amma no one would find out.

I saw that Amma's lips were curved, but she wasn't smiling. "No, no, how could you think that?" she murmured. "She's teasing you. Foolish girl. Omer is going to school, so she picks up a word here, a word there. Nothing to worry about."

"But does her Abba know?" purred Majjo Phuppi.

"She hasn't learnt much. Why bother him?" began Amma. "But you know what, I think Omer will be able to read the remaining news for you when he returns. What do you say? Now sit and have some tea and kheer."

"Really?" Majjo Phuppi's eyes softened. "Thank you. That's all I came for." She settled down on the charpai, her arms folded across her chest, her hand still clutching the newspaper. When Amma beckoned, I sat down to finish peeling the heap of peas.

Hours passed before the door rattled. Before Omer could greet us, Amma instructed him to read the newspaper. Throwing Amma a puzzled look, Omer picked up the paper and started to read. "Baton charge on protesters," he began.

In minutes we had learnt that despite the ban on protests, hundreds of women in Lahore had gathered to march to the Lahore High Court to submit a petition. They were protesting against a law introduced by the Zia-ul-Haq regime that considered the testimony of two women to equal that of only one man in a court of law. Seeing the crowd, the police had charged at the unarmed women with tear gas and batons, injured dozens and arrested nearly fifty women. Escaping the police, a few brave women had been able to reach the High Court and been met by male lawyers, who had handed them garlands.

"They've murdered our leader and now they're slaughtering our rights," shrieked Majjo Phuppi. "Our leader is dead and now it's our turn." Rocking back and forth, she rammed her fists into her chest.

"Stop it," Amma gripped Majjo Phuppi's arms. But a deep wailing noise swelled from Majjo Phuppi's throat. When Amma's dark beetle eyes hardened, Tara and I hurried out. Omer ran to get Abba and returned with him after a few minutes.

I heard Abba trying to soothe Majjo Phuppi, but her cries and moans drowned his voice. Sitting beside Tara, I began to cook the lentils for our evening meal. A sprinkle of stars dotted the dark sky. It was just another evening, or was it? I stirred the curry with a wooden spoon. What did this new law mean? Was I half of my brother? I thought of the notes in my copybook.

1977: General Zia-ul-Haq, chief of army staff, arrests Prime Minister Zulfiqar Ali Bhutto on the charge of murder, imposes martial law and becomes the chief martial law administrator.

1978: Zia-ul-Haq assumes office of President and retains office of army chief.

February 1979: Zia-ul-Haq's regime passes the Hudood Ordinance to establish an "Islamic" system of justice in the country. The new laws focus on many crimes and their punishments, including robbery and rape.

April 1979: Zulfiqar Ali Bhutto is executed.

Was Bhutto's trial rigged? Was Majjo Phuppi right when she said we had no leader now that he was dead, along with the dreams of millions of the poor across the country?

How would these laws affect us? Would they affect us? Abba had declared that General Zia could do what he wanted, but nothing would change in our village. We lived too far to matter to anyone.

I blinked back the rush of tears. Why did I feel like crying? I had done well on my test. Master Saab was proud of me. He thought I had a chance of going to school. Did I?

10

Head lowered, eyes down, I tried to pray. And breathe. But I couldn't. Tara and I sat with legs folded, joined from knees to hips, squeezed into a hot, musty corner. A streak of dim light slanted in through a slit in the wall. My stomach heaved. The stink of sweat and death pushed in from all sides and the keen stares of the 'dealers' made me want to bury myself in the ground.

Our Shaukat Chacha was dead. He was Bari Masi's son and married to Amma's friend Nasreen Masi. Amma had insisted we accompany her because she couldn't leave us home alone, but then she had slipped inside another room to be with Nasreen Masi and left us alone in a roomful of 'matchmaking aunties'. That's what the villagers called them. I disagreed. They didn't make matches. They made deals.

I shrank, feeling them draw in closer to me. When Tara dug her elbow into my side, I picked up the beads but was unable to remember any prayer. The 'dealers' were all around us.

They draped the whitest of chadors around their heads, and with sly smiles and scheming eyes that darted everywhere they watched everyone and missed nothing. They devoured news about any and every single girl in the village, like vultures plucking flesh from bones. They kept track of which girl was single, which girl belonged to which caste, which girl had the right dowry and they dealt out the knowledge they had acquired, to make marriage deals.

Cries echoed and wails soared. More women trudged inside, sniffing and moaning. Remembering my prayers, I began to recite under my breath, but in a few minutes, I lost count. I tried again. My lips moved faster and faster until the end of one prayer merged into the beginning of another. I couldn't help it. Amma had taught us the prayers, but not what they meant. When I had asked Amma for the meaning, she had told me to 'have some shame'. What did shame have to do with it?

"Poor Nasreen," whispered a bony-faced woman. "What will she do? A young widow with three children, the poor soul."

"She has a son, a reason to live for," piped up a sharp-nosed woman. I recognised her as Zubaida Masi, Amma's friend.

"Make room, make room," shrilled a hefty woman with bulging hips, surging forward. Ignoring the dark looks from the women who had to move closer, she thrust herself in between two women, flung her dark veil back, and moaned.

"You are ... ?" questioned Zubaida Masi.

"Family." The woman sniffed, rocking back and forth.

"Ah, but I haven't seen you here before?" persisted Zubaida Masi, leaning forward.

"How would you? I'm from the city. Nasreen's mother is my cousin. It's been years since I saw her. But in such times family is all you have." I flinched at the ear-splitting pitch.

Zubaida Masi nodded. "What a loss!"

"What happened, tell me?" prompted the woman.

"Don't you know?" Zubaida Masi sighed. "God only knows what possessed Shaukat Bhai to go to the city to join the rally. Something went wrong. There was a stampede, the crowd threw stones, burnt tires and set vehicles aflame. The police fired shots, tear-gassed and arrested Shaukat Bhai. He went in alive and kicking, but they found him cold as a fish in a rubbish dump near the police station the next morning."

I shut my eyes: the hanging, the protests and now more deaths. When would it stop? I had read that schools and colleges had closed down.

The woman stared at Zubaida Masi unblinkingly and finally said, "The dead are gone. I hope for Nasreen's sake that her children are all settled."

"Two girls and a boy," another woman piped up.

"Married?" she prodded. I swung my head up.

Zubaida Masi sniffed again. "Just between us, the other day I was advising Nasreen to fix her elder daughter's marriage. She's fourteen after all, and if not now, then when? But Nasreen laughed and said I was a fool."

"She's the fool," muttered the woman. "And she'll realise that soon enough. But tell me, do you think they will serve anything? I left the city at dawn and haven't eaten since. I don't see any sign of food, although it's past noon."

"Ijaz Chacha was spotted walking over to the landlord's haveli early morning," confided another woman. "So many mouths to feed and more squeezing in by the minute. I hope he got the loan." The chant of prayers echoed out from the inner room. For a few moments there was silence, and then shrieks and cries burst out of the room.

I locked my fingers with Tara's. The prayers were over. It was time for the burial. I imagined the men hoisting Shaukat Chacha's body, covered in white cloth, on their shoulders. Only men went to bury the dead; the women stayed home. I could still hear muffled sobs. A low hum filled the room. The door opened and Nasreen Masi's eldest daughter, Zohra, stumbled out.

"Tell me, who's that pretty thing?" probed the large woman over the babble in the room.

"I thought you said you were related?" answered Zubaida Masi.

"That's Zohra, the eldest daughter."

"It's been some time," murmured the woman. She blinked and then raised her hand. "Zohra," she cried. "My girl, come here and meet your old aunt."

I gaped. What was she going to do?

"What are you doing?" hissed Zubaida Masi. "It's her father's funeral."

When the girl drew near, the woman clasped Zohra's hands and drew her down. "Oh you poor little thing, left fatherless so young. But you don't have to worry anymore. I'm here now. I'll take of everything. Come to the city with me and I'll get you married to a nice boy in no time. Your mother won't have to worry about a thing."

Zohra choked back a cry and disappeared inside the room. I gripped Tara's hand. Shaukat Chacha's body hadn't even left the house, and this woman was talking about marriage.

"Shy little thing. She'll do well," murmured the woman.

"What do you think you're doing?" demanded Zubaida Masi.

"Doing what has to be done," muttered the woman. "I know a good family in the city. The boy manages a grocery shop. They're looking for a pretty but simple girl from the village. One who doesn't have the demands that a city girl does. If Nasreen is keen, I could take her and Zohra to meet them."

"God bless you," gushed the bony woman.

"I'll try my best, but it's not like I earn any money from such arrangements. Of course, gifts are always welcome." The woman grunted. "These are hard times, I tell you. But speaking of girls, who's that one over by the wall with that milky white skin? My cousin is desperate to find a daughter-in-law with a complexion fairer than fresh cream." I shivered. The woman's eyes had sunk into Tara like fish hooks.

"Ah, her, she's Mariam's daughter, Tara. She has a twin, you know," said Zubaida Masi.

"Twin? Where?"

"By her side, the one who just turned away."

"Let it be," muttered the woman.

The walls spun. Chatter faded. A low buzz filled my ears. I remembered it like it was yesterday. Amma had taken us to Zubaida Masi's to learn how to make sweet vermicelli with milk. A group of girls had run up to us.

"You're not really twins?" a girl with buckteeth had probed.

"You're so, so different!" chirped another girl with pigtails.

"Like day and night," chanted another. I had wanted to slap her.

"No, like salt and pepper."

"No, no, like mud and milk."

The girls had burst into peals of laughter. We hadn't gone back to Zubaida Masi's again.

"Let it be? Why?" probed Zubaida Masi.

"Waste of a good-looking girl," muttered the woman. "Her mother should do something about it."

I felt the women's eyes on me. My face felt hot.

"Well, at least she has a brother," murmured Zubaida Masi.

"Huh? What do you mean?" she prodded.

"Watta-satta," explained Zubaida Masi. "You know, an exchange, one sibling for another. Her brother's doing well at school. He's a good boy with a bright future. Everyone knows that. Many families want a son-in-law like him. And it helps that she's a clever girl. A brother and sister married to another set of siblings is a good settlement."

"Well, you villagers have it all sorted." The woman's voice rang out. "All this talk of marriage is making me hungry. I'm going to go and find out what's happening about the food." The other women drew back as the hefty woman struggled up and shuffled away. I tried to move, but my limbs jammed. My breath squeezed into a knot. I wasn't going to be traded.

A shout announced that the food had been set out. Women heaved and elbowed each other to reach the rice platters. Seeing an opening, I shot up.

"Zara?"

Without answering, I yanked my chador over my head and zipped through the courtyard.

"Wait," called Tara, but I was already across the street. Inside the door, I pressed my head against the shaded wall. Why had I run out? I should have faced them and stood up for myself. I wasn't going to be married off by any 'watta-satta' contract. I wasn't going to be traded off. I didn't care if the crops burnt down, or an earthquake flattened our hut, or a tornado swept our village off the earth, but I wasn't going to be married off. I had a chance to go to school. How could they stop me? They couldn't. Was it a crime to go to school?

"Zara!" Hearing my twin, I swung back and saw her dangling my shoes. When I stayed still, she dropped them. "Why did you rush out?"

"I need to study." I gazed back steadily. I needed her on my side.

"Study for what? Omer's not even home."

"For school."

"School?"

"Yes. Master Saab said to try for the admission test for the school in Khalid Chacha's village."

"And you're telling me now?" Tara's eyes flashed. When I nodded, Tara turned away.

The rest of the day passed in a haze. Sitting next to my crate, I studied until Amma returned, and then hurried to help Tara wash clothes. We worked without talking. After dinner, Amma and Abba left for Shaukat Chacha's house. Omer sorted the livestock feed outside.

At night, lying on the charpais, my thoughts churned like milk and water whisked into lassi. Why hadn't I told Tara before? She was my twin, a part of me. She snuck food to me when Amma sent me to bed without dinner. She rubbed my head when it felt heavy as a rock. There was no one like her. She played thumb wrestling with me when I couldn't sleep. We always slept with our fingers curled together. We told each other everything. We had never kept secrets from each other. She was right to be angry. I leaned back, feeling Tara's warmth and inhaling her scent. The tight knot inside my chest melted.

"That woman, what she said, it's all rubbish," whispered Tara. "You know that, right?" Her hand curled around my shoulder. "Not now, but in a year or two, I always thought we would get married together." I froze. What was she talking about? Tara shifted closer. "Zara?"

My breath jammed. I shook my head. "No, not now, not in a year, or even in two years." I pulled away. Why didn't she understand? If she didn't, who would? She had to understand. I took a deep breath. "I want more."

"What more?" Tara was up on her elbows. "Marriage will give us so much, our own homes, our own lives. Amma says so."

"Amma's wrong." I shot out. I shut my eyes. Was I wrong to want more?

"Zara, don't," urged Tara. "Haven't you learnt enough? Who's putting these ideas into your head? And what if Abba finds out? We've already lost so much."

I stared into the dark, trying to push the memory away. A few years ago Amma had been eager to grow vegetables on the patch of land behind our house. Amma's friend, Shakeela Masi, who ran a vegetable shop with her husband, had told Amma they were looking for suppliers. One afternoon when our Nani had been visiting, Amma had asked us to clear the weeds and plough the land, since the planting season was near. When Abba returned home, Amma had led him to the plot, held out the packet of seeds and voiced her idea. Abba's brows had fused like a giant centipede. He had snapped that the women in his family didn't work.

When Nani had tried to reason that the extra income could help with our dowries, Abba had growled that his family had to learn to live with what he earned. Stammering, Amma had tried to explain that she had only been thinking about how to help him. But Abba had cut her off and roared that if Amma wanted to help, she should think about how she could please her husband. And she might do a better job without her mother around. That had been the end of Amma's vegetable garden and Nani's visits.

11

A few days after Shaukat Chacha's funeral, Abba discovered an army of pests chewing on our cotton crop. We prayed, sprinkled potions and sacrificed animals, but nothing worked. Finally, Abba, along with the other farmers, rushed to our Pir with sacks of wheat. The next morning, the pest sprays that had mysteriously disappeared from the market were back in the village store.

Master Saab set a date for my exam for Class VI, giving me ninety-one days to prepare. Was it enough? I didn't know. I had never sat for a proper exam before. It could change my life. Amma had agreed to speak to Abba about my lessons if Omer promised to rank first in his class. I knew it was important for Amma that Omer topped. I pretended not to care.

A week after the storm I slipped out into the grey morning. The rooster that I throttled many times in my dreams had stopped crowing, and the baby's cries that had woken me had subsided into gurgles. I had an hour at least. Setting my book on the wooden crate, I bent my head.

A shadow fell over the open copybook. I jerked up. The sun was up in the sky. Amma peered over my shoulder with a frown. "You'll ruin your eyes with studying so much."

"I'm nearly finished." I shut the book.

"And what's all that?"

"Mathematics. I didn't have enough pages in my copybook and

needed to draw different types of shapes. See." My hand skimmed over the lines I had sketched on the dry ground.

"Rub them out before Abba returns. And what have you done to your hair?" Amma tugged at the knot. "Take it down immediately and put your books away."

"But Amma, I only have a few pages left," I protested.

"Do as I tell you. Close your books, get on with washing the clothes and then help me pack. And don't forget to put out the scraps. The cats must be hungry." She turned back.

I stiffened. The cats. Why didn't she just take them to Khalid Chacha's? Gripping the book, I flipped through the pages; at least ten questions left before the end of the chapter. But catching Amma's warning look, I jumped to put my books away.

We were going to Khalid Chacha's place for the festival of Eid-ul-Adha. Khalid Chacha was Abba's cousin and close friend since Abba had arrived in Pakistan. After marriage, Abba had moved to another village, but they had remained close.

An hour later I hung the freshly washed clothes on the washing line, careful not to tear the fraying fabric and helped Tara to pack the clothes, shoes, pickle jars and gifts heaped on the charpai. Following Amma's instructions, we knotted the bundles with thick twine. We had to pack the gifts and clothes tightly. If nothing moved, nothing would break.

Sweat dripped down my face and neck. "Let's bathe," I urged. "Omer will finish the water if he goes first, and I just hauled up a bucket this morning."

"Good idea," said Tara.

Yanking a change of shalwar-kameez from the rusty nail, I dashed into the narrow stall with Tara. After I had caught a cockroach scuttling up my calf, we kept a watch for roaches and other bugs while we bathed, taking turns.

I took one mug of water to soap myself and three mugs to wash off. Done. I slipped into my old clothes. They were fraying at the ends, but the neck was loose and sleeves short. I could breathe. The new shirt that Abba had bought for Tara and me to share this Eid had long sleeves and a high collar that bound my neck like a noose.

"Let's go stand by the door," I urged.

"Wait, take these before you go," called Amma.

I turned back and froze. Amma held out the long dark folds of two burkas. We had never worn the burka before, so why now, and in this heat? What was wrong with the chadors we took? And why the burka? It was the worst. I wasn't going to wear a burka. Never. Trembling, I turned towards Tara, but she had slipped the burka over her head. She looked like a witch.

"Why are you waiting? Hurry." Amma tugged the veil over my head and tied the strings under my chin. The heavy cloth slithered over me, and down to my feet. Within seconds I was trapped and caged. I couldn't move. It was dark and stuffy. Everything blurred into grey. Where did my hands go? I couldn't see. Or breathe.

"Amma, no," I tugged at it. She couldn't do this.

"Take it off, and you won't get another minute to study," hissed Amma.

"But why?" I whispered.

"For your own good."

"Amma, they take chadors, they don't need this," protested Omer, walking in.

"Nonsense," Amma shot back. "What do you know? Hurry and put on your shirt."

At that moment, Abba walked in, and telling Amma he had to bathe and change, he disappeared. Amma got busy laying out his new clothes.

My head was going to explode. Rushing out, I bumped into

the tonga wheel. Gripping the side, I traced my fingers over the faded wood. The invention of the wheel and axle had changed the world. I jumped aboard. Dreams were like fireflies, Nani said. They sparked and flashed in the dark. We had to grasp them, catch them. Otherwise, they would fly away. And it would be dark again.

I shut my eyes. I hiked on the narrow, winding Silk Route, passing the dense cover of the pine trees to reach the rugged terrain of the Himalayas and the Karakorum. I climbed the luminous peak of K2, jutting nine thousand meters above sea level. I sailed past the white foaming waves that rolled on the coastline of the Arabian Sea from Baluchistan all the way to Sindh, a distance of over a thousand kilometres. I flew over the glistening sands of the Cholistan desert, bordering my village, and paid homage to the silent killer. Over the centuries, the gentle waves of golden sand had dried up many rivers and destroyed many villages outside the bastions of Derawar Fort. I ran away from fields that fenced me, and the mud hut that buried me. I had speed and strength. I wasn't going to let a burka beat me.

"Hey girl, are you all right?" asked the tonga-walla as the horses reared and the tonga tilted. I nodded, leapt down and walked around. Flies buzzed around the horse's nose. Bothersome pests. Large brown eyes stared back. I ran my knuckles down the long mane. My chest tightened. Strapped to the harness, the horse followed the path chosen by the tonga-walla. About to ask if it was necessary to strap the horses, I stopped when the door banged open.

"You'll get us all into trouble," muttered Amma. "Thank God Abba didn't see you going out."

"Sorry," I murmured. Omer grinned and opened his mouth to say something, but Abba was out and bolting the front door. Seeing Omer squeeze in between Abba and the tonga-walla, I nudged Tara into the middle seat. She hated the rolling motion;

it made her sick. I sank down and jumped immediately. The plastic was hotter than burning sand.

"Zara," warned Amma. I dropped back into the seat, shut my eyes and in my mind, ran. When I ran, I could be someone else, somewhere else and far away.

"Let's go," said Abba. The tonga walla flicked his rod. The horses broke into a trot. The rickety wheels rolled past the narrow drains littered with paper and plastic. Stray, flea-infested dogs napped in the shade of the mud walls. In minutes, we had left the village behind. I opened my eyes. My backside was numb.

The mud-baked houses and bullock carts receded. Sunlight streamed clear and bright and dust particles hung in the air. The mud track ended abruptly. The tonga climbed onto the thin blade-like road cutting through the fields. At the flick of the rod, the horses quickened their pace.

It looked picture perfect. Leafy trees with knotty limbs arched over the grey, paved road. Sunlight streamed through the canopy of leaves. Beyond the woods, the fields swayed like a sea. Tufts of spiky grass bordered the road. The unfamiliar chirping sounds added a mystical touch to the otherwise silent morning. Small furry creatures scurried along the way and disappeared into the forest, out of a fairy-tale. It looked perfect, but it wasn't. Like the menacing hag who stood at the corner of our street cursing everyone who crossed her, the forest held dark secrets. Last year a young girl had taken the dare to cross the woods after sunset. She had never made it home. Abba had joined the search party. They had found her close to sunrise with her clothes half-torn and repeating silly rhymes. Some villagers whispered that the jinns that lived in the forest had possessed her.

Soothed by the rolling motion I dozed off and woke up as the tonga slowed and turned onto a paved track. Khalid Chacha's village had a gated park with swings and even a small market. Tall, slightly crooked brick houses with adjoining walls lined the winding road. I craned my neck, trying to spot the girls' school Master Saab had mentioned, as the tonga sped through the paved lanes.

The tonga stopped, and we helped Amma down. Khalid Chacha came outside, and after responding to our greeting, beckoned us to go inside. I followed Tara into a large, cobbled courtyard. Two buffaloes chewed grass and swatted flies in the near right corner and an armful of chickens pecked at scattered grain in the far right corner. In the centre of the courtyard a goat with deep eyes bleated, restlessly tugging at the rope tied to an iron hook.

I had overheard Amma say that Khalid Chacha had built four rooms in his house to please his wife. Kulsoom Chachi and Khalid Chacha had two daughters and two sons. We were close to their daughters, Saima Appi and Nazia, but only met them once or twice a year. Hearing a throaty laugh, I spun around. Kulsoom Chachi sauntered towards us. Her long, henna-dyed braids spilled over her loosely draped chador.

"Salam, Chachi," I echoed, a beat behind Tara.

"You're here, finally. We've been waiting since morning," gushed Kulsoom Chachi, clapping her hands. She trailed a finger over Tara's cheeks. "Getting fairer by the day my dear, and what's this? How pretty!" she murmured, eyeing the paisley pattern of henna on Tara's palms.

"Thank you, Chachi," said Tara. "We bought some henna for Saima Appi and Nazia too."

"You're such a sweet girl," murmured Kulsoom Chachi, "But what's this, Zara, no henna for you?" I lowered my lids as Kulsoom Chachi raised my chin. "Still running wild under the sun, I see," she said and laughed when I squirmed. "Come and meet your cousins. We'll have lunch later." I scowled as she pinched my cheek and swung away.

We settled down on the mats. Chachi had cooked pulao with chickpeas and prepared jugs of frothy lassi. Abba and Khalid Chacha discussed how to get rid of cotton pests, the hike in prices, soaring temperatures, and the preparations for the sacrificial ritual for Eid the next morning. I looked up, hearing Khalid Chacha offer Abba a job on his lands. But Abba laughed and brushed the offer aside.

After lunch, Omer escaped to the fields with the other boys. And seeing Amma's nod, I rose to help our cousins. Stacking the dishes in our arms, we walked to the washing pit.

"What? When? Congratulations!" boomed Abba, slapping Khalid Chacha on the back.

"It was rather sudden," admitted Khalid Chacha.

Amma hugged Kulsoom Chachi. "It's wonderful news, and you've shared it on such a special occasion." Kulsoom Chachi beamed.

"It's a father's dream to see his daughters married," declared Abba. "Saima Beti will live like a princess." I swung towards my elder cousin, but she looked down. How could she have agreed? She was elder to us, but only by a year or even less.

"That's what I said," chirped Kulsoom Chachi. "Such a surprise it was. I had no time to prepare. But when they proposed, I knew we had to answer immediately."

"That's not …" began Khalid Chacha.

"And how could we not?" interrupted Chachi. "The tension of young daughters ripening in the house is enough to …"

"That's enough," cut in Chacha.

"I was only saying," began Chachi.

"We have much to celebrate," Amma cut in. "Tell me what

needs to get done." Tugging Kulsoom Chachi's arm, she led her away.

Early next morning, Abba and Khalid Chacha left for Eid prayers, taking the boys with them. I came out to help Amma, but after watching the goat tug and bleat restlessly, I slipped back inside. Why wasn't I more excited? I hadn't tasted meat for months. We had received a whole raan from our landlord before the local elections last year, but nothing since his win.

Hearing Abba and Khalid Chacha return, I curled into a tight ball and closed my eyes. Silence. I heard my heart pound. Suddenly frantic, high-pitched bleats cut the air. Shouts. More bleats. And then silence. I scrambled up, peered outside and saw Chacha raise the glinting silver blade of the skinning knife, I lurched back. My gut heaved.

We had to sacrifice. But why always the poor goat? Couldn't we sacrifice what was important to us? Abba and Chacha could stop chewing the tobacco they loved. Amma and Kulsoom Chachi could stop applying the henna they loved, to darken their hair. Was I crazy to think like this? I had more questions, but no answers. When I asked Amma, she told me to be quiet and to obey my elders. It would keep me out of trouble.

Within the hour, a smell of cooked meat filled the house. When Tara came in to check on me, I doubled over, feigning cramps. When Amma opened the door, I pretended to sleep. Finally, Amma returned and insisted I come out to join the family for lunch. Unable to spin any other excuse, I trailed out behind Amma, ignoring Chachi's knowing smile. Abba urged me to taste the meat, but haunted by the image of a round nose and deep eyes, I even found it difficult to swallow the soft vermicelli pudding. After lunch, Abba and Khalid Chacha retired for a nap, while Amma and Kulsoom Chachi went into the kitchen to prepare the evening meal. Omer sprinted out with the boys again. I gave up any hope of running out and eventually Tara and I joined Nazia and Saima Appi inside their room. We sprawled on colourful blankets strewn on their charpai. Saima Appi folded her legs and laughed while her younger sister Nazia twirled around the room.

"I've got a surprise. Can you guess?" chirped Nazia and winked. Before I could reply, she had hauled out an old hookah from under the charpai. "It's all ready," she said, offering the long pipe to Saima Appi. "Come on, take a puff."

"Are you mad?" hissed Saima Appi, flushing beetroot red. "Take it back. Abba will kill you."

"He won't. It's an old one. There's hardly anything left," coaxed Nazia. She pushed the pipe towards me. "Come on, Zara, it'll make you feel better after all that food. Tara?"

Tara shook her head, but I curved my palm around the pipe and drew in a puff. Nothing. I inhaled the smoky air again and felt a rush to the head. I took another puff.

"My turn," declared Nazia and pulled the pipe back. We took turns under Saima Appi's stony glare, and in minutes there was nothing left. I grinned, feeling a heady rush melt my limbs. No wonder the men smoked it all the time. Nazia slid the hookah back under the charpai.

"No, don't keep it under my charpai," snapped Saima Appi. "And I hate that stench. Stay away from me."

Laughing, Nazia shoved the hookah under the other charpai. "It was just a few puffs." She clasped Saima Appi's hand. "Please don't be mad. I'm going to miss you when you're married and gone."

"Will you really?" asked Saima Appi, her voice softening.

"Yes," declared Nazia. She turned to us and grinned. "I must tell you that Amma became a bit hyper when she learnt that a family was coming to see Saima Appi. She insisted we had to purchase a new tea set."

I winked at Tara. Chachi had said they had no time to prepare for their visit. Why the pretence?

"For days, Amma taught Saima Appi how to pour and serve tea and make sweetmeats," continued Nazia. "But when the groom's family came to visit, and Saima Appi walked out, wearing Amma's rose coloured dupatta, everyone forgot about the tea and sweetmeats. I couldn't tell if Amma was happy or furious."

"Is that when you met him?" I interrupted.

"Who?" asked Saima Appi.

"The boy," I said. Saima Appi and Nazia giggled.

"That's funny. You think she met the boy?" asked Nazia.

"Well, you said his whole family visited," I murmured.

"No, she's never met him, but I nicked his picture from Abba's pocket," explained Nazia. "He's tall, with a long curling moustache. You know what the moustache means, right? Their family has land, lots and lots of it."

"But ..." I began.

"That's wonderful!" exclaimed Tara, and leaned forward to hug Saima Appi. I followed slowly. How had Saima Appi agreed to marry someone she hadn't ever met?

"Do you want to see Saima Appi's dowry?" asked Nazia.

"Yes," said Tara.

"You've already seen a part of it," began Saima Appi.

"What? Where?" asked Tara.

I glanced out and shook my head. Were they still going on about the dowry? I shifted forward. The sunbeams bounced in the treetops. The leaves beckoned. I wanted to run out and feel the wind on my face.

"The buffaloes," said Nazia, "One each for us. Abba bought them last month. Hey, careful. Are you hurt?"

I sprawled on the floor. My hands and feet were ice. The buffalo. It was part of my cousin's dowry. The picture of our glass-eyed, ink-black buffalo swelled and bulged inside my head. Why had Abba really bought Kullo?

12

"Phitteh muh." I muttered under my breath in annoyance as the pencil nib slipped and streaked the page. I would have to wait for Omer to return before I could sharpen my pencil. We owned one sharpener between us. Master Saab had forbidden us from sharpening the pencils with a knife blade. I rubbed my palms on my knees, shut the book, and silently mouthed the words to "Subh ki Aamad", a poem by Ismail Merathi. I continued till the end, and then again. One more time with the translation. Done. I knew the poem and its translation word for word, like a parrot. Omer had warned me not to even think of adding or deleting a letter or a full stop, because it could cost me a full mark. The exam wasn't the time to share my thoughts; it was the time to show the examiners how much of the text I had memorised. And I had done that. But I felt cheated. If the poem was all about the joy and thrill of discovering knowledge, why did the examiners want to jail my thoughts? Why couldn't I write what I really felt?

"Take a break," said Tara, applying a cool paste on the angry rash on the back of my neck.

"Can't." I shut my eyes. "But thank you."

"You're welcome. And why not?"

"Amma's there."

"So?"

"So …" I trailed off.

"Well, at least clean the sweat off your face and neck."

"Why? It's so hot I'll be sweating in seconds again."

"The heat's not good for the crop either," murmured Tara. Hearing the odd note in her voice, I glanced up. Miles and miles of lush green spanned the horizon. What was she talking about? Since our visit to Khalid Chacha's, Tara had taken over most of my chores, giving me time to study early morning and once again when Omer returned. But I still had to put my books away before Abba returned.

The earth dried up, the shadows lengthened and then receded. The village slept. I hung out the last of the damp clothes and joined Tara to knead the dough for the chapattis. Amma said the dough had to be just right: moist but not wet, soft but not fluffy, gooey but not sticky. Sometimes Amma's instructions were tougher than those in my Chemistry book. I frowned. Amma was lying on the charpai. That only meant one thing. Phitteh muh. I still needed to review two chapters of Mathematics before Abba got home.

"Oh, good you're done," said Amma. "Tara, rub my feet, and Zara, massage my scalp. My head's about to explode in this heat."

Muttering under my breath, I obeyed and perched on the edge of the charpai, trying to squash the hissing sound inside my head. I needed time to study. I dug my fingers into Amma's thick coil of hair and began to knead her scalp. Hearing a noise, I looked up. Omer had puckered up his nose and pulled his lips into a frog face. He smacked his lips like he had caught a fly. Trying to swallow my laugh, I burst into a cough and lost my balance.

"Zara!" warned Amma.

"Sorry," I muttered, not meaning it. Straightening up, I began to knead Amma's head again.

"Pranks and laughs won't take you far in your in-laws' house," said Amma. "You're not children anymore. If you're good, you'll marry well. Once you're married you have to keep your husband and in-laws happy and give them no reason to complain. You must do what they say, with a smile and without questions. That's your duty and responsibility. The sooner you understand that, the better." I rolled my eyes as Amma carried on with her favourite topics. Marriage. Duty. Responsibility. All traps. I wasn't going to fall into any of them. Why didn't Amma talk to Omer about them? Why always us? Why was Tara nodding her head in agreement? What was wrong with her?

Amma finally turned to her side. I shifted, thinking she would nap. But she sat up. "Come, we must hurry. Your Khalid Chacha is coming for dinner tonight. We need fresh vegetables. Here, take your veils. We'll go to Shakeela Masi's."

Starting to protest, I caught Tara's warning look. It was better not to say anything when Shakeela Masi's name came up. Shakeela Masi was Amma's childhood friend who ran a grocery shop with her husband, Akbar Chacha, in our village.

I had heard their story from Nani. At my parents' wedding, Akbar Chacha, Khalid Chacha's younger cousin, had stolen into the women's tent, spotted Shakeela Masi dancing to the beat of the dholak, and fallen in love. Vowing to forget her glistening skin and light eyes, he had thrown himself into card games, brawls and potent drinks, but nothing helped. When he finally mustered the courage to declare he wanted to marry Shakeela Masi, he discovered that his father had arranged his marriage to Majjo Phuppi. His father had threatened to disown him if he married out of caste, but they were unable to dissuade him, and Akbar Chacha and Shakeela Masi were married just three months after my parents' wedding. But even after fifteen years, relations were strained. Shakeela Masi and Amma remained close, but Abba kept his distance from Akbar Chacha. The story went that Majjo Phuppi started eating as consolation and vowed never to marry.

I trailed behind Tara and Amma, trying not to trip and fall. How was I supposed to walk straight under the dark folds of the burka? Amma had said I had to wear it for my protection. But I wasn't convinced. I was going to toss it into the cooking pit as soon as my exam was over. Why did I have to be protected? And from whom? The landlord? His thugs? And how were thick folds of black going to protect me? What about my family, the police or the government? *What government?* There hadn't been one for years. Master Saab said martial law was military rule that suspended the ordinary law, but others in our village whispered that martial law was a watchdog gone mad.

Crossing the lane, I walked on one side of the narrow track, staying away from the straggly beggar woman on the corner of our street. Men loitered by the tea stalls, crooning popular Punjabi lyrics. At the end of the lane, we turned right.

"In the name of God, have mercy," called a hoarse voice. I looked up and stared. A scrawny girl cowered like an abandoned kitten in the street corner. Dark, matted hair covered her pale face. She raised her hand, baring a skinny arm.

"Look away and keep walking," hissed Amma, and quickened her pace.

I stole a look. It had to be Chiragh. The gossip had spread like wildfire through our village. Chiragh had run off with a boy, Anwar. He had promised marriage but abandoned her when his parents had tracked them down. There were rumours of an abortion. Chiragh's family had disowned her and moved away. Anwar had married a girl chosen by his mother. Moulvi Saab had tried to stop Chiragh from returning to the village, but our Pir had intervened and allowed her to return, saying that if she had no man or family to protect her, he would be her protector. Nobody knew what that meant. He had two wives and half a dozen children.

Amma and her friends blamed Chiragh, saying there was no place
in our village for third-class girls, and Bari Masi had declared that
Chiragh should drown herself if she had any shame. Majjo Phuppi
had muttered something about what men got away with, and then
noticing that Tara and I listened, had hurriedly told us to make tea.

Closer now, I noticed Chiragh's jade green eyes and her dirt-
smudged face under a ragged chador.

"Have mercy," Chiragh's voice trembled as she shook the tin
bowl. "In the name of God." The bowl tipped over.

It was empty. My gut squeezed into a tight knot.

"I haven't eaten since yesterday," whispered Chiragh.

"Hurry," called Amma, turning the corner.

"Come on," Tara pulled my arm.

"Uh, wait," I wavered.

"Have mercy. In the name of God, have mercy," Chiragh's voice
shook.

I stood still. Unsure.

The jade green eyes flared for a second, and in the next instant,
dulled. "Go on, walk away," she hissed.

But I couldn't move, caught by the glint of tears in Chiragh's
eyes.

"Come on," Tara tugged my wrist. "Amma will have a, uh,
what are you, uh ... Here, take mine too." In a heartbeat, Tara
slipped her silver bracelet into my palm.

Bounding forward, I dropped our trinkets into Chiragh's open
palm and rushed after Tara. My heartbeat slammed in my ears like
a race horse. What had I done? Had anyone seen?

Reaching the corner, I twisted back. Hands clenched, Chiragh
rocked back and forth on her heels. I looked away and rounded
a bend, just missing clumps of dung. Why had I given her our
birth bracelets? They had been a present from our Nani and the

only jewellery we owned. But I couldn't have walked past without doing anything.

It wasn't enough. What was going to happen to Chiragh? How far would our trinkets take her? She was being punished. No one in our village would forgive her. I had heard stories of girls being buried alive or being set on fire for bringing dishonour on their families. Those weren't accidents. Was I part of it? I shivered, suddenly drenched in cold sweat. I had to stop thinking before I made myself sick.

Amma stopped near a vegetable stall. A dark cloth, tied to four bamboo poles, shaded the crates of vegetables stacked on a cart. A pedestal fan whirred, blowing warm air. "Salam, Masi," called a deep voice from the left. Knowing Amma watched from her 'third eye' on the back of her head, I lowered my head.

"Salman beta, you're all grown up and look so much like your father. How are you?" There was a lilt in Amma's voice.

"I'm well, thank you Masi. Amma will be out in a minute. Here, please sit."

Amma turned to us. "Not much room for all of us under this tree. Go and stand under the tent. And take your veil off your head, there's no one here and I don't want you fainting in the heat."

I lifted my veil and sighed, feeling a breeze brush my face. I tilted my face. Deep hazel eyes slid past me. Following them, I froze.

Tara and Salman gazed at each other, unaware of everything and everyone else. Their stares fused and sparked heat. If eyes could eat, they would have swallowed each other. Was she crazy? Amma would thrash her, or worse. I pinched her arm, but she stood still, staring at Salman.

"Mariam!" rang out a musical voice. "It's been too long. I didn't even see you on Eid. Where have you been?"

"Oh, it's so good to see you," gushed Amma. "We were at Khalid Bhai's for Eid. And after that, the weeks flew. I don't know where the days go!"

"Excuses, excuses," chided Shakeela Masi. "I know I'll only get time with you when we're withered, wrinkled and without any teeth. And have you thought about how we will chat then?" Amma and Shakeela Masi burst into chuckles. Stepping forward, Salman bumped against the wooden cart. The crates creaked. Vegetables rolled. I quickly pinched Tara's wrist again. Gasping, she swung towards me, her cheeks red like tomatoes.

"Are those your daughters? How they've grown!" Shakeela Masi murmured, walking over. "It's been a long time since I've seen you both. Have you met my son, Salman?" Shakeela Masi curved her arms around us.

"Salam," said Salman. I nodded, head lowered. I knew I wasn't expected to answer. I hoped Tara had the sense not to, either.

"Salman Beta, will you help me choose the vegetables?" called Amma.

"Huh, yes Masi," said Salman. He hesitated and then stepped out from behind the stall.

"Good idea," said Shakeela Masi, "And I can show your daughters some baby chicks, if that's all right with you, Mariam?"

"Yes, of course," said Amma.

Everyone moved at once, but I caught the spark between Tara and Salman. It was hot enough to fry pakoras!

"What's going on?" I whispered as Tara turned away.

"Nothing," murmured Tara.

"Girls!" called Shakeela Masi.

We scrambled after her.

13

I scooped a ball of rice into my fingertips, swallowed and chewed furiously. Abba and Khalid Chacha still argued over the new variety of seeds. Gulping the last mouthful, I looked up and frowned. The dish of rice was empty. Only a spoonful of yogurt left. I reached out, but hesitated. Omer had already put his plate down. Catching Amma's stare, I also put away my plate, ignoring my growling belly. It wasn't worth it. I squashed the urge to lick my fingers like Omer was doing. Amma never said anything to him.

"Enough of farm talk. I have some news," said Khalid Chacha. I looked up, hearing an odd note in his voice.

"What news? Why didn't you say so before?" asked Abba.

"We've fixed the date for Saima's wedding."

"Congratulations. For when?" Abba slapped Khalid Chacha's shoulder. I stared down at the tin plate. My distorted reflection always made me smile. Not this time. Had Saima Appi even met her future husband yet?

"Soon. The boy's mother insisted we keep it in late August. I know it doesn't give us too much time, but I've been saving for years."

"I've already started sewing the bed linen," said Amma.

"Thank you." Khalid Chacha smiled and shook his head. "Everyone keeps saying how lucky we are. The boy comes from an influential family with large land holdings, and is the only son. But ..." he flicked a rice grain off his shirt.

"But what?" said Abba.

"I wonder if that's enough," said Khalid Chacha. Catching Amma's hard stare, I began to stack the dishes. Tara followed.

"You said yourself it's a good family with large land holdings?" said Abba.

"Yes, it is," said Khalid Chacha. "But the boy hasn't gone to school. The times are changing, you know."

"One doesn't need to go to school to be a good farmer," declared Abba.

"I knew you'd say that," interrupted Chacha. "And I also know Saima Beti hasn't gone to school, but she's still young. I had decided to say no, until Kulsoom reminded me that she was expecting our first child at her age."

"She's right," said Amma.

"It's an excellent match, Bhai. God willing, everything will be fine," said Abba.

"We'll celebrate this news with a sweet dish," said Amma. "I'll bring out the kheer."

"Yes, do that," said Abba, and turned to Khalid Chacha. "And stop worrying. You are doing what's best for your daughter."

Watching Amma pass out the milk-rice pudding in red clay pots, I hoped there would be some left for us. I sat across from Tara and filled two large bowls with water. Tara took out the black washing soap and began to scrape and soap the dishes while I rinsed and dried them. I tried to catch her glance, but she stared down. Abba and Khalid Chacha still chatted.

"I'm glad Omer Beta is continuing his studies," said Khalid Chacha. "He'll go far."

"You think so?" said Abba. "I could do with his help in the fields."

"There's still time. Let him finish secondary at least."

"Yes, I know," replied Abba. He grinned. "As you say, 'The times are changing.'" He laughed, and Khalid Chacha joined in.

"Mariam Behen," said Khalid Chacha. "This kheer is outstanding. And the vegetable pulao was excellent. You have to teach Kulsoom how to make it."

"She makes it well enough, Bhai, but thank you." Amma smiled.

Khalid Chacha laughed. "There you go, you two, always praising each other. I'll tell her that. She'll be pleased, hearing it from you."

"Did you buy the vegetables then?" asked Abba.

"Yes, I took the girls with me and left Omer home."

"How much did you pay for the onions?" asked Abba. "The prices have spiked because of a rumour that there's a shortage."

"It's the same with sugar," said Khalid Chacha.

"I got a good rate at Shakeela's," said Amma. "It was the same as last month."

"Ah, Shakeela," drawled Abba. "Is she still flitting around like a queen bee? I don't know how her husband puts up with it."

Glancing up, I caught Tara staring at Abba. Catching my eyes, she lowered her head.

"She's not like that," protested Amma. "She's my childhood friend and married to Khalid Bhai's cousin, after all."

"A marriage that nearly destroyed our elders," growled Abba. When Khalid Chacha shook his head, Abba grunted. "All right, I won't tease, but tell me, how are they?"

"They're well," said Amma. "They've expanded their shop."

"Damn traders," said Abba. "Of course they'll do well. They cut our rates to increase their profits. No ties to the land."

"How can you say that? They work hard like us," protested Amma.

"Work hard?" Abba's jaw tightened. "What do you know about that? Hard work happens in the fields and under the hot sun. Our sweat is the proof of our hard work. We don't sit under the cool shade multiplying profits."

"Let them be. Why do you care? We have nothing to do with their family now," soothed Amma.

"Yes, thank God we don't," muttered Abba. He stretched his legs. "Now, are you going to get me a second helping of the kheer, or sit and listen to us talk the whole evening?"

Amma got up. "Khalid Bhai, would you like another helping too?"

"No, none for me behen, feed your husband. He works hard under the hot sun," quipped Chacha, laughing. Abba grinned.

"You okay?" I murmured. I watched Tara pick up a freshly rinsed plate and dip it into the bowl of soapy water. She nodded without looking up. "What's wrong?" I pressed.

"Nothing." Tara glanced up and dipped another clean plate into the bowl of dirty water.

"I do have eyes," I said.

"Not human eyes," shot back Tara, "You have these eagle eyes." She yelped as I pinched her arm. "Stop it, your hands are soapy."

"Then stop putting the clean plates back into the dirty water," I shot back, and Tara gasped.

"Is everything all right?" called Amma.

Nodding, we straightened up.

I waited until Amma had joined Abba and Khalid Chacha again, "Tell me what happened."

Tara squeezed her eyes and shook her head. "I don't know."

"Tara," I prodded.

"Okay, okay," Tara pushed her breath out. "I think I'm going crazy. What did happen, nothing, right? We went to the shop, bought the vegetables and came back. But something …"

"Salman?"

"I don't know. Yes, maybe, or something about him." She turned a plate over and began to trace circles along the rim. "We didn't even talk, you know. It's crazy. But ..."

"But what?" Keeping an eye out for Amma, I leaned forward.

"There was something, a click. I felt a rush. It felt right. For a few moments there was nothing in the world except him." Tara set the plate down and locked her fingers. "I better stop. What am I saying?" She took a deep breath. "I felt ..."

"Like eating kairis?" The words were out before I could stop myself.

"What?" Tara stared at me.

"Nothing," I mumbled. "Listen, I think he felt the same. He couldn't take his eyes off you. Even when you turned away."

"Did he? I don't know. Leave it. Didn't you hear what Abba said? It's clear he doesn't like their family."

I glanced at Abba. Tara was right. If Abba made up his mind about someone, he rarely changed it. "I can't believe it," I murmured finally. "Saima Appi's agreed to marry a man she hasn't even met."

"Why strange? That's the way it has been and will be. Hurry. Amma just looked over again." Tara started to stack the clean dishes.

"But imagine going to live with a stranger, a family you don't know? It's creepy. What if Khalid Chacha and Kulsoom Chachi have chosen someone whom Saima Appi won't like?"

Tara shrugged. "They're her parents. They know her. I'm sure they've chosen someone she'll like."

"But getting married to someone you don't know at all? Haven't talked to or spent time with?" I continued. "Our religion gives us that right, you know."

"Shush, you'll get into trouble," warned Tara. She paused. "Didn't you see Chiragh?"

"She looked awful," I whispered.

"She did," nodded Tara. "But why did you have to give her our bangles? They were the only jewellery we had, and what will we tell Amma if she asks about them?"

"I was giving only mine. She looked like she hadn't eaten for days."

"She was with that boy, Anwar. He dumped her."

"He betrayed her."

"Zara!"

"He did. I'm not saying what she did was right but …"

"Exactly," said Tara. "It's up to us. We can get married like decent girls."

"Or what?" I narrowed my eyes. "You sound just like Amma. You do," I insisted when Tara scowled. "Yes, Chiragh was with that boy, but he was with her too. What about that? We're celebrating his marriage, but shunning Chiragh like she has a disease. That's not right."

"She was with him; she did things she shouldn't have."

"She loved him."

"Love?" scorned Tara. "Love is a sickness. That's what Amma says. It makes you sick."

I stared back. What did I know about love? Nothing. Amma said love was a sickness. Like malaria. It gave shaking chills, high fever, sweats, headaches, nausea, vomiting and pain. We had to stay away from it. "Well, Akbar Chacha fell in love with Shakeela Masi, didn't he?" I began. My thoughts raced and stumbled. I shook my head. "I'm not saying our parents don't know better than us, perhaps they do. But what happens if they're wrong? What if they make a mistake?"

"They won't. Why do you keep saying that?"

"Because."

"There is no because." Tara shook her head. "It's better to let our parents decide. They've seen life and they know people. What do we know? We're lucky we have parents who care about us and want us settled."

"But still, what if they don't choose the right person for us?"

"Shush, what's gotten into you?" Tara glared.

"No, tell me," I pressed. "If our parents choose whom we marry, do they support us or take us back if it doesn't work out? Or are we forced to live with the mistake that they've made? Look at our neighbour, Samina Masi. How happy is she with her arranged marriage? Her husband beats her nearly every day. We hear her cries, her pleas, begging him to stop. We pretend nothing is wrong and she goes on making excuses about the bumps and bruises on her face and arms. Remember how he accused her of tempting the landlord's thugs and beat her in front of the whole village? He's a madman. Everyone knows it. She's left many times, but her parents always send her back."

"Nothing like this will happen to us," began Tara and tugged my arm. "And our parents are different. Now come and help me alter the wedding clothes. And we need to practice our kikkli. It's the first wedding in our family. We'd better enjoy it."

I hesitated, wanting to say more, but gave in. Tara was right. We had to practice our kikkli. We performed the kikkli at every wedding in our village. I loved spinning round and round to the drum roll. We held each other's hands tightly, not letting go. For minutes, many minutes, our feet flew, our heartbeats thumped, our rhythm were in sync and the universe spun until there were only Tara and me in it. It was our dance. We were better than all the other girls at kikkli. No one could beat us at it.

14

The sun roved the sky like an angry dragon. Even at night, the air burnt. Nothing moved, and it hurt to breathe. Sticky and sweaty the whole day, I was unable to get rid of the stink that clung to my skin. The lemon halves I stole to rub in my armpits didn't help, and I sucked on raw onions to cool my parched mouth. But despite the heat, I smiled when I saw fields of white cotton puffs stretching to the horizon. It was going to be a full harvest. Abba told Amma he would be able to purchase a goat.

A week later, we awoke to a growling rumble and rushed out. Dark clouds hovered on the horizon like winged demons. Rumours of black magic flew through the village. Abba slaughtered a goat and scattered the raw meat around the fields to ward off evil spells. Amma sprinkled brewed potions on the crops. At mid-morning the clouds burst open.

Abba, along with other farmers, hurried to our shrine to donate a ration of wheat from the depleting stock. But even the Pir had no control over the downpour, and by early evening Abba was trying to salvage what he could. By dusk, rumours of another failed harvest gripped our village. The next morning, the sun was out again. Abba said it was too early to tell whether the downpour had ruined the crop.

A week later, we left for Khalid Chacha's village to attend Saima Appi's wedding. Lulled by the swaying motion, I slept through the journey and only woke when our tonga, heaped with bags and bundles, rolled to a stop outside Chacha's front door, decorated with gold and orange garlands.

After a heavy lunch, relatives and friends gathered in the courtyard. I sat with other girls on the floor while the elders sprawled on charpais. Amma went inside to help Kulsoom Chachi, Abba stepped out to finalise the details of setting up the marriage tent, and the boys ran out to play in the streets. Relatives shared old anecdotes and spun puns and jokes until the air pulsed with a buzz.

"I ask you, do we have any reason to celebrate our Independence? It's been thirty-six years. Where do we stand? What have we achieved?" boomed a voice. I swung up to see a bald man in a dhoti, shaking his fist.

"What do you mean?" questioned an old bearded man, lounging on the charpai.

The bald man snorted and looked around. "I mean here we are, still travelling on donkeys and horses, while some countries have sent missions into space. What then have we gained independence from?"

"Our neighbours are no better," countered the bearded man.

"*That's* our problem. Why do we always look only to our neighbours? What about the rest of the world?"

"Why are you getting so excited? God would have given us wings if he wanted us to fly," muttered the bearded man.

"God did better, he gave us brains to think!" declared the bald man.

"Didn't the American space station crash?" piped in another man with a moustache.

"See?" smirked the bearded man. "We have forgotten our limits. God punishes those who forget their limits."

"The Americans have already landed on the moon." I froze. Had I spoken aloud? I couldn't have. I had. The words were out. They floated in air for a split second and then rushed back at me, drenching me with icy water. I froze as Amma's hand clamped my wrist. Where had she come from? Had she heard? My face flamed.

"Huh, who spoke?" The bearded man looked around.

"Mariam Beti, was that your daughter?" The bald man leaned forward. "Did she say something?"

"No, nothing, Ramzan Chacha," reassured Amma. Her nails dug into my wrist.

"She should know better than to interrupt her elders." The bearded man frowned.

"Oh, let her speak," persisted the bald man. The murmurs died. I stared down, willing the ground to open up and swallow me. What had I done? What if someone told Abba?

"There's no need," began Amma.

I pushed my breath out. I hadn't done anything wrong.

"There is," urged the bald man. He looked at me. "Zara Beti, Tell us what you said."

"You're spoiling her," hissed Kulsoom Chachi, watching the bearded man shuffle away.

"Go on, tell us what you said." The bald man smiled.

Someone grunted. I shut my eyes, feeling like a prisoner in front of a stoning squad. They would blame me no matter what I said. But I had to speak. I couldn't let them think I couldn't talk. I had things to say for myself and for other girls. "One small step for man, one giant leap for mankind." I opened my eyes, looking up at the bald man. "These were Neil Armstrong's words when he stepped on the moon ten years ago."

"That's enough," snapped Amma.

"Well said," exclaimed the bald man. "Something to think

about, no?" Some heads nodded, but others shook and muttered disapprovingly.

"And how does she know all this?" questioned the man with the moustache.

"My son, her brother, he tells her what he learns in school," said Amma quickly.

The man frowned. "And you allow it? That's not wise. There's a reason we don't send our girls to school. They start to think for themselves and …"

"Everyone can think what they want to," interrupted Kulsoom Chachi. "But not at my daughter's wedding. Let's talk about more cheerful things." She turned to Amma and shook her head. "Take charge before she ruins your name. Better to nip such thoughts in the bud," she murmured.

Mango-gold rays flooded Khalid Chacha's courtyard the next morning. Girls laughed and chatted, but I sat alone, convinced that I had a talent for annoying everyone. Even Tara had looked at me accusingly. When a friend of Saima Appi's, dressed in a fussy peacock dress with a matching headband, had wheedled us to play a game, I had cringed. What a stupid game. Some of the girls weren't even ten years old. Could they think of nothing else except marriage?

The game had begun. The girl who picked the most original colour would be the winner. In turn, each girl shouted out the colour of the bridal dress she wanted at her wedding. The girls played enthusiastically, calling out "pink", "red", "maroon", "orange", "yellow", "green", "crimson", "fuchsia", "purple", "light blue, no, midnight blue". Hesitating for a split second, I had shouted "white", and in the next instant, catching the horrified faces, knew I had gone too far. White was the colour of death. Stuttering, I had tried to explain they had misunderstood. I meant a school uniform, I had said it as a joke, but the girls had stared blankly, turned their backs on me and moved closer, leaving me alone. Even Tara left me to join the girls.

Now, I watched the girls gather around the dholak, a curved, wooden drum we had decorated the night before with shiny gold ribbon. We only heard the dholak playing at weddings. Amma declared that all music was haram. She had made Abba give away his radio to the village tea stall. But every time I heard the strum of a musical instrument and caught a tune, I couldn't help but feel a thrill. The fast rhythm made my heart beat faster and my blood rush inside me.

I gazed around. We had worked the whole night to decorate Khalid Chacha's red-brick house. A canopy of gold and orange flowers stretched over the charpai where Saima Appi would sit. A bright tent cloth, supported by bamboo poles, divided the courtyard into two halves, one for men and the other for women. Shouts and laughs filled the air. Chatting and smiling, women hurried in through the doorway. The crowd swelled. Naheed Akhtar's "Tu Turu Turu Tara Tara" blared from the record player. Chacha had rented the player at the request of the groom's family.

The chatter ceased as Saima Appi appeared in the doorway. Someone shut off the record player and the girls sprang into action. One girl beat the two-sided drum. Another girl struck the wooden sides of the dholak with a spoon and the remaining girls, including Tara, burst into a popular wedding song. Suddenly wanting to be part of the group, I tried to edge towards Tara, but a crowd blocked my way.

Kulsoom Chachi tossed one end of a chador to her mother and they held the chador over Saima Appi's head. The crowd of women parted as Saima Appi took faltering steps towards the charpai set in the middle of the courtyard.

My gut churned. What had they done to her? She resembled an evil clown. The ghost-like foundation had cracked. Blood red lipstick smeared the side of her lips and her lowered lids glinted like two eerie, blue half-moons. A thick gold chain looped from her nose to her ears, reminding me of a buffalo being led away by its owner. Her red and gold dupatta was plastered to her forehead and strands of frizzed hair had escaped from the sides. Women elbowed each other, trying to close in on her. Between the beat of the drums and loud singing, shrill voices rang out.

"The shirt, too tight."

"The clothes can't be new. Did they alter her mother's clothes?"

"She has gained weight, hasn't she?"

"The lipstick is too bright."

"Look at the gold. How many tolas?"

"Her family's or the groom's?"

I shrank back and was swept into a surge of women moving forward.

"Come, come," they urged, "The dowry's on display."

Swept into the crowd, I reached the back of the tent and gaped. More than half a dozen metal trunks crammed with clothes, shoes and bed linen were lined up on the tables. Gold jewels heaped inside shiny casings glinted in the bright light. Boxes of glasses, dinner sets and pots and pans were stacked beside a sewing machine, a washing machine and a water cooler. A bicycle and a water buffalo were tied to a tent post.

But something was wrong. The groom's family huddled to one side, with heads bent close together. The groom's mother shook her head, whispering agitatedly. The family members nodded their heads, listening to what she said.

Kulsoom Chachi, with Amma close behind her, hurried forward. "Is anything wrong?" she asked, with a bright smile pasted to her face.

For a second, nothing happened. Then, pandemonium.

"Anything wrong, you ask," hissed the groom's mother, wheeling to face Kulsoom Chachi. "You tell me! Did you call us over to insult us?" She pointed towards the table. Her lips thinned into a tight line.

"What?" stammered Chachi, her voice trembling.

The chatter stopped. Everyone shifted closer and whispers spiralled as the groom's mother, with her eyes flashing fire, walked up to Chachi. "Our elders insisted on this match, so I went along. You should be grateful we didn't give you a list for a dowry, but this," She pointed to the tables again and spat on the ground. "Why, for generations brides have brought bricks of gold and plots of land into this family. My father gifted ten cattle, ten gold bricks and even a motorcycle for my dowry. And you dare to dump a grocery store on us?"

Gasps erupted. Twitters swelled. Amma caught Kulsoom Chachi as she swayed. Chacha stepped up, a dark flush staining his face. "Please," he began. "Don't say this, not at this time. We'll give you whatever you want, just accept our daughter." A shout announced the arrival of the Moulvi Saab. It was time for the Nikah.

When the groom's father beckoned, Khalid Chacha sighed and followed the Moulvi Saab to the women's side of the tent, for Saima Appi's consent. Head lowered under the heavy dupatta, Saima Appi nodded three times to the Moulvi Saab's question and burst into tears. Boys cheered, men thumped each other on the back, and girls and women clung to each other, crying and sniffing. A woman with a shrill voice began to stuff Saima Appi's trembling mouth with sticky sweetmeats.

Hearing the call of food being set out, I slowly followed

the crowd towards the heaped tables. Khalid Chacha had hired caterers to provide biryani, naan, chicken korma and purchased mangoes as a special treat. I grabbed two mangoes to share with Tara. We hadn't tasted a ripe mango in years. The landlord's thugs guarded the orchards like their women.

After lunch, the women retreated to sit on the charpais. Tara and I stood behind Amma. "Kulsoom Behen," called out a plump woman wearing a deep purple, sequined chador, ambling over. "Congratulations! Sorry, I'm late. But why do you look so glum? It's your day to rejoice and dance. What a catch, and so much land! Hearts must be burning with envy. Protect yourself from the evil eye, I tell you."

"Thank you Sakina Behen," Kulsoom Chachi sniffed and clasped her friend's arms.

The woman turned to Amma, "Mariam Behen, how are you?"

"Thank God, all is well," answered Amma. "How have you been?"

"I'm well, all's well," said Sakina Masi. "Ah, and are these your daughters?"

Amma glanced back in surprise. "What? Uh yes, Tara, Zara."

We stepped forward. "Salam," I said, a beat after Tara. My skin crawled under the woman's lingering gaze.

"Pretty," murmured Sakina Masi with her eyes still on us. She smiled at Amma. "Tell me, Behen, have you started talks anywhere?"

"Talks?" asked Amma.

"Yes, about their marriages. You have started thinking, haven't you? And what better occasion to talk about marriage than at one." She chuckled. "They look old enough. Good height and slim. And thick long braids, I see. Can't stand girls who primp and fuss before marriage."

My breath squeezed. Not again.

"Marriage," echoed Amma looking at us. "But they're only …" her voice trailed off.

"If you're interested, I could bring my sister to your village. We're looking for a girl for my nephew." Sakina Masi beamed. "I like the look of the fair one."

"Is this the nephew who works in the factory?" probed Kulsoom Chachi.

"Yes, the same one," said Sakina Masi.

"Hmm, I've heard good things," said Kulsoom Chachi.

"I'll talk to their father," said Amma slowly.

"Yes, talk to him," interrupted Sakina Masi. "We are close to Khalid Bhai. Why, our family ties go back for generations."

"Their father will be pleased," said Chachi.

"Yes, but …" Amma paused.

"It's best to marry them off before they start thinking too much," declared Sakina Masi.

"Yes," murmured Amma.

The pale sun had begun to sink when Khalid Chacha, along with the rest of his family, departed, to escort Saima Appi to her in-laws. Amma and Abba had gone to rest inside, leaving us to clear the courtyard. I rolled up one mat after another and stacked them all in one corner.

"Let's take a break," I said and sank down on the last mat. We had won the kikkli competition, but suddenly it didn't matter. Without a word, Tara dropped down, close to me.

"Did you have fun?" I asked, after a pause.

"Today?" whispered Tara and when I nodded, she shrugged. "I don't know." She paused. "Fight for your dreams, Zara, go to school."

"Huh?" I swung round to face her.

"I mean it. You will, right?"

I nodded and squeezed Tara's hand. "Yes, but tell Amma."

"Tell her what?"

"About Salman."

"You're crazy," murmured Tara.

I shook my head. I wasn't crazy. The day before we had left, Salman had come to deliver a jar of pickles. Amma had gone inside to empty it, and I had stood guard while Tara had rushed to the door to meet Salman. They had less than a minute before I had warned them that Amma was coming out. Turning away, Tara had tried to hide her flushed face and had hurried inside.

"She'll understand," I urged now.

"Understand what? What can I tell her? There's nothing to tell. If only I'd met him sooner!" Tara's voice trailed off.

"There's still time," I said.

Tara shook her head.

Silently we watched the sun sink into the shadows.

"I should light the oil lamps," said Tara.

"I need to take the floral strings down," I said.

We sat still. Finally, Tara shifted closer and rested her chin in her cupped hands. "Promise me," she whispered urgently.

"What?"

"Promise me, we'll always be close, and be there for each other after marriage, even after children, and when there's no one else."

"Yes." My voice cracked. I tried again. "We will. I promise." I reached for Tara's hand. It was ice cold. I held it tightly, afraid of my thoughts.

Were our lives a race from our parents' house to our husbands' house? Done and over, even before we had started to run, understood what we were capable of, or what we wanted from life?

15

I crooked my head, sniffed, and rushed to the wall. Clusters of bright mustard flowers dotted the fields. Perfect. I was in the mood for a feast. I inhaled, savouring the sharp whiff of mustard greens. Amma would cook them with makai ki roti if Omer asked her to; that was the only way to get anything out of Amma these days. After topping the class exams, Omer was slacking off on his chores, yet getting whatever he wanted these days.

But I owed him. He had defended me when Amma declared she would not tell Abba about my lessons and it would be better for everyone if I stopped them altogether. He had threatened to quit school when Amma announced I couldn't take the exam. On the day of the exam, he had waited for Abba to depart for the fields before rushing out with me, leaving Amma muttering that I would bring nothing but shame to our family.

Master Saab, a tall man with silver hair brushed back against dark weathered skin, had been waiting for us. Since it was a school holiday, there was no one around. "It's good to put a face to a brain," he had said with a smile, and told me to follow him inside the well-lit room with two large windows. I had stared at the rows of desks and chairs. Where had they come from? Beckoning me to sit behind a desk, he had set out the paper in front of me.

Trying to sit comfortably on the wooden chair, I had stared at the lines of typed questions in black ink, and broken into a sweat. And then without warning, my mind shut off. Dark waters crashed into me, and smothered my breath. Black. Cold. Clammy. I had looked around blindly. What had I been thinking? I had been a fool to think I could ever go to school.

I had shut my eyes and heard Nani's voice: *Dreams were like fireflies. We had to grasp them. Catch them. Otherwise, they would fly away. And it would be dark again.*

Drawing in a deep breath, I had read the first question and begun writing.

ॐ

"Zara." Hearing Tara's voice, I jumped down from the wall.

"The change in the wind, do you feel it?" I burst out.

"Yes I do, but why do you have that funny expression on your face? There's a ton of work to finish. Come and help me." Tara dropped the freshly peeled potato into a bowl of water and reached for the basket, but I slid it away. "Hey, stop that!" Tara protested.

"Let's run out," I urged, gripped by a current. I wanted the fields all around me. And the bleeding had finished. I was free for some weeks.

"Run out?" Tara rolled her eyes. "Didn't you hear Amma? We have to peel the potatoes, air and mend the winter blankets, and prepare the room for …" she stopped abruptly.

"For Sakina Masi's visit?" I shook my head and grasped her arm. "Tell Amma about Salman. You have to tell her."

"No." Tara looked around quickly.

"I think he loves you." There, I had said it. Amma would thrash me for saying it.

"Love is a sickness, Amma says." Tara's voice wavered.

I paused, aware of her eyes on me. Amma did say love was

a sickness, but was it? Authors had written about it. Artists had painted it. Poets had sung it. I had seen a flash between Tara and Salman. Was that love? I didn't know. Did Tara? Didn't she have the right to find out? "I think he's serious," I whispered.

"Why? Because he sent a foolish poem?"

I shook my head, remembering the tightly folded paper note tied to a small rock that I had spotted in our courtyard the day we had returned from Saima Appi's wedding. It must have been tossed over the wall. Ignoring Tara's warnings, I had dashed to unfold the paper.

Come, my love, take care of me,
I am in great agony.
Ever separated, my dreams are dreary,
Looking for you, my eyes are weary
All alone I am robbed in a desert,
Waylaid by a bunch of way words.

"It's one of Bulleh Shah's poems," I had exclaimed, and gripped Tara's hands. "It has to be from Salman."

"He said he would write when he came to give the pickles." Tara had clasped the note to her chest.

"But Bulleh Shah? He knows Bulleh Shah?"

"It doesn't matter," Tara had muttered before tucking the note inside her shirt.

Now, catching the strain in Tara's eyes, I shook my head. "It's not foolish. You have to tell Amma. I will support you, and so will Omer. If Amma knows how you feel, she will help you. She will have to. Salman is her childhood friend's son."

"You think I should? You really think there's any chance?" whispered Tara. Her eyes searched mine. "I try not to think of him, but it's impossible not to."

"You have to believe there's a chance," I began, and tugged at her arm again. But come, let's get out. It will be fun. And we haven't been out in months."

Hesitating for a split second, Tara sighed, "Okay, but only if we finish the game of hide and seek that we started last time. And remember what you said, the winner gets away with not doing any work for one day."

I grinned. "Done. You can peel one more potato, while I take out the blankets. We can mend them once the musty smell has gone."

Minutes later, I raced out, with Tara behind me. Amma had gone over to Nasreen Masi's with a platter of rice, hoping to cheer them up. The village grapevine had been feeding on the constant clashes between Nasreen Masi and Bari Masi, her mother-in-law. We knew Nasreen Masi didn't stand a chance.

I sprang up, feeling lighter and taller. I jumped higher, wanting to brush the leafy treetops. I couldn't ask for more. I had taken the exam and given my best. I didn't care what Amma said. I would go to school and win a scholarship to college in Lahore. No, Karachi. It was a bigger city. I knew I could do it. Then what? Work? No, I would go for my Master's degree. I wanted to be a scientist, an astronaut; to discover, and explore. How would my village look from space?

"What's the plan?" asked Omer as we ran up to him.

"Hide and seek," I said. "We never finished playing." I nodded at Tara, who had caught up.

"That's babyish," protested Omer. "Let's cross the river instead. The water has gone down, and there are enough rocks for us to make it across."

"I'm not going anywhere near that river," I declared. I still had nightmares about the time I had accepted Omer's dare to cross the river. Following him, I had leapt over the rocks and slipped. The current had swallowed me in seconds. I had gone down until I felt Omer's hands hauling me up. Now I shook my head. "It's two against one, and you're IT! Count up to two hundred before you come to look for us. No, three hundred. Turn around now."

"Fine," Omer frowned. "But this is the last time. And stay clear of the orchards. The landlord's men are out today. Understood?" He swung back and began to count, "One, two, three, four."

I spun around to run, but before I could take the lead, Tara caught my arm. "I have an idea," she whispered.

"Huh?" I wheeled back.

"Let's hide by the water tank near the landlord's haveli, but take different routes to get there. I'll run through the forest, and you cross the fields."

"Alone?" I stared at Tara in surprise. We never ran alone.

"Yes. When Omer sees only one of us running through the fields, he'll start to search here. He'll never think one of us has dared to cross the forest alone. And that will give us time to meet by the water tank and find a good hiding place."

"Shouldn't we stay together?" I frowned.

"Come on, it'll be an adventure," urged Tara. "And you keep on saying I should learn to be more adventurous."

"Okay, but I'll go through the forest. It's longer, and I run faster."

"Sure? You don't like the woods."

"I'm sure." I wasn't. But I ran faster than Tara. I nodded. "It's still light, so it should be okay. Let's go." Seeing Tara take off, I swung towards the forest. I raced through the dark woods, zigzagging to dodge low hanging branches and vines. I flew over dark shadows and deep ditches. I felt the chains break and the shackles dissolve. The air roared in my ears. My lungs blew fire. I could do anything I wanted. Coming out of the forest, I dove into the springy tuft of grass by the water tank.

My breath came out in spurts. My heartbeat slammed in my ears. Rolling on my back, I stretched my arms and legs. Cotton clouds floated in the azure sky above. The ground shifted, and I tilted with it. My feet touched the sky. I shut my eyes. I felt light as a cotton puff floating in the wind. Free.

"Come out. Where are you? I know you're here," called Omer.

I jerked up. My head reeled. How had Omer gotten here so quickly? Where was Tara? I made my way around the water tank.

"I know you're here, so come out," yelled Omer. I stayed still. He had to catch us. I wasn't going to make it easy for him.

"Ah there! Got you!" Omer grabbed my braids.

"Ouch, don't pull."

"Where's Tara?" Omer eased his grip.

"I don't know. I was waiting for her."

"She ran with you."

"No, I came through the forest. She took off through the fields and was going to meet me here. Didn't you see her?"

"No," snapped Omer. "I overheard you two whispering about 'forest and water tank' so I followed, without even looking at the fields. Why did you run alone?"

I stared at him. "Tara wanted to, she said she wanted to trick you. Let's look around. She must be hiding." I pulled away. Goosebumps popped up on my arms and neck. Where was Tara?

I raced around the water tank. Omer ran to the boundary line of the forest calling Tara's name. Within minutes he had turned back and caught up with me. "She's not here. She would have come out by now. Let's go back to the fields. Are you sure she didn't follow you?"

I swallowed the lump in my throat and nodded. "I only took off when I saw her racing across the fields."

"Well, she's not here. We have to get back. She could have fallen and hurt herself. Hurry."

I nodded. "Tara!" I yelled, beginning to run.

"Shush!" warned Omer. "Do you want the entire village to come out? You walk along the path, and I'll cut through the fields. Don't worry, one of us will find her."

I rushed over the narrow dirt path, my eyes searching for Tara, my ears straining to hear her voice. Within minutes I had reached the end of the track. I stopped, and my eyes blurred. There was no sign of Tara. No sound.

Omer had stopped crisscrossing the fields and was staring at the swaying crop. I hurried over to him. "Where is she?" I burst out. My chest felt hard and tight. I could barely breathe. Where was Tara? Where had she disappeared? Was she trying to trick us?

Omer's eyes swept the fields again. "Run to the house. Tell Amma we can't find Tara."

"What?"

"If Amma's not home, go to Nasreen Masi's. But don't tell anyone else, only Amma. Now run."

"No, I'm not going back without Tara."

"You have to. Amma will know what to do. Hurry. Tara might be hurt. The quicker you go, the faster we'll find her."

"But ..."

"No buts. Do it for Tara's sake."

I swallowed my protest. Omer was right. Eyes pinned to our hut, I raced back and burst through the door.

"Where were you?" snapped Amma. "I came out and there was no one. What's wrong?" Amma had leapt up from the charpai and gripped my hands.

"Tara, we can't find her. Omer is calling you."

"No!" cried Amma. "No, please, dear God." She moaned and

shut her eyes. Murmuring prayers, she pulled her chador across her head and shoulders. "I'll go. You stay here." She pushed her feet into her slippers. "Bolt the door and open only for Abba, no one else. You hear?"

"I want to come too."

"No, just do what I tell you." Giving me a hard stare, Amma rushed out.

I shut the door and stumbled inside. I thrust my head into our blanket. It smelt of Tara, of me, of us. I draped the blanket around my body, clenched the river stones in my fist and began to pray. The magic would work. It would bring Tara back. I murmured the prayers over and over again and then shot up. What was I saying? I didn't know what I said. I began to pray again, but this time in my own words. I would be good; I would do anything God wanted me to do. Anything. Everything. In exchange, I just wanted Tara back, safe.

I lurched up, hearing a banging on the door. How much time had passed? "Who is it?" My voice broke as I ran to the door, still clutching the river stones.

"Zara?" called Abba. "Open the door." I fumbled, trying to open the latch, and lurched back as Abba shoved the door. It slammed against the wall and splintered. Heat stung and slid down my cheeks. "What's wrong? Why are you crying? Tell me. Zara! Stop it." Abba slid the bolt back as far as it would go and grasped my shoulders. "Where's your mother? What's happened? I can't help if you don't tell me."

"Tara! We can't find her."

"Since when?" A vein throbbed in Abba's neck.

"Afternoon. Amma's gone to help Omer search." I shivered.

Abba clamped his hands on my shoulders. "We will find her, but do as I tell you." His eyes scanned the horizon. "I have to go out after them. Keep the door bolted and stay inside. Don't open it for anyone. If someone knocks, pretend you're not home. You hear me?"

"Yes," I whispered, but Abba had already disappeared. After fastening the door, I leaned against the cold wall. Darkness flooded the sky like water soaking parched earth. I sank to the ground and locked my arms around my knees. My head throbbed.

"I have an idea. Let's surprise Omer," whispered Tara. I opened my eyes. It was deafeningly quiet. I was hot and damp. The river stones had fallen to the ground. Dazed, I stared at the empty courtyard. Where was everyone? Chickens scurried around looking for the feed. Kullo grunted and tugged against the rope restlessly. Kittens meowed. Pins and needles stung my feet as I struggled to my knees. Where was Tara?

16

Thud. Thud. The pounding. Was it in my head? Why was I on the floor?

"Open the door," yelled Omer.

Leaping forward, I flung back the latch. Abba rushed inside and I sagged against the wall. Abba had found Tara. She was back.

The next instant I spun around. Why was she in Abba's arms? Why was Abba's shirt covering her? Abba hurried inside, with Amma right behind him. The door shut.

"What's going on?" I burst out.

But before Omer could answer, Abba was out again, his face darker than dusk. His eyes blazed at me. "Where's the water? Didn't your mother tell you to get some?" He swerved towards Omer. "I'm going to Amjad Chacha's place. Follow me." He strode out.

"What's going on?" I repeated. Words stuck to my throat.

Omer shook his head.

"Tell me."

"You don't want to know." Omer shut his eyes.

"I do." Suddenly I didn't. Fear crawled over my windpipe like a centipede.

"Tara … she … there was blood, around her mouth. I thought she was dead, but then she moaned. They raped her, said Abba, but she's alive. Thank God! Are you okay?" Omer's hand was on my shoulder.

"Raped?" I clutched Omer's arm. "Who?"

"Don't know. Abba found her. I'd better go. He's waiting. We'll talk later."

17

Seconds after falling into the dark waters, my mind had flashed like lightning. On Omer's dare, I had leapt across the rocks and missed. I had sunk into the rushing current, blinded by a red-hot glare, until Omer had hauled me up, swearing at me for jumping like a girl. And then everything had blurred until I coughed, spat out water and gulped mouthfuls of air. Now, it was happening again.

My mind flashed over the jumbled bits of the afternoon in slow motion, then faster and faster. I had urged Tara to run out. Tara had zipped off through the fields. I had raced through the forest. How long had I watched the clouds drift past? How long had we searched for Tara? Amma had cried out when I had said we couldn't find Tara – had she had a premonition?

I shuddered and squeezed my eyes. I couldn't have heard right. Not rape. It happened elsewhere, in other villages, to other girls. Not in my village. Not to Tara. Not to my twin. It was a mistake. I hadn't heard right. Not rape.

I drifted, surfaced, drifted off again, and woke with a jolt. I was hot and clammy. The sky was inky black. I edged towards the door and pushed, but it was bolted from the other side. There was no sound. When the sky lightened to the shade of an onion peel, I finally slept. A hand was on my shoulder, shaking me. I pulled away and burrowed into the charpai.

"Zara, wake up," urged Omer.

I winced at the morning glare. How long had I slept? I scrambled up. "Tara? How is she?" I searched Omer's face, willing him to say there had been some mistake, and that Tara was okay.

"Still inside," said Omer. "Amma's saying we can't see her. Abba left early, so I let you sleep, but you should get up before he returns. There's work to be done."

I nodded, and struggled to stand up. Seeing darkness, I took a deep breath. It would be all right. Abba must have gone to the police to register a case. They would hunt out the beasts that had attacked Tara. Waiting for Abba to come back, I swept the floor, cleaned the chicken coop, and bathed Kullo.

It was early afternoon before Abba returned alone. "I'm going to Khalid Chacha's," he told Omer. "Go to the market and get some vegetables for dinner. I'll be back before evening." I stared at his back. Had he gone to the police? Where were they? Why was he going to Khalid Chacha's? I dared not ask. We never asked Abba where he went or what he did.

"Abba, Tara?" My voice broke.

Abba stopped and stiffened, but didn't look back. "Your Amma is taking care of her."

"I want to see her," I whispered.

"Me too." Omer stepped forward.

"No, she's not strong enough. You can help by doing what your mother tells you." Without another word, Abba strode out.

"Tara must be better, or he wouldn't have left," said Omer.

I nodded, feeling my throat tighten. Why wasn't Abba saying more? Why the silence and secrecy? Had he gone to the police? They must be trying to find the men. I forced myself to get back to the chores: I folded the clothes, fed the animals, and sorted the rice grains. Someone banged on the door, but I ignored it, remembering Abba's warning. I was cooking the evening meal when I heard the door creak open.

"Fill this with water," called Amma, and slid the tin pail outside. "Leave it by the door when you're done."

I tilted the water drum to fill the bucket and hauled it to the door. Thinking fast, I called out, "Amma, I've got it."

"Leave it outside," shouted Amma.

I stood silently. Hearing the latch lift, I pushed against the door. "I want to see Tara," I began.

"Are you mad?" Amma shoved the door back. "Stay out. Didn't you hear your Abba?"

"Amma, please." My voice shook. "I have to see her. She's my twin. She needs me."

"No. Go away. I have enough to …" A low moan muffled Amma's voice. Was that Tara? Before I could call out, Amma had pulled the pail inside and shut the door.

Flames burst in front of my eyes. No one was going to keep me away from my twin. I pounded the door and kicked it.

"Amma," I cried. "Open the door, open it."

"Zara, don't," warned Omer, coming up behind me.

The door opened an inch. "Stop this madness," hissed Amma. Her eyes were bloodshot, and her lips pulled back in a snarl. "Tara doesn't want to see you. You made her go out; you made her run alone. Should I tell your Abba that?" The door slammed shut.

Staggering back, I stumbled. It wasn't because of me. My mouth tasted of ashes.

"Zara," said Omer. His voice came from a distance. His hand curved around my shoulder, but I wrenched away. It wasn't because of me.

Abba returned late afternoon. "Zara," he began, his hawk-like eyes searching my face. "Clean the family room and make something for dinner. We have guests coming."

The crimson moon hung low when the guests gathered in the courtyard. The men ate in silence, except for Abba, who said he wasn't hungry. I looked around and released my breath.

All these men knew us. They were like family. It was going to be okay; they would make it okay. Tara and I were like their daughters. They had said that so many times. Amjad Chacha was our old neighbour. He had carried us on his shoulders when we were younger. Tara and I had always marvelled at his wriggly moustache that curled like two worms. Riaz Chacha was our relative. He had always brought us candy. He sat opposite Abba, who was squeezed between Khalid Chacha and Moulvi Saab, a religious scholar who led the Jummah prayers in the mosque.

I squirmed, thinking of the times Tara and I had mocked Riaz Chacha's tinted glasses and his tight T-shirts. He worked as a driver in the city but returned for holidays and family gatherings. Riaz Chacha had been married to Kulsoom Chachi's sister. I had heard that the death of his wife during childbirth had driven Riaz Chacha to the city. When they finished eating, the men strode inside. The door shut. At Omer's nod, I darted forward. It was okay to eavesdrop. I had seen Amma do it when Abba went inside with his friends. We had a right to know what they said. Tara was my twin, closer to me than anyone else. I pressed my forehead against the door and peered through the crack in the door.

18

"It was important we meet tonight," began Moulvi Saab. His gaze settled on Abba. "We will hear Yaqoob Bhai and then decide what to do." He paused. "Yaqoob Bhai?"

"Uh." Abba glanced up, and without meeting anyone's eyes, looked down again. He began to talk in a flat voice. I strained to hear.

I shivered. My belly twisted like a wet cloth being wrung dry. Tara had been raped and rolled into a shallow ditch. If the wind hadn't puffed out the corner of her kameez, Abba might never have found her. Why hadn't I heard her cries? Why hadn't I known something was wrong? I was supposed to know. She was my twin.

Abba stopped talking. The men muttered and whispered. Someone recited a prayer. Moulvi Saab murmured something, but Abba shook his head.

Moulvi Saab cleared his throat. "You said there were two?" When Abba nodded, everyone started talking, but Moulvi Saab raised his hand, and they stopped. "So we agree there's no use in going to the police now?" I gasped as everyone nodded. Not go to the police? What were they going to do? "Then we must find the culprits. I'll make an announcement tomorrow. Every man and boy over twelve years old must come to the mosque to take an oath on the Qu'ran that he knows nothing about this heinous crime. We will investigate anyone who refuses to comply. We will find the criminals and then take them to the police. We will make sure our daughter gets justice." He thumped his fist on his knee.

"Yes, we must," said Khalid Chacha.

"Yes," murmured Amjad Chacha.

"Moulvi Saab," began Riaz Chacha. "I hold you in the deepest regard, but there's a hitch."

"What hitch?" demanded Moulvi Saab.

"Well," said Riaz Chacha looking around. "I agree that we must punish the criminals. I pray they burn in hell, but you must understand that Yaqoob Bhai has more to lose."

"More to lose?" echoed Khalid Chacha. "What has happened is not Yaqoob's fault. We can't let these dogs get away."

"If we don't catch them, they'll strike again," added Moulvi Saab.

"Listen to me," said Riaz Chacha. "Do you know anything about what's happening in the country? There are reports of new laws. I don't have the full details, but there are rumours."

"Rumours of what?" demanded Khalid Chacha.

Riaz Chacha looked at Abba steadily. "New laws that say the victim has to prove rape. Otherwise, he or she can be found guilty."

"What are you talking about?" Abba frowned.

"I'm saying Tara Beti will have to prove she was raped or they can accuse her of zina," Riaz Chacha burst out.

A sharp shiver grazed my arms and neck. Cold and clammy, I pressed against the door. Zina. It was part of the Hudood Ordinance. I knew that much, but what did it really mean?

"I don't believe you," spat out Abba.

Riaz Chacha shook his head. "It's not up to me. It's the law. If we can't prove rape, the criminals can accuse Tara. She can be convicted. You know, zina is a crime against the state. And there are new laws – about the testimony of one woman only being half of that of a man in a court. Even if Tara Beti testifies she was raped, it will not be enough."

"Don't worry Yaqoob Bhai, I'll make sure that never happens. We have our own justice system here; it will go in our favour," declared Moulvi Saab.

Riaz Chacha frowned and shook his head. "It's risky. New courts are being set up. And if we do as you say, what guarantee is there that anyone will own up? Can we force anyone to come to the mosque and admit to this crime? You say you will investigate, but what can you do against them? What can you prove?" He glanced around, but no one spoke. "Sorry, Moulvi Saab, but an oath will make no difference because the criminals won't think twice about lying. What's happened can't be changed. We need to think about the future."

"There might be some truth in that," began Amjad Chacha, and pulled at his moustache when Moulvi Saab and Khalid Chacha stared at him. "My wife was saying that if this news gets out, Yaqoob Bhai won't be able to hold his head up. People will make up stories."

"I don't care about people," burst Abba. His eyes blazed.

"You need to care. You have a responsibility to your family name and to your other children," reproached Riaz Chacha. "What's happened has happened, but think about your other daughter. She can marry anyone now, but who will want to marry her once you speak out? Even close relatives break off relations at such times. Have you forgotten what happened to Chiragh?"

My mind reeled. Chiragh? What did Chiragh have to do with this?

"Riaz Bhai has a point," declared Amjad Chacha. "Once the news gets out, people will manipulate the story and draw their own conclusions. There is no better example than Chiragh's parents.

Such good people, but they had no choice except to disown their daughter and leave their village. The villagers don't forgive or forget such matters. Samina said that there's a rumour brewing."

"What do you mean?" Khalid Chacha frowned.

"People saw Yaqoob Bhai leave the village in a hurry," said Amjad Chacha. "No one has seen Mariam Behen since yesterday. And anyone on the street can see Yaqoob Bhai's door is half broken. When someone banged on the door, no one answered. People add one and one and come up with four. My wife said it would be different if Tara had died." Abba growled, and Khalid Chacha frowned at Amjad Chacha, but Amjad Chacha continued. "We would have buried her body with honour. But now you risk dishonouring your family name."

"Amjad!" warned Abba.

"How can you say such things?" warned Moulvi Saab. "Our faith doesn't support such thinking."

"I'm sorry," said Amjad Chacha. He wiped his eyes and looked around. "Tara is like my daughter, and I could kill those dogs. But my opinion won't change anything. Our women uphold our family honour. Once it's gone, nothing can bring it back."

"Exactly! That's what I've been trying to say," exclaimed Riaz Chacha.

My breath choked. What were they talking about? We had run out to play. What did honour have to do with it? Omer grabbed my wrist as I sprang up. "Not now," he mouthed. When I resisted, he shook his head and whispered, "Please, we need to listen."

Shakily, I leaned against the door. I wasn't going to let them get away with this. They weren't going to make up lies, not about Tara.

"How can I let it go? My daughter's innocent. How will I live with myself?" protested Abba. "What if this happens to someone else's daughter tomorrow?"

"Think of your own family before thinking of others," advised Riaz Chacha. "Do you want to ruin your other daughter's life?" He pulled out a handkerchief from his pocket and wiped his face. "Once you tell everyone, there will be no turning back. In the end, there won't be many who will support you. They'll find ways to blame your family. Why did you let your girls out? Why didn't their mother control them? What were they doing in the fields? Did Tara know those men from before?"

"How can you say this?" argued Moulvi Saab. "The girl's been wronged."

"You are an exceptional man," said Riaz Chacha, turning to Moulvi Saab. "But are most men like you? No. We have to consider the risks. Remember Tara was found in our landlord's fields. What if the landlord's thugs raped her? Can we force them to come to the mosque and take an oath?" He turned towards Abba. "You will have exposed the incident for nothing and shamed your family. And our landlord will never forgive you. He might send his men after you, your other daughter, or even your wife."

"That's true," murmured Amjad Chacha. "We must think this through."

"You haven't done anything to upset the landlord, have you?" asked Khalid Chacha, looking at Abba.

"No, no," muttered Abba, but then frowned. "I complained about not being allowed to sell my crops in the open market at the tea stall the other day. You don't think?"

"No." Khalid Chacha shook his head. "This was not revenge. How would they recognise your daughter? It was an accident. Tara was alone, and they knew they could get away with it. But it's true, the landlord has eyes and ears everywhere. You need to be careful."

No one spoke. Abba closed his eyes. Khalid Chacha clasped Abba's shoulders and turned to the other men. "We can't do much against the landlord. He has relatives in the army, and we know who rules our country. We can't afford to upset him. We don't know what his men did to Amir Buksh when he tried to pay off his debt. No one has seen that man for weeks. His poor wife and children are too afraid to step out. No one is allowed to bring them food. They are starving inside their own home."

Moulvi Saab turned to Abba. "I can't foresee what might or might not happen. I can't force the landlord's men to come to take an oath. But I can advise and support you. I promise you that I will do my best to ensure your daughter gets justice."

Abba gazed at Moulvi Saab for a few moments, then turned to Khalid Chacha. "Tell me, what should I do?" Khalid Chacha opened his mouth to speak, but then shook his head and looked away.

"I'll tell you," interrupted Riaz Chacha. "I feel your pain. I can help you. There is a way out – a good one, for the whole family. But first, you must understand that you will find no peace if you allow Tara to stay here."

"Huh, what do you mean?" Abba stared at Riaz Chacha.

"Well," said Riaz Chacha and rubbed his goatee. "If the truth gets out, which it will if Tara stays here, you risk losing your honour in this community. You might even be forced to leave. Best is to send her away."

"Send her away? How can I send her away, where?" Abba looked around, but only Riaz Chacha met his eyes. The room was silent again.

"My friend, listen to me," said Riaz Chacha. And with his eyes fixed on Abba, Riaz Chacha began to talk.

19

I reached out, but Tara and Omer vanished. We had been feasting on kairis a few seconds ago. Where were they? Rubbing the grit out of my eyes, I pushed myself up. It was past dawn. Why was it so silent? In a flash, I remembered.

I flew towards the half-open door. The room was empty. Quiet. Nothing was out of place. The blankets were neatly rolled up on one end of the charpai. I gripped the door to stop from swaying. Where was Tara? My eyes blurred, seeing darkness. The sound of bats – hundreds, thousands of bats beating their wings filled my ears.

"Zara?" Hearing Omer's voice, I spun round.

"Where's Tara?"

Omer shook his head. "I tried to stop them, but Abba wouldn't listen. They left early in the morning, taking Tara with them. Remember what Riaz Chacha said?"

Riaz Chacha's stories of the rich and powerful and their mansions, factories, planes, powerful cars and holiday homes had finally caught Abba's attention. Seeing that Abba listened with rapt interest, Riaz Chacha had tightened the noose. The rich needed an army of maids, cooks, drivers, guards and gardeners to run their houses. And if one was intelligent and hardworking, there were opportunities. Abba had nodded, agreeing with Riaz Chacha. And that's when Riaz Chacha had gone in for the kill. His friend's friend worked in one of the best maid agencies, and they were looking to hire local maids. If Abba agreed, and he would be foolish not to, he could recommend Tara. She would be safe, earn money, and even be able to send some home. It was the best solution for a girl in her situation. Listening to Riaz Chacha's smooth voice, I had begun to tremble. Did Abba not know what the rich did to their maids? But wait, Omer had promised to stop Abba.

"Zara?" Omer's voice broke into my thoughts. "Are you listening? After the meeting, Abba and Khalid Chacha left to call the agency. When they returned, Abba insisted they had to leave immediately. There was a maid's position open in a businessman's house. I tried to stop them, but …"

Dazed, I stared back. Did Omer not remember? He had brought home the newspaper from school. The headline had screamed "Girl Dies from Burns". The newspaper reported the story of a twelve-year-old girl working as a maid in the city. Her employer, some official's wife, had tied the servant girl's hands and feet together like they were twigs, emptied the kerosene tin on her, and set her on fire for not sweeping the house properly. The girl had died within minutes. She had been from a village close to ours.

"Zara," Omer reached out, but I stepped back blindly.

"They took her away?" I whispered and shook my head. It couldn't be true. But Tara was gone. We had never been apart before. How could Abba and Amma have taken her away?

Omer shook his head. "You heard what the elders said. The new laws are against us. And if the news gets out, we lose our honour and risk shaming our family name."

"And selling Tara into slavery, that's not shameful?" My lungs spewed sparks.

"I tried to stop Abba," protested Omer. "I blocked his way, but he pushed me aside, saying I was a child and wasn't helping. Then

Amma accused me of upsetting Tara and making her cry. They left without letting me see her."

Unable to stop trembling, I gripped the door. Omer had promised me that he would not let them take her away. I wanted to scream at him. I wanted to race out after my twin. I wanted to thump the ground and shout out what Amma and Abba had done. But I stood, doing nothing. I shut my eyes. Omer was right. Tara would get no justice here. I slumped against the door, wanting to squeeze into a hole and hide. Chickens scurried close to the charpai. Pale light fluttered on my lids. I squeezed my lids tighter. I wanted to jump into the past, shut the lid, and never come out.

I felt Omer's hand on my arm. "Listen, we'll find out where she is. I promise." I looked up, and Omer nodded. "Kulsoom Chachi is coming over. She'll be arriving soon. I'll stay with you until she arrives, then leave for the fields. The crops are in danger of being flooded."

"I don't care. This isn't right," I whispered. Not waiting for Omer to respond, I turned away. I shivered under the hot sun. This was my village, obsessed by honour and shame. Fathers had hacked their daughters into mince, buried them alive, or drowned them for shaming the family name. The men got rid of anyone that threatened their family honour and family name.

Amma and Abba would hide the rape. They would pretend it never happened. But how was I supposed to forget Tara? What if it had been me? What if I had been raped and not Tara? Would Amma and Abba have abandoned me? Would Tara have let them do that?

I had to get Tara justice. Who could I go to? Friends? Who? We had none. We had never been allowed to make friends or get close to outsiders. Family? I could go to a relative. Majjo Phuppi? No. She would tell Abba immediately. Police? There was no police station in our village. The nearest one was two hours away. I had overheard tales of what happened at police stations. And what if

Riaz Chacha was right and Tara was unable to prove it was rape, then what would happen?

I couldn't go to anyone. Not my family, nor the police. There was no help. I was alone and trapped, with dark, gritty thoughts jamming my head.

Kulsoom Chachi arrived later in the day, and complaining that she was exhausted from the journey, went to rest inside. I rinsed the dishes, swept the courtyard, and finally crouched to wash the clothes by the stone pit. I flipped the basket over and gagged, seeing Tara's torn, blood-stained pants. Crawling to the toilet, I retched until my gut stung.

By afternoon, it began to rain, but there wasn't a cloud in the sky. When Amma and Abba didn't arrive by evening, I began to pray they had changed their minds about leaving Tara at the maid agency. I would forgive them. They had to bring her back. She had never been away from her home and her village. She had never been away from us. This was crazy. She was their daughter, their better daughter. They wouldn't get a better daughter than Tara. She obeyed them, did her chores without complaining, and kept no secrets from them. She was part of them. How could they put her to work in a stranger's house? I lay awake unable to sleep, until my thoughts curled like wisps of hazy smoke.

The next morning the sun was out, but it drizzled at the same time. By afternoon, sticky, moist heat flooded the courtyard. Kulsoom Chachi still slept. Omer had missed school, left to work in the fields and returned for lunch. Finished with the chores, I didn't know what to do. I hadn't opened my books for days, but I didn't want to. For once, I didn't care about my studies. Nothing mattered except getting Tara back.

I tried not to feel anything and get on with the chores, but when I opened or shut my eyes, the afternoon flashed to mind over and over again, until my head burst into flames, my limbs jammed up and I couldn't move. I slumped. Exhausted. Was Amma right? Had Tara run out because of me? I shivered in the heat.

Hearing the rattle of the tonga wheels, I leapt up. The door rattled and opened. A figure in a black burka staggered inside. Amma. She was alone. Claws pinched my breath.

"Amma," I burst out, running up to her. Did she still blame me? I gasped as Amma pulled me close, but hearing Abba's voice, she let go instantly.

"See what you can do with these. I'm going over to Moulvi Saab's and then to the fields. Remember to bolt the door." Setting down half a dozen baskets, Abba strode out.

"Where's Tara?" I burst out, staring at the tinsel covered baskets. I swung to face Amma. "You were supposed to come back yesterday. And what are the baskets for?"

"Shush," said Amma. "Not now." She pushed her veil off. Dark shadows smudged her eyes.

"Amma, you're back," said Omer, walking out of the room.

"Yes, thank God," said Amma. She ran a hand over Omer's head. "Abba's also back. He's gone to meet Moulvi Saab."

"And Tara?" I whispered.

Amma glanced quickly at the door and then back. "Your Abba decided that."

"What?" I demanded.

"Amma, sit down. You must be tired," cut in Omer. Handing Amma a cup of water, he led her towards the charpai. "Did you go to the agency then? Has Tara started working as a maid?"

"No." Amma sighed, "But it's all well now. God has answered our prayers." Her knuckles strained as she gripped the cup and took a quick sip.

"So where is she?" probed Omer.

Amma took another sip. "I can't tell you."

"You have to," I shouted, and immediately slapped my hand over my mouth. "Sorry."

Omer threw me a warning look. "Amma, we're worried," he said.

Amma sighed and looked at us. "If I tell you, you can't repeat a word, understood?"

"Yes," said Omer and I together.

"I'll have to stop if your Abba returns," muttered Amma. She murmured a prayer into her cupped hands and blew on us. "It was afternoon when we reached the maid agency. We were exhausted from the journey and waiting to meet with your Riaz Chacha's contact at the maid agency, when someone called your Abba's name. It was Imtiaz, Abba's childhood friend, whom he had recently met over Eid. He worked as a mechanic in the city and his business had been thriving until a month ago, when his wife was run over by a bus, leaving him with three young children, and the youngest one not even a year old. The children wouldn't stop crying for their mother. He had stayed home for a few months, but now his savings had run out. He was in despair because his mother was too old to take care of the children, and they weren't sure they could afford the agency."

"What does this have to do with Tara?" I blurted out.

Amma's voice dropped to a whisper. "We didn't say too much, but Imtiaz's mother was so loving and affectionate towards Tara. She kept saying that Tara reminded her of her daughter-in-law. When Abba finally confided why we were there, Imtiaz and his mother were horrified and most sympathetic. Drained by the journey, Tara was asleep by then. And that's when Imtiaz's mother begged me not to register Tara in the maid agency. I understood then." Amma's voice trailed off.

"Understood what?" asked Omer.

"No," I burst out. They couldn't have. Fear gagged my breath.

"Your father said it was for the best," whispered Amma.

"What are you talking about?" asked Omer.

"How old is he?" I gripped the charpai.

"He's much younger than your Abba, and that's good enough." Amma's eyes flashed.

"Good enough for what? What are you talking about?" Omer burst out.

"They married Tara to Abba's friend," I whispered. I stared at the baskets wrapped in tinsel. There had been similar baskets at Saima Appi's wedding.

"You didn't." Omer clutched Amma's arm.

"Yes, we did, and it's best for everyone," said Amma.

"Why did he want to marry Tara? Why didn't he hire a maid?" asked Omer.

Amma's eyes hardened. "Don't ask stupid questions. A wife will serve him much better than a maid would. He's a man who helped us when no one else did. He's married to your sister now. She is lucky to get another chance. He is a good man, a generous man. There was no need for it, but he even sent gifts. A watch for Abba, a radio, and …"

"I thought he didn't have money," I interrupted.

Amma shook her head. "Try to understand. Your Abba was under so much strain because of the crops, and then with what happened. We have to thank God for this blessing. The Nikah ceremony took place last night, and we caught the night bus back to the village."

"But Tara was just …" began Omer.

"Stop," Amma flung his hand away. "Don't say that word. You have no idea what it means. You don't understand this world. Abba said it was a miracle that a man like Imtiaz had agreed to marry Tara. She's happy now. He lives in the city, has a house, a job."

"He's as old as Abba. He needed a maid, not a wife," argued Omer.

"That's enough." Amma took a deep breath. "Be happy for your sister. She has been given a chance for a new life." Turning to me, Amma beckoned and her voice softened. "Come here, Zara, my daughter. I've missed you so much."

Without resisting, I let Amma pull me close. It had been years since I had been in her arms. Maybe Amma was right, and Tara was safe. At least she wasn't working as a maid and being beaten or abused. But she had just been raped. And now she was married to Abba's friend. My gut twisted into a tight knot. Amma said Tara was happy. Was she really?

"You are so precious," whispered Amma in my ears. Her lips brushed my forehead. Feeling oddly comforted, I pushed my face into her shoulder, soothed by the warmth of her body. I inhaled the childhood scent. The tightness in my chest melted. I was home. This was home.

"You want to make me happy, don't you?" murmured Amma. Unable to answer, I nodded. "Such pretty hands you have," whispered Amma, and lifting my palms, she kissed them. "I'll teach you to put henna on them. What do you say?"

I jerked back, my breath caught. "Henna? Tara loves henna," I choked.

"Yes, but you are her twin, her half." Amma pressed her lips to my forehead. "Life has cheated me from preparing for one daughter's wedding, but I have you." She sighed.

I stared at Amma. What was she talking about?

"It's for the best," murmured Amma. "Your Abba sent word to Sakina Masi. They're coming to see you tomorrow."

20

"Your other daughter's marriage, very sudden, no?" asked Sakina Masi.

Tin cups clanked. "Oh sorry," Amma set the tray down. "Will you have some tea?"

"I will, I will," purred Halima Masi. "First the dessert and then the tea, what are you trying to do, fatten us up before the marriage negotiations?" She laughed, and Sakina Masi joined her.

I dug my fingers into the jute knots. How could this be happening? I was on display, like goods for sale. No, goods weren't covered under chadors. Fury surged from my belly to my chest. I had to do something. Shifting on the charpai, I breathed out. I had rights. Had Amma forgotten? They were printed somewhere in some moth-eaten books, hidden away. I had to find them. They wanted a fight. I would put up a fight.

"Here," said Amma, handing over the cup.

"So your husband must have been in the midst of negotiating Tara's marriage when I met you at Khalid Bhai's?" asked Sakina Masi. "Funny, it didn't seem like that ..." Her voice trailed off.

"You know how it is. I couldn't have said anything until it was final." Amma flapped her hands. "Things happen when they happen. You see, her father had already given them his word." The charpai dipped as Amma sat down.

"True." Sakina Masi nodded. "Why, I was married at twelve.

My grandfather had promised me to his friend's son when I was just five. My mother howled until she lost her voice, but there was nothing she could do."

"Yes I remember," interrupted Halima Masi. "You gave us all such a shock, wanting to ride the groom's horse."

Sakina Masi smiled and cleared her throat. "I know it's soon after Tara's marriage, but I hope we can have your other daughter. You are doing the right thing, and we are in a hurry to negotiate."

Right for whom? I clenched the jute weave.

In exchange for getting to hear details of Tara's marriage ceremony, I had allowed Amma to braid my hair with flowers. Abba had left earlier, saying he had to work in the fields. But that hadn't stopped Amma. She had lined my eyes with surma and draped my head with a heavy maroon chador speckled with gold work. Once Sakina Masi's family arrived, Amma had led me out. The slight pressure on my arm had been warning enough. I had to behave or else.

Seeing me walk out, Halima Masi had lifted the chador to exclaim, "Ah, what pretty eyes, but uh, the complexion, no, no, it won't do."

"It will clear," Amma had assured her. "She spends too much time in the sun. I was the same way."

Halima Masi had raised her hand to pat my cheek and made a clucking sound. "Make sure she stays inside from now on. She won't be getting out after marriage, and really, the groom can't be fairer than the bride, can he?" Everyone had laughed again. I had clamped my lips together to stop myself from nipping her fingers. Now, trying to ease my breath, I blew through my nose, and the dupatta puffed out softly.

"Yes," said Amma. "He has a decent job, and it's a good family."

Lifting my head, I tried to focus. What were they talking about?

"So they're based in the city then?" asked Sakina Masi.

"Yes, the boy is. It was such a rush, and so much to do." Amma coughed.

"Here, have some water, Behen," said Halima Masi.

"Thank you," said Amma.

"So, what were you saying about your son-in-law?" probed Sakina Masi.

"Tara's husband, he works in the city and is well settled ..." Amma trailed off.

"I was hoping for that." Sakina Masi smiled. "He can help then?"

"Help?" asked Amma.

"Yes, with the dowry. I mean you must have married Tara off with one. I've heard how much these city boys demand. But now that he's part of your family, he can surely help out."

Had they seen the fields of damaged crops? My eyes stung. I wasn't going to cry. Not in front of them. My throat itched, and it hurt to swallow. I sneezed.

"I should take her inside," began Amma.

"We should also leave," said Sakina Masi, and looked over. "Halima?"

"Yes, yes," said Halima Masi. "I'm glad we came, so I won't waste time and come straight to the point. I like your family and your daughter, but my son is a rare jewel. One in a million."

"No need to be shy," said Sakina Masi. "Tell them frankly. You have a daughter and a dowry to worry about as well and ..."

"We've made a list. It should make it easier for you," interrupted Halima Masi's husband, speaking for the first time.

"A list?" murmured Amma. Paper rustled.

"It's all written down, for your ease, of course," said Halima Masi. "Now if you think you can manage, we can finalise the details. Right, Sakina?"

"Yes, that's right," replied Sakina Masi.

"Thank you, Behen," said Amma and paused. "I will look at it. I mean we will, when Zara's father returns."

"Do that," said Sakina Masi. "But we want to reach some agreement, and soon. We had hoped your husband would be home, but …" She cleared her throat.

"He had some work, urgent work, but I will talk to him as soon as he returns," said Amma.

Charpais creaked, voices died, and the door shut with a thud. I bolted up, and the chador dropped to my waist. Gulping mouthfuls of air, I drank in the colours around me; they were sharper and brighter than before, the grass greener, the sky bluer. I wasn't going to be caged again.

"Don't you worry," muttered Amma, walking over. "If not here, then somewhere else." She patted my arm. "I've heard your Zubaida Masi's cousin is in despair. The poor man has been married for two years now and still no child."

Zubaida Masi's cousin? Poor man? What was Amma talking about?

"The Pir told him that his wife is all dried up inside. She'll never be able to give him a child. Tragic, but lucky for us. Can you blame him for wanting a second wife? I'll ask Zubaida to come over. Now go on and get changed. You don't want to ruin the dupatta." She gave me a slight push.

I shivered at the look on Amma's face. Not a week since Tara's rape and her forced marriage, and Amma wanted me gone, married to anyone she could find. Silently, I wheeled round and walked away. I wasn't Tara. I wasn't going to let Amma get away with it.

21

Zubaida Masi never came over. Amma learnt that she had picked the daughter of a well-off farmer for her nephew. All the village women attended the wedding but Amma stayed home.

Wary of Amma's hard eyes and fast hands, I kept my distance from her. It was the only way to avoid a shove or a slap. When she came out, I hurried inside. When she came inside the room, I rushed out. Amma muttered and fumed about my lessons. They were a waste. They weren't going to help me in life. She was going to teach me how to cook curries, prepare soft chapattis, mend clothes and embroider my wedding linen. She was going to show me how to be a good wife and a good daughter-in-law. She was going to turn me into the best daughter-in-law in the village. No boy would ever pass me over.

While Amma ranted, I slipped into a safe place in my mind. When I woke up I saw Tara. I heard her voice, felt her warmth, inhaled her scent and clung to her memory like it was a boat in a stormy river. Did Abba, Amma or Omer not miss her? How was she? What did she do the whole day?

Even though I tried, I could do nothing right. Amma complained that I dusted carelessly. When I cooked, I kept forgetting to add salt. I washed the dishes, forgetting to scrape off the grease. I swept the courtyard, spreading the dust and leaves around more than before. I washed the clothes without rinsing out the soap. I made tea forgetting to add sugar, or added double the required amount of sugar.

Amma beat me with her chappli and made me sit on the wooden crate. I didn't care. I was inside my safe place. I wasn't going to get married, and I wasn't interested in hearing about the muggy heat, the pests, the silt in the water, the dust, the hike in vegetable prices, the stench from the rubbish dump outside, or any new marriage proposals she was trying to arrange for me. I wanted to talk about Tara. I wanted to know when she would be coming back or when we would go to visit her. But Amma's steely eyes gave no clues, and she refused to talk about Tara.

Some days I awoke convinced that I had imagined the dark afternoon and Tara was still with us. In confusion, I would start to search for Tara; run to the wall and back. I would hurry inside the bedroom and out, pace around the courtyard and back to the wall, tracing and retracing my steps, until my head spun and Amma's sharp voice snapped me back to earth. Finally I would slump down and wrap my arms around my knees.

I hadn't talked to Tara before she left; I hadn't said goodbye to her or hugged her. We had never spent a day apart. How could Amma and Abba have abandoned her? Some days I felt the walls drawing closer, choking my breath, and I would rush out to gulp fresh air. But Amma never let me go far. I was forbidden to leave the house.

Every evening, leaving Amma to wait for Abba and Omer, I retreated to the room. But lying on my charpai, I couldn't sleep. Tangled bits and pieces of that afternoon flashed like sparks in my head. There had been a flush on Tara's face and an edgy flicker in her eyes. Was Amma right? Had I told Tara to come out into the fields? Who had said what? I couldn't remember.

Two weeks after Amma's return, Zubaida Masi zipped in again, bursting with news. The government had approved a gas pipeline for our village as part of a five-year development plan. A dark jeep with tinted windows had raced into our village at dawn. The villagers had thronged to watch officers in khaki uniforms and long boots march across the village grounds, carrying beeping tools and metal instruments. The officers spoke Urdu, which only a handful of our elders understood. Saraiki was the popular language in our village. Ignoring the crowds and questions, the officers retreated to the guesthouse. The village grapevine blazed that maybe change was coming.

But the following afternoon, the cleaning woman told everyone she met that the officers had woken up past noon and demanded a full breakfast. Their room had reeked of smoke, and when she had poked in her broom to start cleaning, half a dozen dark glass bottles had rolled out from under the bed. After breakfast, the officers had sped off, without tipping anyone and raising clouds of dust.

Amma listened till the end and then spun a lie. I stared at her in disbelief as she told Zubaida Masi that they had married Tara to an eligible city boy. The proposal had come through Khalid Chacha's relatives. The groom's family had insisted on a hasty marriage since their son had to take up a job. They had no choice. The boy was a good catch.

The banging began soon after dawn next morning. I opened the door to a crowd of Amma's friends. Gossiping and laughing, they crowded on the mats and charpais, demanding answers. Under Amma's direction, I distributed small packets of round nutty sweetmeats, but the sweets failed to satiate their appetites and the women pressed her for details. How had we managed to find such a catch for Tara? Who had arranged the meeting? When were Tara and her husband coming to visit? When would the celebrations take place? Amma tried to distract them with chai and more food and withdrew to the cooking pit. Abba offered vague and lame explanations, but some questions had no answers, and after a few hours the women left with pursed lips and angry eyes.

The next afternoon Omer returned from school with torn and dusty clothes. He stomped into the room saying he wasn't hungry. When Amma demanded to know what was wrong, Omer confessed that he had punched a boy for calling Abba a miser for not spending on his daughter's wedding. A fight had broken out, and other boys had joined the scuffle. The boys had backed off when Master Saab threatened them with suspension.

A few weeks later I was back on my crate, punished for burning the sweet rice that Amma had told me to cook for some distant relatives who were coming to see me. I had pleaded with her to stop them, but she had ignored me. When I swore I wasn't going to meet them, Amma said I didn't have a choice. I had to show her that I did have a choice.

"Zara," whispered Omer. "Can we talk?" I swung my head up. Omer wasn't supposed to talk to me while I sat on my crate. Busy studying for his exams, he hadn't spoken to me for days. But he had promised to find out more about Tara. Had he found out something? "Master Saab heard back from the school." Omer gripped my wrist and beamed. "They've checked your paper. You didn't forget, did you? You got ninety-one percent! It's one of the best scores. Master Saab is thrilled. He said that if Abba allows it, you can start the school term in January!"

Dazed, I stared back. What was he saying?

"Zara?" Omer's voice floated near me. "Did you hear what I said?"

I shook my head. "Are you sure?" My voice wavered. I had forgotten about the test. Was he making it up? I hadn't hoped to get over eighty percent. No one ever had.

"Yes, I am sure. Master Saab showed me your paper. And guess what?" whispered Omer.

"Omer, you're back?" called Amma. "Why are you talking to Zara? She's punished. Don't you need to pack?"

"Salam, Amma. I was telling Zara about how to milk …" began Omer.

"She has enough to do," cut in Amma. "She'll be making sweet rice again, once she's told me how sorry she is for what she did. And don't you have to leave for Khalid Chacha's soon? Abba said he has arranged for your travel. Eat something and then finish your work. And for God's sake get the chicks away from there." She walked off.

"Zara," Omer leaned closer.

"Ninety-one?" I whispered.

Omer nodded. "I'll speak to Amma." He lowered his voice as Amma glanced towards us. "But you need to continue your lessons."

"Lessons?" I pulled back. I didn't have it in me anymore. "I'm not ready," I began.

"What do you mean not ready? You've already missed too many days. You'll forget what you have learned." Omer frowned.

"That was before."

"Before what?"

"Sakina Masi said …" I stopped.

"Forget Sakina Masi," hissed Omer. "Have you seen their demands? Amma and Abba can't meet them. And you promised me you were serious about your studies."

"Promised?" I frowned, trying to grasp a drifting memory. I had made another promise. I had promised to look out for Tara.

"Zara, are you listening?" I stared at Omer as a rushing sound filled my ears. What did I want? Did it matter anymore?

At night, I lay awake, unable to sleep. My eyes shot open as Amma and Abba entered. The charpai creaked. "Any word from Tara?" whispered Amma. "We haven't heard anything for some time now, and I've been meaning to ask you."

"I called and spoke to her husband for a short time. He said he was busy with work," said Abba.

"And Tara, how was she?" asked Amma.

"I wasn't able to talk to her. He said she was busy with the children, but well. Go to sleep. She's in her home, and we have other worries now."

"We have to send word to Sakina," murmured Amma.

"We'll say something when we have something to say. With the crop situation, how am I supposed to think of anything else?"

Amma didn't reply. The charpai creaked, and it was quiet.

The next morning I followed Amma to Nasreen Masi's house. In spite of her in-laws' resistance, Nasreen Masi had accepted a teacher's position at a school in her parents' village and was leaving soon.

Once a large woman, Nasreen Masi had shrunk down to her bones. Beckoning Amma to sit on the charpai, she set a bowl of prayer beads between them. Unsure of where to sit, I squatted on the low stool. My eyes followed the scrawny chicks, but my ears tuned into the conversation.

Nasreen Masi was confiding in Amma that out of all her friends and acquaintances only Amma and Shakeela Masi had come to wish her. The rest, fearing her in-laws' disapproval, stayed away.

Amma swore. I looked up. Amma sounded different, her voice stronger. Wiping her eyes, Nasreen Masi sniffed and confided that the night of the funeral, a large woman had come to their house, claiming she was a distant relative, and said she wanted to take Zohra to the city to marry her nephew. Furious, she had driven the woman away. But her mother-in-law, Bari Masi, had found out that she had refused the proposal, and had beaten her with a broom. Then yesterday her father-in-law had whipped the girls for not folding his clothes correctly. She had defended her daughters, and the old man had turned on her with his slipper. Nasreen Masi pulled up her shirt to reveal angry red welts on her arms and back. Amma swore again and then glanced at me. I looked away. I had welts of my own to show Nasreen Masi.

"I shouldn't be talking like this in front of your daughter," murmured Nasreen Masi. "Sabra, come outside. Your friend is here," she called.

Sabra appeared at the doorway and beckoned. I followed her inside a dimly lit room with stained walls and grimy windows. Clothes, chadors, blankets and kitchen utensils were heaped on the charpai. Sabra's elder sister, Zohra, folded clothes and piled them inside a tin trunk. Looking over her shoulder, she smiled. "Zara, it's good to see you. Your mother has been so kind to us."

I nodded. "Sorry I haven't come sooner."

"Wish we could have met Tara before she left," said Sabra. "Your parents got her married in a rush, didn't they?"

"Don't be nosy," interrupted Zohra. "It's always good to see you, Zara, but we would have loved to see Tara too. Lucky girl. She must be living like a queen in the city."

I swayed. Zohra's lips moved, but I couldn't hear her anymore. I tried to breathe, but there was no air. I gasped. It grew darker.

"What's wrong?" Sabra grasped my elbow.

"Amma, Mariam Masi!" cried Zohra.

"Zara?" Amma was hurrying towards me. I took a deep breath, trying to fight the darkness.

"She nearly fainted," said Sabra.

"Zara, what happened? Are you all right?" Drawing me close,

Amma turned to Nasreen Masi. "We should go. She's not been keeping too well. There's too much illness going around since the rains."

"Yes, of course. Take care, my friend." But before Amma could make her way out, Nasreen Masi had sidled up to Amma and clasped her hand. "Before you leave, I must tell you. There's a rumour going around about Tara, about why you took her away. Tara is happily married, isn't she? There's nothing more, is there? You can tell me."

I froze. Would Amma tell the truth and confide in her friend? She had to. Nasreen Masi could help us get Tara back.

Amma was shaking her head. "People have nothing better to do than to make up stories," she hissed. "There's nothing more. Tara is happily married. Thank God."

I shut my eyes. Lies. Again.

"Truth has a rotten core," whispered Amma as we walked back. "They say they want to know, but they don't. Nobody can take too much of it. You remember that."

22

A week later, the sands of the Cholistan desert stormed over the horizon like angry waves. In a few hours they would be upon us. But I wasn't afraid anymore. I could do anything if I put my mind to it.

Seeing Amma's lips tighten like a stitch yanked too hard, I began my chores. I sorted grains, kneaded the dough for chapattis, peeled and chopped vegetables, swept the floor, dusted, washed clothes, and bathed and fed Kullo. For the first time in weeks, I did everything right. My brain ticked like Nani's hand loom, clicking, crossing, warp and weft. Nani had sat in front of it for hours, working away. Like threads closing gaps, my thoughts fell into place.

I needed answers. Where was Tara? I had to find out. I had promised her. By afternoon, the fields had vanished, and all evening and through the night the wind howled, lightning crashed, and rain pounded our mud roof like hoof beats of armies in battle. I jammed my fingers into my ears to muffle the roar. I needed to think.

I opened my eyes to pale light streaming through the half-open door. Sparrows cheeped on damp branches. I reached out, but as always, I was too late. Tara disappeared each morning. Before I knew it, tears would run down my face, hot and fast.

Enough. I sprang up. I wasn't going to let the pain break me. It was the enemy. I was going to jab, cross, and hook it. Rolling over, I pulled out my notebook and pencil from under the quilt, flipped to the last page, and wrote: "335 days". I had a target now, to reach the city and find Tara. A month had already gone by. I had less than a year left before next autumn, the time of assu, to find her. Below "335 days", I wrote the date. Done. I flicked back to the first page.

"Don't count the days. Make the days count." Muhammad Ali's words leapt at me. Why hadn't I opened my notebook before? I had been keeping a journal of my heroes, the men and women who stood up, spoke out, and fought for what they believed in. Master Saab had told us to start a hero's journal much earlier, before the exams. On the first page, I had pasted Muhammad Ali's picture from an old newspaper and written about his wins, losses and struggles. Born in Louisville, Kentucky, in 1942, the son of a black billboard painter, Mohammad Ali started boxing at the age of twelve. He trained hard, and practiced even when he wasn't fighting. He won the gold medal in the 1960 Olympics and heavyweight championship in 1964, and became a boxing legend. He was banned from fighting in America, and even sentenced to prison. But he had not given up and had fought back to reclaim his title in the famous 1974 boxing match named Rumble in the Jungle, in Zaire.

A little before mid-day, I was rinsing the last few clothes when the door rattled and Omer rushed inside, his face flushed. "Salam, Amma," he burst out, shooting me a quick look. "Master Saab wants to meet you to talk about my studies. He's waiting outside."

"Why? You're not in trouble, are you?" Amma turned away from Majjo Phuppi, who had come to visit, and with whom she had been chatting, and frowned.

"No, it's not that. But will you meet him? Can I call him inside?"

"Shouldn't he talk to your father instead?" said Amma, pulling the chador around her shoulders and over her head. "This isn't a good time."

"You know that Master Saab doesn't step out after Maghrib prayers, and we don't know when Abba will come home. Can you meet him now, please? And Majjo Phuppi is also here. It's better that you meet him while she's here."

"Oh, all right, if you insist." Amma sighed and turned to me, "Go inside and shut the door."

I slung the last few clothes on the line, tipped the bucket of soapy water, and hurried into the room. I shut the door, dropped down, propping myself up on my elbows to peer through the chink in the door. I wasn't going to miss out on anything Master Saab had to say.

"Salam, I'm sorry for barging in like this," began Master Saab, walking over. "And thank you for seeing me." Amma bowed her head in greeting. When Master Saab shifted, I sensed another movement. A lanky boy in a white shalwar-kameez stood behind him. I edged closer to the door. The boy shifted, and the sunlight slanted over his deep eyes and full mouth. He looked straight at me. I ducked.

Master Saab hovered, and finally settled on the charpai across from Amma. When Omer nudged Amma, she raised her head for a quick nod, and Master Saab began to speak in the low modulated voice that I remembered.

He was confident that Omer had passed his exams for entrance into the secondary school but wanted to discuss Omer's future. Since enrolment had shot up in the primary classes, he had no space or time to teach the higher classes, and if Omer wanted to continue his studies, he would have to apply to other schools. When Amma protested that there was no other school in the village, Master Saab reassured her that she had nothing to worry about. Omer had an excellent chance of being admitted into a good school outside the village, and of even getting a scholarship. He was a top student. The nearest school was in Multan, but the best school for boys was in Lahore. However, since there wasn't much time, they had to decide quickly. Leaning forward, Master Saab waited for Amma's response. Amma looked down and finally murmured that she would have to ask Omer's father.

Master Saab urged Amma to decide soon and then recommended that Saleem, the boy who sat beside him and whom he had adopted, and Omer should not waste time and instead should begin to review their lessons while they waited for their results, since they were already a class behind for their age. Omer could help Saleem in Mathematics and Saleem could help Omer in English. When Amma murmured something about Abba again, Master Saab cleared his throat. "Now that we're done talking about the boys, your daughter Zara, is she here?"

"Why?" Amma's head shot up. Her gaze flew to Majjo Phuppi. I dropped down.

"She's a brilliant student!" exclaimed Master Saab. He leaned forward. "I couldn't believe her exam results. With such informal and irregular studying she scored extraordinarily high marks, enough to get her into any school in the District."

Majjo Phuppi gasped.

"Master Saab," began Amma shaking her head, "I don't think …"

"And you'll never believe it," interrupted Master Saab. He beamed. "The school in the neighbouring village has offered her a scholarship for Class VI starting January. What do you think of that?"

Trembling, I pushed hard against the door. Any harder and the door would break. A scholarship? Charged with a current, I wanted to break through the door and race out. I clenched my fists.

"A scholarship?" whispered Amma. She shut her eyes and shook her head. "I'm sorry, but Zara won't be able to continue her studies."

"Not continue her studies? But …" began Master Saab.

"We've decided," began Amma. "We are thinking about …" she paused.

"Thinking about what?" asked Master Saab.

"Nothing, but no more studies. I want her home with me," said Amma.

"But Amma, it's not fair to her. She deserves to go to school. She's studied so hard." Omer was up on his feet.

"Who said anything about what's fair?" interrupted Amma. "Thank you for helping her, Master Saab, but no. If studying was in her destiny, she should have been a boy."

"But if she's as good as any boy, she deserves a chance," interrupted Majjo Phuppi.

"What?" Amma gaped at Majjo Phuppi.

"I said if she's good as any boy then she deserves to go to school," repeated Majjo Phuppi, looking at Master Saab. She turned to Amma. "I knew something was going on when I heard her read. She's sharp. And if she's as good as Master Saab is saying she is, then don't stop her, Behen. Let her go to school."

"You don't know what you're saying. Her father will never allow it, especially not after …" Amma's voice faltered.

"Bibi?" questioned Master Saab.

Amma sniffed and shook her head.

"I can talk to him," offered Majjo Phuppi.

"No," declared Amma. "Nobody tells him anything."

"That's a pity," said Master Saab. "What about Omer?"

"I can't say no," Amma shifted her head slightly. "But I can't say yes either until his father agrees." She locked her hands, unlocked them, and began to twist the chador around her fingers.

"I understand. Well, let me know when you've talked it over. The boys are intelligent and hardworking. Given a chance, they'll do well." Master Saab stood up and nodded to Saleem. "We should leave now, Khuda Hafiz, Bibi." He dipped his head.

Amma rose after them. "Khuda Hafiz," she echoed, following them to the door.

I couldn't move. Or breathe. All the lessons and all the studying had been for nothing. The viper was back, coiling around my windpipe, crushing my dreams.

I dragged in a deep breath. No. I wasn't going to let them knock me down. I had to fight back. I had won a scholarship. I wasn't going to let Amma snatch it away. I wasn't going to give up. Others had fought for what they believed in and won. Like Nur Jehan, the 'Light of the World', a brilliant leader in the seventeenth century. She had been the wife of Emperor Jahangir. She had ruled the court and led her army to victory.

At night, after washing dishes, I stood at the doorway ready to sleep when I heard the door creak. Catching Abba's hawk-like eyes fixed on Amma, I swallowed the "Salam" on my lips, and scurried into the room.

"Omer," growled Abba, "go inside now."

"But …" protested Omer, glancing up, but then fell silent. He gathered his books and came inside. As soon as he shut the door, we crouched to peer through the slit in the door. Abba sat hunched up on the charpai, and Amma hovered over him with her back to us.

"I'm telling you I called," said Abba. "The ring went through, but no one picked it up. I had the operator dial the number half a dozen times."

"Are you sure you gave the right number?"

"Of course," Abba frowned. "They're probably out of town. Don't worry."

"But someone should have been home. What about the servants?" Amma's voice shook.

"He could have given them leave."

"And his mother?"

"She must have gone with them."

"Can you try next week?"

"I said don't worry." Abba closed his eyes.

"Someone has to," murmured Amma.

"What?" snapped Abba.

"You close your eyes and pretend everything is well, but I know it's not. I haven't spoken to Tara for weeks." Amma's voice trembled. "They haven't come to visit us like he promised. First, he was busy with work, and now no one answers the phone." Turning away, Amma wiped her cheeks with her chador.

"Well, worrying will not help," snapped Abba. "I'm sure they're just on holiday. If he doesn't call back, I'll tell Riaz Bhai to go and check on them. I still have the card he gave me." When Amma didn't answer, Abba leaned back and began to smoke his hookah.

I stood still, seeing nothing. Why wasn't Abba able to reach Tara? Did she not want to talk to us anymore? But wait. Hadn't Amma told us that Abba's friend didn't have any servants? "Omer," I whispered seeing him open his books again. "We need to talk."

Omer shook his head. "Two more chapters. We'll talk soon. I promise."

"When? And aren't you done with your exams? Why are you still studying?"

"I have to study. The city schools are tougher than the village ones. We're already behind for our class. I have a lot to cover before the term starts. And you need to get back to your lessons too. It's been over a month now. You can't forget what you've learned. We'll talk tomorrow."

☙

I caught Amma's frown when I sat for my lessons with Omer the next afternoon. Was she going to stop me? She hadn't said anything about Master Saab's visit. I tried to focus on the work Omer had set out, but it was impossible. Thoughts simmered and boiled. Why had Abba's friend married Tara if he had servants? Had I misheard Abba? Abba said he had Tara's husband's card. Where had he kept it?

The essay and sums made no sense, and finally Omer lost patience. He slashed a red line across my wrong answers. He made me redo the whole paper twice and beat his pen on the notebook like a cane.

As soon as the lessons were over, Omer opened his own books and bent his head to them. I hesitated. I had to wash Kullo and then milk her. But there would never be a right time. I grabbed his books.

"What are you doing?" snapped Omer.

"We need to talk."

"And we will. I told you. But now I need to study. Give my books back." Omer reached out for them.

"No," I dodged. "When you studied for the exams I couldn't talk to you. Now your exams are over but you still don't have time. You do have time. And we need to talk now."

"About what? You don't understand anything. Give my books back!" Omer scowled.

I gripped the books even tighter. "Understand what?"

Omer jumped up. "Zara, stop this. I have to study. I need to."

"Why? You're going to school whether you study or don't study."

"I need to study to become someone important," hissed Omer. "We're nothing! We lost Tara because we're nothing. I couldn't do anything to help her. Now I have a chance to change my life, to change our lives. I need to succeed and become someone important, so no one can ever do this to us again."

Silently, I set the books down. Omer was fighting in the only way he knew. I was doing the same.

A few days later, Saleem came over to study with Omer. Abba had announced that it didn't matter whether Omer studied with his friend or went to school. There was not much to do in the fields these days. But when he needed Omer, he would have to return to the fields. That was his future. He had better understand that.

After warning me to stay away from Omer and his friend, Amma retreated to the room to nap. Setting the pot of bubbling lentils aside, I leaned over the wall overlooking the expanse of green fields. They stretched to the horizon and maybe beyond. Would I ever cross them?

When the door creaked, I lowered my head. "You've finished? So quickly?"

"No," grumbled Omer. "Not finished. We're stuck, and thought we would go for a short walk to clear our heads."

Turning away, I gripped the wall. Amma had forbidden me from stepping out.

"Do you want to come with us?" asked Omer. He stood right behind me.

I wheeled around to stare at Omer. Go with them? I hadn't stepped out since that afternoon.

"We won't tell anyone," said Omer in a rush. "I know Amma has stopped you from going out, but I don't want to leave you alone. And there are two of us." He beckoned.

I took a step, but then hesitated. The fields? No. Omer had said they would walk along the river. Flowing for nine hundred miles, the Sutlej was the longest of the five arms of the Indus. It started from about 15,000 feet above sea level in the Himalayas and swooped down to gush through deep gorges, to enter India and then Pakistan. I had seen the full waters glide meek as a worm, or rear up like a maddened beast. I had nearly drowned in the waters. But maybe it was time to face them again.

"Hurry up. We can't take long, just twenty minutes at the most," said Omer. "Come on." He beckoned again. Without glancing back, I followed.

Over the next few weeks, the afternoons fell into a pattern. When Amma went inside to nap, I waited for Omer and Saleem to walk out, and tagged along behind them, listening. The discussions ranged from what they had learnt in history to English novels to science experiments and math formulas, as well as the daily yield of eggs and milk, about which I knew more.

Walking close to Omer, I kept a distance from Saleem, remembering that Amma had told us to keep away from strangers. But Saleem didn't behave like a stranger. He told jokes and made me laugh. He shared how he had come to live with Master Saab. He talked about his parents' deaths, the months he had lived in his uncle's house knowing that his aunt didn't want him around, and how Master Saab had stepped in to adopt him. He talked about leaving the village to finish his studies. He wanted to become someone famous.

One afternoon Omer ran ahead because he wanted to jump over the rocks but Saleem stayed back. He had a cut on his foot and didn't want to risk getting it wet. When Saleem walked over and sat beside me, I nearly slipped off the log. I stared down hard, my heart pounding. What was he doing? What if someone saw us? But wait, what was he saying?

Why did I want to study? What did I want to become? Did I miss Tara? He had heard about her marriage. Had I met her since? Would I be married off soon as well?

For a few moments I stared at Saleem. No one ever asked such questions. But unable to look away from his searching eyes, I began to answer, the words tumbling out, when, suddenly remembering Amma's warning, I shut up again. What was I doing? My cheeks flamed.

And that's when, without warning, Saleem curled his fingers over mine. My heart flip-flopped to my throat. What was he doing? Before I could say anything, he started talking. Whatever happened, I shouldn't give up studying. And if I had promised to look out for Tara, then I had to keep my promise. And I should keep studying. Master Saab believed in me, and so did Omer, but I had to believe in myself. That was even more important.

I couldn't look away from him. Why was he telling me to study and to keep my promise to Tara? Why did it matter to him? Did he really mean it?

Hearing Omer shout out to Saleem, I scrambled up, but Omer had yelled something about catching a fish. Giving me a quick smile, Saleem got up. I stared at him walking away and continued to feel the warmth of his hand on mine, hours after we returned home.

Over the following days, I found myself thinking of Saleem, and caught myself looking at him. When he looked back, I lowered my head. But when he turned away, I felt an unexplainable feeling of loss. I missed the feel of his hand over mine and his dark searching eyes looking into mine. I missed his smile that made my heartbeat race.

I'd never felt this way before. It didn't make sense. I didn't know him. But when I thought of him, feelings stirred, melting my limbs and filling me with heady heat. I felt like a pupa swathed inside a cocoon, about to burst out. How could I feel so much and not know him?

Saleem was just a friend. I had to keep telling myself that.

23

"Zara!" called Amma.

I burrowed into the quilt, trying to grasp Tara's hands, but she faded into pale light. Hearing Amma call again, I jumped up and pulled out my notebook. My fingers clenched the pencil. One hundred and twenty days had already gone by, and I still hadn't found Tara's husband's card. Where had Abba hidden it? I had no time to look for it; Amma's sharp eyes always followed me.

We were going to visit Khalid Chacha and then to see the mela. The news of the mela had spread like wild fire in our village. Tonga drivers flocked to our village square and lured us with promises of discounts, mouth-watering foods, foreign merchandise, and thrilling feats.

It was late afternoon by the time we set off. Amma had forced me to wear the burka. When I protested, she declared I didn't have a choice. Smothering the urge to toss it off and walk out, I had reluctantly worn it. She was right. I didn't have a choice. I couldn't walk out. Where would I go? Who would keep me? How would I support myself? I didn't have an education, a degree or any job skills. Abba and Amma had made sure of that. The stories of my heroes were just stories and not real, unless I made them real.

The tonga picked up speed. Dark swollen clouds reminded me of jinns and demons. The clappity-clap of hoof beats and the whirring sound of wheels echoed in the still afternoon. It was twilight when the tonga swerved from the main road and onto the track that led to Chacha's village. Oil lamps flickered in the distance.

"We're late," muttered Abba. "No lights and no men in the fields. Not a good omen. We should have started earlier."

"We're nearly there," said the tonga-walla. "It would have been worse if we were still on the main road. You've heard about the dacoits?"

"Not in front of the women!" warned Abba.

"They hit a party travelling to Multan last week, and spared no one, not even the women and …"

"Worry about getting us there, baba," cut in Abba. "Your horses are growing old."

"My horses, no Saab, they're not old," protested the tonga-walla. "My Shehzadi can run faster than any horse in this district." He whooped, cracked his cane, and the horses broke into a gallop.

"Stop now!" a voice thundered. The tonga-walla cursed, and the tonga lurched. Thrown back, I clutched the sides of the vehicle. "Stop!" shouted the voice again. Murmuring prayers, Amma grasped my shoulders.

"Who is it?" shouted Abba. "What do you want?"

"Be careful, Saab," warned the tonga-walla.

"Abba, stay back," shot Omer.

Voices muttered.

"Yaqoob Bhai, is that you?" called a familiar voice.

"Khalid Bhai? Oh, thank God," exclaimed Abba.

"Thank God, thank God," echoed the tonga-walla. Amma slumped. The men hooted and backslapped each other.

"You had us worried," said Khalid Chacha. "You said you were going to leave early morning, so I expected you to reach hours ago.

I came out with my boys to look for you. It's not safe to be here at this time even if we're together. Can we all fit in?"

"Yes, of course." Ignoring the tonga-walla's protests, Abba beckoned to Omer to sit with us in the back. Khalid Chacha and my cousins squeezed into the front with Abba. The tonga sped forward, and Amma continued to pray until we drew up outside Khalid Chacha's house. I helped Amma down and followed her inside. A semicircle of oil lamps cast a warm flickering glow.

"Mariam Behen!" exclaimed Kulsoom Chachi, swooping out from the dark. "Thank God you're here. We were worried." She clasped Amma by her shoulders and turned to me.

"Salam, Chachi," I murmured.

Kulsoom Chachi tilted my chin under the lamp's glow. "Still going out in the sun, I see." She frowned. "You know, Sakina was asking me the other day."

"Let it be," interrupted Amma.

"Let it be? Never! Think about it, Mariam," urged Kulsoom Chachi. "A good proposal is like a pearl in an oyster shell. Better to marry her off before …" She sighed. "You won't get a moment of peace with an unmarried daughter in the house." She gave me a slight push. "Go meet your cousin Nazia. Your Saima Appi is visiting, but don't bother her, she needs to rest."

I made my way to the room, hoping Nazia had been able to pinch the hookah again. I was dying for a few puffs. Seeing a slight figure huddled on the charpai, I paused at the doorway. Was Saima Appi really unwell?

"Zara," called Nazia. I spun round and saw her approaching.

"Ah Zara," called Saima Appi. "When did you get here?"

"Just now," I murmured, unable to tear my eyes away from Saima Appi's hollow face. How much weight had she lost? Was she pregnant already? She couldn't be.

"Let Saima Appi rest. We can go out to help Amma," suggested Nazia. I nodded and followed my younger cousin out again.

We gathered around the mat in the courtyard. When Kulsoom Chachi brought out a dish of steaming rice, Khalid Chacha enquired about Saima Appi, but Kulsoom Chachi muttered under her breath and looked away. Chacha repeated the question, but Kulsoom Chachi still didn't reply. Abba and Amma glanced at Khalid Chacha curiously, but he shook his head, and with forced gaiety urged us to start eating.

I tried to catch Omer's eye, but he ignored me, something he had started doing when there were other boys around. Once done with eating, I looked around: no one spoke, shared a joke, or even an anecdote. Chachi and Amma began to gather up the dishes. Why had Chacha invited us over? After dinner, Khalid Chacha asked Abba to join him on the charpai. Signalling to me to follow her, Nazia disappeared into the room with a plate of rice.

Saima Appi sat up when I walked inside. "Come, sit," she said folding her knees. "How are you?"

I dropped down beside her and took her hand. It was cold and clammy. "I'm all right," I said, looking at her closely. Her eyes were dull and her skin pale. Something was wrong.

"And Tara? How is she? Happily married?"

Had Amma not told Chachi? "She's fine," I whispered.

"She's lucky, then." Saima Appi's voice broke.

"You're lucky too," burst out Nazia.

I shivered at the look on Saima Appi's face. "What's going on?" I asked.

"Nothing," mumbled Saima Appi.

"Tell her. It'll make you feel better," urged Nazia.

Saima Appi shook her head.

"Tell me," I pressed.

Saima Appi shut her eyes. "Fine. You want to know. Then I'll tell you." She pushed out her breath. "I have a shadow."

"What?" What was she talking about?

"I have a shadow. I'm cursed." Saima Appi sighed. "It's true. A few weeks after our wedding, two of our buffaloes died, then the rains wrecked the crops, and my sister-in-law lost her baby in the third month. It was a boy. My in-laws accused me of bringing them ill luck."

"That's crazy. How could you have done anything?" I began.

"That's what I've been telling her," interrupted Nazia. She grasped Saima Appi's arm. "You had nothing to do with this. Dozens of buffaloes died in your village because of disease. And you never went near the fields. The floods ruined half the district's crops."

Saima Appi shook her head. "My mother-in-law said I was unlucky. I had brought this misfortune upon them. Everyone believed her. What could I do?"

"And your husband?" I asked.

"My husband said nothing. He believed his mother. He stopped coming near me."

"Did you try to talk to him?" I leaned forward.

"Talk? I pleaded and begged him to believe me. It was so good between us in the beginning. I thought he loved me. He took me out, bought me juice and ice cream. When the first buffalo died, his mother and grandmother declared that my shadow had killed it. I thought they joked. I hadn't even gone near the livestock. But they were serious. They said I was the only change in the house. They said my shadow was cursed. When I told my husband he laughed and told me to forget about it. A few days later, the second buffalo died. There was a terrible uproar. My mother-in-law accused me again. This time my husband beat me and forbade me from entering the kitchen. He moved out of our room. I could only come out to eat meals."

"You put up with it?" I whispered.

"What was I to do? Could I walk out? I wanted to, but where could I go? I couldn't go back home. When the rains destroyed the crops, my mother-in-law told me I couldn't come out at all. No one talked to me. They set a plate of food inside the room for me. I thought I would go mad. Finally, when my sister-in-law lost her baby, they whipped me and locked me in the storeroom. I was there for days."

"No!" I burst out.

"Then Abba's friend visited," interrupted Saima Appi. "I didn't see him, but I heard them talking. Abba had sent sweets for me. They told him I was unwell. He must have suspected something was wrong because the next day Abba stormed in. He refused to leave without seeing me. I heard him running through the house, calling my name. That's when I began to scream." She shivered. "I'll never forget the look on Abba's face when he saw me. He threatened to get the police if they didn't free me. My in-laws just stood and watched me leave. Even my husband, he just stood there. Abba brought me straight back home, didn't say a word to anyone, and told Amma that my marriage was over. Amma was furious. Said I must have done something to upset them."

"You did nothing. It wasn't your fault," insisted Nazia.

"They said it was," murmured Saima Appi.

"It always is," I murmured.

"What do you mean?" Saima Appi stared at me.

"I mean," I stopped, afraid of my thoughts. Pins stung my neck and arms.

My aunt. Chiragh. Tara. Saima Appi. Each and every time, it was always our fault.

24

"There's no need to take the girls, I tell you," Kulsoom Chachi thumped the platter of grains on the floor. "There's work to be done, and …"

"And what?" demanded Khalid Chacha, halting at the door. I bumped into Saima Appi and Nazia, who had stopped behind him. Omer had already left for the mela with the other boys. Chachi hadn't stopped fuming since Khalid Chacha had announced he would take us to the mela after the morning chores were done.

"How can you parade the girls with the disaster on our heads? What will people say? That we have no shame?" Kulsoom Chachi shook her fist. "You forget that I'm her mother. Better for my daughter to be dead than divorced."

I winced. Saima Appi didn't need to listen to this. And who was going to recognise us in our black burkas? It hid us from our heads to our heels. It covered our faces. It buried our voices. What more did Kulsoom Chachi want?

"I promised the girls. It will do them good," said Khalid Chacha.

"Good?" screeched Chachi. "You talk about good. It would be good if my daughter was back in her husband's house."

"Kulsoom!" growled Chacha.

"Go then. But when people talk, don't say I didn't warn you." Kulsoom Chachi turned away.

Nearly an hour later our tonga rolled into the fair grounds. Ice-white mist shimmered against the blue sky. I hurried after my cousins and Khalid Chacha through the maze of stalls set up on the campground, but couldn't stop glancing back. Tara had always been there, behind me, following me. My eyes blurred. I didn't want to remember Tara, not all the time.

We walked past carts stacked with glass bottles full of neon coloured drinks. Sticky sweetmeats floated in platters of thick sizzling oil. Hearing the shouts and laughs from the merry-go-round, I stopped to gape at the animal-shaped swings whizzing higher and higher. Tara had loved such rides, and we had planned to see the carnival together. Children laughed and squealed as the swings flew past. A dizzying lightness filled my limbs. I longed to join the crowds that lined up for the ride, but Khalid Chacha had walked ahead. A boisterous group of boys rushed forward, chatting about snake dances, acrobatics, and cockfights.

I inhaled the scent of spicy chaats, roasting channas, and gola-gandas in the air and hurried past tables loaded with plastic ware, chinaware, glassware, clothes, old books and magazines, soaps, towels, odd bottles filled with murky potions. I giggled with my cousins, spotting the heap of women's underwear stuffed with foam.

Shopkeepers crooned limericks to entice customers over the low hum of chatter. Reaching the end of the first row of stalls, I stood unsure of which way to turn. Abruptly, Khalid Chacha pointed to a corner stall. "I know what we need to get."

"Shoes?" I asked.

Saima Appi nodded. "I've been wearing Nazia's old ones since I returned. Abba got me out so quickly that I didn't have time to grab mine."

Half an hour later, I was following my cousins out of the shoe stall, carrying my first pair of maroon khoosas wrapped in newspaper. I had gaped at the variety of slippers, sandals, khoosas, and boots available in an overwhelming range of colours and designs, and immediately thought of Tara. She would have loved the embroidery and the sequins and sparkles. She loved everything that shone and glittered. I hoped her husband had taken her shopping. She hadn't taken much from home.

We hadn't walked far when Nazia tugged Chacha's arm. "Abba, I want the anklets, the ones hanging over in that stall."

"Don't you have enough at home?" asked Khalid Chacha.

"But Amma said I need another pair." Nazia pouted. "And I don't have the ones that make a tinkling sound."

"Oh, all right," conceded Chacha and turned to Saima Appi and me. "What about you two, do you want them too?" He paused, seeing Saima Appi look down. I flushed. Divorcees and widows didn't wear jewellery in our villages. Had Khalid Chacha forgotten?

"I don't," murmured Saima Appi.

"You do," contradicted Khalid Chacha. "I'll get one each, for you all."

"I want the ones with bells," chirped Nazia, browsing through the display.

The spiky-haired boy flashed a toothy grin and waited for Nazia to decide. "That's an excellent choice," he declared, seeing her choose one. "It comes to rupees thirty for three, but for you, a special discount, only rupees twenty-five." He dangled the anklet, laid it out on his palm, and held it out.

"What, rupees twenty-five for such frivolous trinkets! You can't be serious. Rupees twenty, that's it!" declared Khalid Chacha.

"Saab, please, you insult our treasures. We use the original moulds that were made for the royal family of Bahawalpur. Rupees twenty-three. That's my final price."

After a few minutes of haggling, Khalid Chacha set rupees twenty-two on the table. The boy grinned, wrapped the trinkets in paper bags and handed them over.

On the way back, Saima Appi drifted off to sleep and Nazia grasped my arm. "We'll try on the anklets with our new shoes once we get home," she whispered. I nodded. A warm rush ballooned my chest. I couldn't wait to reach home and show Amma my new shoes and anklets.

"I was lying, you know," Nazia whispered. "Amma didn't say anything about getting anklets."

"Huh?" I turned towards Nazia.

"I've met a boy," confided Nazia. "He's a shoe-keeper at the shrine. Nobody knows about us. I'll meet him when we go to the shrine next Thursday wearing my new anklets." She flushed.

"Be careful," I whispered, and squeezed her arm. The flush on Nazia's face and the spark in her eyes made my heart race, and made me think of Saleem. I had been thinking too much about him.

When we reached Khalid Chacha's house, I jumped down and followed my cousins inside. Amma sat sorting grains by the cooking pit, across the courtyard from Kulsoom Chachi. I waited for them to stop talking. When Kulsoom Chachi got up to rinse the clothes, I peeled off the newspaper and held up the khoosas. "Amma, look, aren't they beautiful?" I said.

"Very nice." Amma smiled and nodded. "Better put them away for your dowry before they get spoilt. Here, wrap them in this." She bent to pick up the newspaper.

I broke into a cold sweat. Marriage. Did Amma think of nothing else?

"No," croaked Amma, staring at the paper she had picked up. "No, it can't be."

"Amma?" I went forward to steady her.

"Him, it's him, Kamran. But how?" Amma's voice was hoarse.

"Huh? Who? Where?" I tried to peer past Amma. "Amma, what's wrong?"

"I don't understand. It's him, Tara's husband," whispered Amma.

"Tara's what?" I steadied my voice. What was Amma talking about? "You mean Imtiaz, Abba's friend." I tried to reach for the newspaper, but Amma dodged.

"Yes, no, I mean ... your Abba made me promise." Amma shook her head. "He said we couldn't reveal his real name in case anyone made a connection. Tara's married to Kamran. We met him at the maid agency. He was a friend of Riaz Chacha's contact."

"You lied?" I cried and yelped when Amma struck my cheek.

"It wasn't a lie," hissed Amma. She thrust the paper towards me. "Read it. Tell me what it says! Why are the police there?"

I stared at Amma in horror. Police?

"Read it!" commanded Amma.

"Amma, shush," I said, trying to tug the newspaper from Amma's grip. Without warning, Amma's head lolled, and her body sagged.

"Is everything all right?" called Kulsoom Chachi.

I slipped the newspaper out from under Amma's elbow and shifted her to lean against the charpai. "Stay here until I get back." I stood up. "Chachi, Amma's not feeling well. I'm going to get her some water." I called out and without waiting for an answer, I hurried towards the cupboard and ducked behind a pillar to study the paper. It was from two weeks ago. I stared at the black and white image of a thin, bearded man being handcuffed by two officers. Tara's husband? A shiver ran down my spine.

The headline ran: "Police Raid. Man Arrested on Suspicion of Operating a Brothel."

My vision blurred. I pressed my forehead against the wall, trying to pull air into my tightening chest. I heard the sound of shuffling feet. Footsteps sounded, and voices bounced. Someone shouted. Amma cried out my name.

"Impossible! You're hallucinating," growled Abba.

"I'm not. I'll show you. Where's Zara?" cried Amma.

Before I had taken even a few steps, Abba seized the paper from me. He stared at it, with Khalid Chacha looking over his shoulder. He straightened up, snorted and shook his head. "See, I told you. How can you tell? The picture is hazy. You're mistaken. It can't be him. It must be someone who looks like him. All this uproar for nothing." He flung the paper down.

"Read the paper, Zara," ordered Amma. Kulsoom Chachi's mouth fell open. "Read it," repeated Amma. I shrank back. Amma wanted me to read. Now? Not before, not when I had a chance to go to school, but now, and in front of everyone?

"What do you mean, read? Have you gone mad? She can't read," said Abba. No one spoke.

"What have you done, Behen?" whispered Kulsoom Chachi, and shook her head.

"She can read," murmured Amma, not looking up. "I was going to tell you about the lessons, but then ..." Her voice hardened. "Read, Zara. Read what's written."

"Inside, now!" warned Chachi, turning to Saima Appi and Nazia, who watched.

I picked up the paper, read the headline, and paused. My face and neck were damp with sweat. My heartbeat hammered in my ears. I forced myself to read on.

"Kamran Sultan," pounced Amma. "That's his name. Do we need more proof? Oh God, help us. Why didn't we just kill our daughter?"

"Mariam, stop," Abba snatched the paper from my hands. "It's lies, rubbish. I'm going to call Riaz Bhai right now. He told us he knew this man. There has to be some mistake."

Amma shrieked and began to beat her chest. Kulsoom Chachi rushed towards her. I couldn't move. A dark sandstorm was growing inside my head. My eyes stung. Abba was right. There had to be some mistake.

I crouched in the shadows, waiting for Abba and Chacha to return. The sun was setting before I heard a noise outside. When the latch snapped, I shot up and saw the truth written on Abba's face even before Khalid Chacha began to speak.

At first Riaz Chacha had been outraged at the accusation. He knew Kamran because of some work he had done for the maid agency, but he had no idea that he was involved in anything illegal. He insisted he had always heard good things about Kamran Sultan and had promised to call back. Then, he had called back to beg for forgiveness. Everyone who knew Kamran Sultan was shocked. He was reputed to be a quiet man who worked hard. No one had suspected more. The police inspector had him in custody, with all the evidence required for conviction, but was under pressure to let Kamran go. And he would if he wanted to keep his job, because Kamran Sultan had close contacts with influential people in the city.

"God has punished us," whispered Amma. "We betrayed our daughter. Not even our saints can save us."

"Behen, please," murmured Kulsoom Chachi. "Tara's married to him. She's his wife. Whatever he is, he will protect her. And it's better if she never finds out. Have you talked to her since her marriage?"

Amma opened her mouth, but Abba raised his hand to silence her, and spoke. "No, Kamran said he would bring her over, but he never did."

"What about the Nikah Namah, you have a copy?" asked Khalid Chacha. "If Tara Beti is unhappy, we can file for divorce."

Abba shook his head. "He said he would bring our copy over when they came to visit. But Kulsoom Behen is right. Tara is safe as long as she's married to him. We must remember she's looking after his children. She probably knows too much by now. He'll never let her go, and might harm her if he suspects that she wants to leave or tell others about him."

Amma moaned and rocked back and forth. Kulsoom Chachi grasped her shoulders.

"Mariam, control yourself," rebuked Abba.

"Take her inside and look after her," commanded Khalid Chacha.

"Yaqoob Bhai," began Khalid Chacha. "We can still try. Have faith. We won't give up."

"No," said Abba. "We can't do anything."

"He runs a brothel. How can we let Tara stay married to him?" protested Khalid Chacha.

Abba shook his head, his face stone hard. "We can't risk anything else. He has contacts. If this news gets out, it will shame us and dishonour our family name. We must forget about Tara. She's in her husband's house. It's her fate."

Shivering, I shrank from Abba's words. It was dark and still outside, but inside my head, I howled and screamed. This was not Tara's fate. She had been raped and then forced into a marriage to protect their 'honour'. This was what Abba and Amma had done to her. Even now, he could think only about family name and honour. What family? What honour? I wrapped my arms around my knees, trying to stop trembling. I had to break away from the lies. I wasn't part of this. I couldn't be.

25

It was late afternoon when the tonga swung into our lane. Amma and Abba hadn't exchanged a word on the way back. Hearing a shout, I craned my neck to look ahead. Saleem jumped up and down, waving his arms across the street. Suddenly I wanted to talk to him; he was my friend too. I watched Omer leap down and dash over before the tonga rolled up to the door.

"You've done it," shouted Saleem, but I couldn't hear the rest because Amma had pulled me inside. Telling me to boil the rice and soak the lentils, she hurried out.

I wavered, tempted to eavesdrop, but spun back. Dropping a handful of rice into a pan of water, I raced into the room. I had to hurry. Amma could come inside any second. I ran my hand along the narrow shelf. Nothing. I pulled up the bedding from my parents' charpai. Nothing. I rummaged through the pockets of Abba's shalwar hanging on the wall. They were empty. I pushed open the metal chest, groped through old clothes, bags, chadors, and spotted Abba's money pouch. My fingers fumbled, untying the knots. I thrust my thumb and forefinger inside and touched paper. I pulled out a card. Kamran Sultan. I had him now. I flipped my notebook open and scribbled the address. Done. I slid the card back, tied the strings, tidied the chest and rushed out to see Amma walking in.

I flushed and looked down, waiting for Amma to catch me, but Amma only murmured that dinner would be late since Abba had left for the fields and Omer had left for Master Saab's. Lowering herself on to the charpai, she pulled her chador down to her chin and began to pray.

I crouched by the cooking pit, pretending I had never left. My hands shook as I drained the rice, set the pot of water to boil and began to cook the lentils. Near dusk, when the dull orange light split into embers, Amma pushed her chador back and shared that Omer had received an offer from a prestigious boarding school for boys in Lahore and would leave at the beginning of the summer term.

Spring's warmth retreated, and a wave of grey cold seeped inside. Amma wilted like a parched stalk. She woke only after Abba left. Refusing even a cup of tea, she dragged herself to the charpai. She lay on her back with her eyes closed. I pretended not to see the tears that slid down her cheeks. What was the use of crying now? She had played her part in Abba's deceit and dragged us all into it. When I roused Amma for a mid-day meal, she swallowed a few bites and then lay down again. She went inside to sleep before Abba returned.

Abba stayed out, trying to salvage the crops from the flooded fields. He bartered our chickens to buy food supplies. A few days later, two men came to take Kullo away. He skipped meals and didn't come home some nights. I didn't know where he ate or slept. I didn't dare ask.

I stuck to my chores. I cooked, washed, dusted, swept and ran the house, to stop myself from thinking. But like arrows, thoughts stabbed my head through the day. Abba and Amma had lied. I had let them. I had let them take Tara away. I had helped them to hide the rape. And done nothing to help my twin. I had given up on my dreams. I was so far from where I wanted to be. And it was too late.

In the passing weeks, feeling lost, I walked into the rooms not knowing why I was there, or stepped out into the courtyard not knowing what to do next. I talked to the kittens to make sure I still had a voice. At night my mind twisted like a tornado, memories surfaced, spun and sank into a haze. Some nights I woke up sweaty and clammy, thrashing my arms, fighting off the gold stalks closing in over me. I hid inside the room to smoke Abba's hookah. The smoky taste loosened my nerves. I didn't care if Amma caught me.

Omer zipped in and out of the house, saying he had things to do, but insisted we continue my lessons. We worked for a few hours each day. I heard from him that Saleem had also received admission in the same school and planned to leave with Omer. I would lose them together.

A few weeks after we returned, I squatted to start washing clothes in the courtyard when the door rattled. Amma tried to get up from the charpai, but after a few tries she slumped and nodded to me to open the door. Omer was studying inside the room.

"Mariam," called Zubaida Masi, elbowing me aside. "What's this I hear about you being unwell? But have you heard? It's awful." Hurrying over, she whispered into Amma's ears. Amma gasped and quickly swathing a chador around her head, hobbled outside with Zubaida Masi's help. When the door shook again, I called to Omer to open it.

"Salam, no, she's not here," answered Omer. A shrill voice rose and threatened. Omer quickly bolted the door and swung back.

"Who was that?" I asked.

Omer frowned and shook his head. "Chiragh's dead."

My chest tightened, remembering the flash of jade green eyes and the dark matted hair crouched on the street. What had they done to her? "How?" I whispered.

"Raped and strangled. Amjad Chacha discovered her body in the fields. Bari Masi just came to stop Amma from going to the funeral prayers. You should have seen her face when I told her that Amma had already left." He shook his head. "That woman scares me."

I had finished rolling the dough for chapattis when the door rattled. Amma staggered to the charpai, sank down and beckoned. Suddenly afraid, I walked over. Without a word, Amma pushed a tangle of thin silver into my hand and turned away. I stared down and squeezed my fist around the silver trinkets. Why hadn't Chiragh sold them? Why wasn't Amma angry?

Later I learnt that Moulvi Saab had requested the village women to prepare the body for the funeral since Chiragh had no family in the village, but they had refused under Bari Masi's orders. Only Amma, Zubaida Masi and Surriya Masi had turned up to wash the body. When Moulvi Saab had begun to read Chiragh's funeral prayers, a mob had gathered and threatened to set the mosque on fire. Moulvi Saab had been forced to send Chiragh's body to the shrine. I shivered. The villagers never forgot and never forgave. They prayed to God for mercy and forgiveness but had none to spare.

A few weeks later, I stood on my crate, leaning against the wall. The chores were finished, at least until sunset. Springtime lurked, and the freshly washed earth glistened. Suddenly I pushed back and shut my eyes. It was happening again. The air was still. The walls were moving in closer. The fields loomed over me. They would bury me. I was trapped. I gulped a deep breath. I had to run out and get away. Hearing the door rattle, I spun around. Omer walked in, balancing a stack of books in his arms. He did little else except study these days.

"Omer," I called. "Can we talk?" Omer glanced at me in surprise, but when I tilted my head towards the charpai, he nodded. Abba was out in the fields, and Amma napped inside. Once we sat across from each other, I stalled. "All ready to leave?" I asked lightly and balled my hands into fists, suddenly wishing I had the magic stones. But they had disappeared. Like Tara.

"I guess," said Omer and clasped my arm. "You know I have to go. I want to make something of my life. It's the only way to escape this." He looked around.

"Yes," I mumbled. I needed his help, but I couldn't let him guess that. What if he said no? I drew in a breath and squared my shoulders. "I want to go with you." The words were out.

"Go with me?" Omer stared. "But how? It's a boys' school and …"

"No, not to school, take me to Lahore to find a job." I took a deep breath and steadied my voice. "We need the money. Abba's lost everything. We're in debt. Remember Saleem told us that Master Saab's nephew works at a maid agency? Can he help in getting me a job, any job?"

"You want to work in the city? But you were against it. I don't understand, why now?" Omer shook his head.

I looked at him steadily. "I was against it after reading the news about the maid who was burnt to death. I was afraid of what might happen to Tara. But there's nothing left for me here now. I've lost the scholarship. I can't study or get married unless I have a dowry. I need money for both. But I'm stuck. I can't go forward and can't go back."

Omer continued to look at me. "All right. Let me talk to Master Saab and find out if he's okay with it and if his nephew can arrange a job. And you're right. It's not a bad idea. Maybe it can work. I will be in Lahore and look out for you. And the money will help." He grasped my hand and smiled. "If Master Saab can convince Abba, we'll leave for Lahore together."

☙

"But what about her marriage?" countered Abba. "She needs to get married soon. The time will pass, and then ..." His voice trailed off.

Abba, Khalid Chacha and Master Saab sat on the charpai in the courtyard. Amma had a fever and rested inside. After giving Amma medicine, I crouched by the cooking pit, brewing tea.

"Let her work for some time," began Master Saab. "She will be safe and will earn good money. Once the news gets around that she's earning, proposals will pour in. Believe me. That's the way it is these days, not like the old times, when the family name mattered, when values mattered and when the girl mattered."

"Khalid Bhai?" asked Abba.

"She does have to get married," agreed Khalid Chacha. "And Lahore is far away." He sighed. "But then times have changed, and maybe with Master Saab's connections it can work."

"I'll take full guarantee of where she works. My nephew Shafique has been providing maids to respectable families for years now. And Omer Beta will be there to check on her as well," said Master Saab.

"Yes, we wouldn't even consider it otherwise," said Khalid Chacha. He turned to Abba. "Have you heard back from Sakina?"

"Heard back?" Abba's hawk-like eyes narrowed. "They sent another list. As if we have the money even for the first one! She said they would visit again, once we gave them the go-ahead. I didn't know what to say."

"Bad news spreads fast. Everyone knows about the crop failure." Khalid Chacha looked grim.

"I'm facing a disaster. I don't know how I'll manage," said Abba.

Khalid Chacha nodded. "Send Zara to the city. It's her fate. We'll arrange her marriage when she's earned her dowry."

I woke up early on the morning of my departure. Everything was the same, for the last time. I wouldn't be there tomorrow.

Amma lay unmoving on the charpai. After the morning chores, I wandered around the courtyard and, drawn to the wall, I leaned over and stared hard. Not a stalk or a leaf moved in the muggy heat. The fields were a mirage.

An hour later, I had packed two changes of clothes and my comb in a bag. I drew the zipper and clicked the lock shut. I stepped outside, my eyes on Amma's limp body. Who would cook and clean after I left? Who would look after Amma?

"Khuda Hafiz," I whispered to Amma, leaning close. I caught a flicker in Amma's eyes and for a moment was tempted to tell her everything, but then Amma's eyes dulled, and I pulled back, my words zipped and bolted inside me. No one needed to know. This was my journey.

Abba went to drop us at the nearest bus station, a small shack in front of a dusty parking lot. A mob of boys and men crowded around the bus. It stood tall, a glistening beast, painted in bright colours, with drawings of birds, hearts, flowers and calligraphy, ready for flight.

Book Three

LAHORE

26

Hearing footsteps, I turned round. The sky was flushed gold. How long had I stood by the window reminiscing?

"You'll get into trouble staring out like that," said Bushra. "Our time isn't ours in this place. Hurry, or you won't get anything to eat. Not the best way to start your first day."

Without a word, I followed Bushra to the kitchen. Since we were late, all we got was a mug of tepid tea, and curious looks from three maids in dark chadors. Bushra made no introductions, and the maids' stares made my skin prickle. Finally, they turned to whisper to each other. My chest tightened. In my village, I had Tara. No one bothered us when we were together. But I was alone here.

Before I had finished my tea, Gloria appeared with a list of chores. I was to wash the clothes, dust and polish the furniture and silver before lunch; iron and starch the washed clothes and hang them back in the closets before dinner; and put out coils for mosquitoes and lock the windows and doors in the evening. I had to stick to the schedule and keep my meals short.

A few minutes later, I was staring at the line of detergent bottles and the baskets heaped with soiled clothes. How many pieces of clothing did three people manage to get through in one day? After hanging out the clothes to dry, I armed myself with an assortment of sprays for dusting and polishing wood, silver, marble and glass, and set to work. By evening my body hurt and my belly growled.

Lunch had been a few spoons of lentils with half a bowl of rice. I had a few minutes to swallow the mush under the cook's creepy stare before it was time to get back to work.

Over the next few days, careful to avoid other servants, I explored the house whenever I got the chance. It was grander than anything I had seen in books. In tiled bathrooms, I turned on the gold taps engraved with H and C and cupped my hands under the clear water that gushed faster than the river. Drawn to the panel of gold switches and unable to stop myself, I clicked the buttons on and off, again and again. I got giddy staring at the hundreds of shimmering crystals that hung from the chandelier. I ran my hands over the smooth glistening marble shelves. I gazed at the photographs in gilded frames. Happy, shining faces smiled and laughed from hilltops, oceans and distant lands. They were free. They went to places I had only dreamt of visiting.

In a few days, I knew I wasn't going anywhere. There was no escape. Time ran with the ticking of clocks, not the stars. I woke before dawn to start work and continued working past dusk. Outside, the sky changed: it swirled tea-pink each morning, blazed sea-blue in the afternoon, and glimmered coal black at night. But I was trapped in a maze with hard floors and concrete walls. When I finished one chore, I found another added to my list. When I stepped out, the guards sent me back inside. I had to stay inside the house at all times. They had their orders. How was I going to get out and find Tara? When?

Following Gloria's warning about the male servants, with bold eyes and bolder hands, I learnt to make my way through the dozen rooms and halls that sprawled over an acre. I remembered the rooms by their colours. The brick-floored patio with wicker chairs and table opened into the gardens. It was where Jameel Saab, Sehr Madam, and their son had breakfast by turns, and alone. Sehr

Madam nibbled a solitary lunch in the pantry with the chequered floor on the days she chose to stay home. There were other rooms: a silver-and-gold gilded dining room, a drawing room filled with pale silk sofas, and tables set with silver and crystal ornaments, a sitting room with velvet sofas and a television which blazed with bright colours and sounds at the push of a button.

Uneasy under the glassy stare of the tiger mounted on the wall, I avoided Jameel Saab's smoky study. There were guest rooms too: a green room, a blue room, a red room and a white room. It was a house full of rooms, most of them empty. There was too much space and silence. Jameel Saab, Sehr Madam and Babur Saab spent their time in different parts of the house through the day. I never saw them together.

A week passed, and then two. I waited, but Omer didn't call or visit. I missed him. I missed Saleem and our talks. Had I imagined how he looked at me and listened to me? I had to get out. But how? Restless, I began to calculate sums, recite poems, and review math formulas while I worked. It helped to quiet my mind, but I missed my books. And my hands and feet hurt. My palms hardened and my knuckles bled from washing heaps of clothes. The balls of my feet toughened into leather. I missed the smell of mud. I missed the feel of the loose earth under my feet. Lying down at night, I missed Tara. I missed whispering and giggling with her. I missed the part of me she had completed. I had no friends, except her. We were different, but more similar than different. I had to find her. But how?

To soothe my gnawing thoughts, I dug my nails into the hardened pads of my feet and tore off flakes of dead skin. It felt good to rub the raw tender skin. Dreaming of running back to my village with Tara, I slept restlessly and woke with my heart pounding, drenched in sweat.

Bushra didn't speak to me until the end of the second week. Then she took charge. She gave me a drawer for my belongings. She drew my charpai closer to hers. She allowed me to listen to gossip with other maids, who let me be.

Our Saab, or Jameel Sheikh, owned many houses. He had moved back from Dubai to Pakistan to set up a textile mill with the help of his first cousin, who was a high official in the army. Sehr Madam was his first cousin. Under family pressure, he had married her when she had turned seventeen. In their family, business and marriage stayed inside the family.

I caught Sehr Madam flitting in and out of the house. She was beautiful but as translucent and fleeting as the shadows that shifted through the day. Bushra confided that unlike other homes where she had worked, in this house Jameel Saab took a keen interest in the hiring and firing of staff. He had hired Gloria in Dubai and brought her back with him. Bushra whispered that Gloria had instructed all the other maids to address her as "Ma'am". It upset Sehr Madam, and quarrels flared up quickly. It was better to stay out of Sehr Madam's way then.

Bushra whispered that Gloria was the real madam. She ruled over the servants, and her stature was beyond question, even above Jameel Saab's bodyguards. Gloria had nurtured a clan of servants in the house; they were her eyes and ears in the house, and in return, they were allowed to bully any servant they wanted, whenever they wanted.

In a few weeks, I realised that Bushra was right. Gloria was the real madam. She stood at the top of the hierarchy. Apart from the guards, drivers and cook, there were the other maids: one for cleaning the windows, one for oiling Sehr Madam's hair and massaging her, and one for taking Babur Saab to the school and picking him up. Bushra was Sehr Madam's personal maid and she had to stay close to her at all times, starting from the morning when she brought her tea in bed. Nanny was Babur Saab's maid. I was the maid for 'oopar ka kaam', which meant dusting and polishing the furniture and shelves and washing and ironing the clothes. My position was just above the maid for 'neechay ka kaam' – Surriya, a young, scrawny girl who wore clothes a size too small, who swept and scrubbed the floors and driveway, and returned to her home, a shack in a slum behind a shopping plaza, by dusk each day.

Surriya and I ate last and after the other servants had eaten. The cook gave us the smallest portions, saying that was all there was to eat. Sometimes we went without dinner. She had to leave and I, exhausted from the chores, would fall asleep. Bushra told me not to worry. She had a plan.

One afternoon, she led me to the refrigerator in the pantry and nodded. I stood still and unsure, knowing I could be fired. I had been warned to stay away from the food that was cooked for Jameel Saab's family. About to turn away, I paused, seeing Bushra open the refrigerator door. A scent of pulao wafted out. I inhaled and shut my eyes. My mouth watered, my tummy rumbled. Without thinking, I grabbed the plate that Bushra held out, reached inside and scooped a handful of rice onto the plate. I chewed hungrily and grasped another handful. I was hooked.

The refrigerator carried more food than the family would ever need. Watching me eat, Bushra said that if I did as I was told, I could take my pick of what to eat, because cook napped every afternoon and the other maids snuck off to the lounge to watch TV. But in return, I had to give Bushra her share, and do as she said.

A few weeks later, Bushra whispered that there was a stash of snacks in Sehr Madam's cupboard. Most of the treats would spoil before Sehr Madam even opened them. The cupboard was locked, but she could teach me to pick locks. Did I want to learn?

Wavering for a heartbeat, I nodded. Sehr Madam would never miss them. In a few weeks I had learnt to steal packets of nuts, supari or betel nut, and chocolates from the stock of dozens of boxes in Sehr Madam's cupboard. Bushra urged me to nick other things. Tempted by shiny clips, scarves, jewellery, and wads of money, I hesitated, but put them back. I wasn't a thief.

After a few weeks of catching me browsing through Babur Saab's books, Bushra confided that there was a treasure trove of books in Jameel Saab's study. And he rarely read. Unable to stop myself, I began to sneak Jameel Saab's books up to my room. I read about history, geography and the technology that was fast shaping the world. Every time I read, I felt whole and closer to the girl who had cleared her exams and won a scholarship. I marked the diary each morning and waited for Omer to call me. Where was he? He had to have some news by now.

∞

In the late afternoon, hearing the doorknob turn, I shut the book on boxing that I had taken down to browse. The door swung open and Babur Saab, dressed in jodhpurs and riding boots, pulled away from Nanny. "Zara," he called, running up to me. Scotty followed him. "I want to play the tez-gari game." Babur Saab, Scotty and I had become friends after I had started slipping them stolen treats. The tez-gari game involved Babur Saab climbing onto my back, while I scampered around the room imitating the tez-gari, or Jameel Saab's Ferrari, parked in the garage. Scotty ran after us barking, with his tail wagging.

"Hurry," snapped Nanny, dropping a blue and red costume on the bed. "He has to get ready for a birthday party. Get him changed. We must leave by four fifteen."

"Oh, is it time already?" I stooped to allow Babur Saab to jump off. He was ten years old but acted like a six-year-old. Or did children in villages grow up faster?

"It's past four, girl. At least learn to tell the time while you're here." Nanny rolled her eyes.

"Zara can't tell the time," chanted Babur Saab. Throwing his hand up, he jiggled his new watch.

"Of course she can't," said Nanny. "Poor village girls don't go to school, Babur Saab. They live in mud houses and play in the dirt."

"I want to play in the dirt," chanted Babur Saab.

"Hush, or no birthday party," warned Nanny. "And you," she turned to me. "Get him changed into his costume before I come back."

"I'll teach you to tell the time and we won't tell Nanny," whispered Babur Saab after Nanny had left. He pulled out a book, jumped on the bed, and waved at me. Scotty bounded up beside him. I hesitated, and squatted on the floor. "No, up here with me," insisted Babur Saab. He thumped his fist on the bed. Keeping a watch on the door, I perched on one side.

Babur Saab flipped the pages and ran his finger over a familiar picture. He began to talk. I stared at the image of an ink-black buffalo. Kullo. Where was she now? Once I had dreamt of earning money from selling milk. I had dreamt of going to school.

"You're not listening," whined Babur Saab.

"Sorry," I said. "Tell me again." I pretended to learn how the short and long hands of the clock worked, and then I helped Babur Saab to change into his Superman costume. Babbling about his hero's x-ray vision and his power to fly faster than a bullet, Babur Saab darted around the room, and hearing Nanny's voice he ran off. Scotty rushed out after him.

I picked up the dirty jodhpurs and riding boots and crouched in the bathroom. We all had heroes. I had my heroes – women and men. I had read about them. I remembered them. They lit up my world and sparked hope. They fought for what they believed; they fought for their dreams. I believed in them and their struggles. There was Razia Sultana. Belonging to a slave family, she had impressed her father with her brilliance. Astute and brilliant, she became the first woman ruler of the Delhi Sultanate in the thirteenth century. She ruled India, fighting for justice. Refusing to wear a veil, she led her army to battle on an elephant. She hadn't given up her throne until her death.

I gripped the brush and ran it over the leather boots. Fast. Faster. Again and again. The dirt flew out onto the floor. My heroes. They had not given up on their dreams.

27

The telephone screeched like a frenzied chimp. Rushing into the hall, I looked around. Where was everyone? I wasn't allowed to pick it up and answer. Although sometimes, after checking that no one was around, I cradled the receiver between my ear and shoulder, and pulled at the round dial, pretending to talk to Omer.

Hearing a shout, I pushed open the kitchen door and gaped. Why was Surriya cringing, with everyone crowded around her? Surriya raised her head, her eyes flashing from behind her straggly plait. My head spun. Chiragh. It was Chiragh looking up at me.

I shot forward, but Bushra caught my wrist and I stopped with a jolt. Gloria stamped her boot close to Surriya's head. What was going on?

"I'll give you five seconds to give a name," snapped Gloria, rapping her polished nail against her watch dial. Cupping her hands, Surriya begged for another chance. She'd thrown up because of a stomach infection. There was no other reason. She was the only earner in her family. She had four smaller siblings to feed. Gloria swore, barked an order, and in seconds the guards leapt to haul Surriya out into the alley. Ordering everyone to get back to work, Gloria strode out. The servants dispersed, and the kitchen emptied.

"She didn't deserve that," Nanny spat out. Her eyes scanned the room. "Why do we let that skinny shrew rule over us?"

"You know why," Bushra rolled her eyes.

"Men!" Nanny swore.

"Shush," hissed Bushra, watching the cook saunter inside. He'd been missing before.

"That was no reason to throw her out," grumbled Nanny. "The girl said she'd take care of it."

"She's plain stupid," muttered the new maid, hired for cleaning the windows.

"I bet he forced her." Bushra glowered at the cook.

"Forced or not, she should have taken care of it. Why wait so long? What was she waiting for? For the baby to drop down? Her mother's going to kill her." The new maid sniffed. "It's our fate, to be lumped or dumped."

"No, it's not," I began. But catching Bushra's frown, I stopped.

"What do you mean?" Nanny pushed the spectacles up her hooked nose.

"We have to fight for our rights," I began, feeling my chest tighten. "We've forgotten our history. We fought alongside men during the Partition. We've had women professors, warriors, rulers, leaders from … ouch, ouch." I trailed off as Bushra dragged me away.

"That's enough," she hissed. "Are you mad? Do you know what happens to men when they hear that kind of talk?"

Silent, I stared back. I hadn't said anything that was untrue.

"You'll be sorry," muttered Bushra, "I've seen the way the cook watches you, you with your warm skin and gold eyes. You're flinching now, but remember. Don't fall for his promises, you hear me? He's already got two wives back in the village and look what he's done to Surriya. They lie, they all lie."

I knew more about lies than Bushra would ever know. I had learnt to lie from my parents.

28

"Quick, I hear footsteps," warned Bushra. She tossed Sehr Madam's dupatta that she had been modelling, on the ironing board, and began to fold the clothes. I grabbed a sheet from the laundry basket and flung it over the heap of chocolate wrappers left over from my raid on Sehr Madam's cupboard last night.

"Pantry. In five minutes." Gloria blocked the light. Her eyes skimmed over the room, resting for a second on the charpai before she strode out.

"That was close," muttered Bushra, pulling her chador low over her forehead. "It must be payday. Just as well, since I go on leave today. Have to get our roof repaired before the monsoons land on our head. Come on, we can't keep her waiting."

In a daze, I pulled up my chador and followed. A month had gone by already and I was no closer to getting out of the house.

We entered the tiled pantry. Sunlight streamed in through the framed windows that opened onto the red-brick patio. Bright blossoms spilled out of rows of flowerpots lining the square space. This room was the closest I came to getting out. Gloria perched on the stool behind a counter. She beckoned to Bushra and slid a wad of notes across the gleaming surface.

I stared at the fire-red bundles. Money. And heaps of it. In my village, I'd seen smudged brown five rupee notes and pale green ten rupee notes, but never the fire-red hundred rupee notes. My heart raced. I looked up, hearing Gloria's voice. Bushra had walked out, and Gloria's eyes were on me. "Are you listening? Hurry and count. I've already deducted the amount we have to pay to Shafique. What are you staring at?"

My fingers tingled. I counted once, and then again. Twenty fire-red notes. Two thousand rupees. A fortune.

"Any problem?" probed Gloria.

"No, Ma'am," I whispered. It was mine. All of it. Heat flushed my cheeks.

"Go on and sign then. Do you know how?" She rapped the pen against the notebook. Taking a deep breath, I leaned over to write my name. "Do you have any family here?" asked Gloria once I looked up. Her eyes were on my face again.

I nodded. "Yes, Ma'am. My brother."

"Well, your *brother* is waiting for you by the guard hut. I'll give you ten minutes to meet him. Then back to work."

I stared at the swing doors. Why hadn't she told me before? How long had Omer been waiting? I glanced towards the pantry clock. Breakfast was not for another fifteen minutes. I darted out and drank in the fresh air, free of the sickly-sweet smell of Arabian jasmine that flooded the house. Bushra had whispered that it was Gloria's favourite flower and dozens of bouquets were bought weekly and arranged in crystal vases throughout the house.

I raced towards the guardhouse. Omer leaned against the wall in his familiar way, with his shoulders pulled back and his head slightly bent to one side. I stopped. My breath stuck in my throat. It had been too long. I couldn't cry. Not now. Brushing the back of my palm over my eyes, I hurried towards him.

"Zara, thank God." Omer hurried over. "You're all right, aren't you? Amma is furious at me for not checking up on you sooner. I've been calling every day, but that donkey of a guard always said you're working. And then I got caught up with schoolwork and couldn't get away."

His voice. It was the same. I swayed, suddenly feeling I was back home, in my village.

"Hey, are you all right?" Omer clasped my wrist.

I nodded. "I'm fine," I whispered. He was really here.

"You sure?"

I nodded and held up my other hand. "Look, I got my first salary."

Omer shook his head. "This is crazy. You shouldn't be working. You deserve to go to school." He paused. "Tie the money in your chador or keep it somewhere safe. Don't tell anyone where you've kept it."

"Forget the money. Have you found out anything about Tara?" I interrupted.

He looked around. "Is there any place we can sit and talk?"

I searched his face and then nodded. "Follow me." I led him to the wooden bench, set under the drooping branches of a willow tree in the side garden. "What about Tara? Have you found out anything?"

Catching the look in Omer's eyes, I gasped. "You have. I know you have. Where is she?"

29

"Have you met her? Is she all right?" I asked.

Omer shook his head. "I don't know. I checked the address you gave me. It is Kamran Sultan's house. He lives there with his mother, who's very ill. But his wife died years ago, and he's never remarried. Tara's not there."

"She has to be there. That's where Abba said she was." I stopped. My chest tightened. "Then where?"

"Did Amma or Abba ever mention Tara's Nikah Namah?" interrupted Omer, his eyes pinned to my face.

"Abba did. He told Khalid Chacha that Kamran was supposed to give him a copy when he visited. But he never did."

Omer closed his eyes and winced. "Do you think the marriage might be a sham? A hoax?"

"Sham? No! How?" I leapt up. "Amma and Abba saw Tara get married. They even attended her wedding remember, they …" My voice stuck in my throat. I stared, unseeing. How much had Amma and Abba known about this man? How much had they bothered to find out?

"You can rent a Moulvi these days," muttered Omer.

"If Tara's not in the house, then where?" I knew even before I finished speaking. I moaned, feeling splinters of blistering heat rip the skin off my flesh.

"We don't know for sure, but …" Omer broke off and looked

away, avoiding my eyes. He knew too.

"We have to get her out!" I shrieked and clenched the bench.

"How? It's too risky. It's impossible." Omer shook his head.

"We can't let her stay there."

"Not we." Omer's face was grim. "I can't let you have anything to do with this. It would be different if she was married to him and living in his house. But she's …" He paused and flushed. "You can't go near that place. I won't let you go near that place."

☙

I hurried to the kitchen, my chador flapping behind me. Near the door, I checked my slippers. Damp, but clean. I pulled my chador over my head. Pushing the door open, I stepped inside. A gust of heat slammed into my face. A crowd of servants chatted at the far end of the table. The cook poured the sizzling tea into tin mugs.

"You're late for breakfast," growled the cook.

"Sorry," I murmured. My stomach churned at the sight of the grey mush on the plate. I shivered. My hands and feet were blocks of ice.

The cook thumped the tray on the counter. Bodies thrust forward, shoulders jammed and arms shot out. Suddenly longing for the hot tea, I tried to squeeze through the bodies.

The windows rattled as the door banged shut. Seeing Nanny charge forward, I stepped aside, but Nanny gripped my chador. "Where is it?"

"Where's what?" I struggled to break free.

"Where is Babur Saab's Disney watch? You cleaned his room this morning, didn't you?"

"I cleaned it, but I never saw the watch."

"Tell the truth, girl." Nanny tightened her grip and turned to the other servants. "Last week, that poor boy taught her to read the time, and she goes and repays him by stealing his watch. He's been crying ever since he woke up."

What was she talking about? I swerved towards the others for support, but immediately shrank from their cold, accusing, dead-fish eyes. "I didn't take it, I promise. You got him ready."

"Me?" Nanny narrowed her eyes until they were slits of steel. "Are you trying to blame me?" She squeezed my arm hard.

"You're hurting me," I cried. "No, I just …."

"Not so fast," cut in the cook. He folded his heavy arms across his chest. "You met someone just now. Your brother, right?"

"Yes," I breathed out in relief. Omer would confirm my story.

"Ah," pounced Nanny.

"So you gave it to him," declared the cook.

"What? No, that's not what I meant," I stuttered. Why didn't they believe me?

"Tell the truth," said Nanny.

"It's the truth."

"How do we know it was even her brother?" added the cook.

"You gave it to him, whoever he was," insisted Nanny. "Tell us, if you know what's good for you."

"She'll tell us after I'm done with her," declared the cook. He turned around. "Everyone out."

Feet shuffled. I broke into a cold sweat. They couldn't leave me alone with him.

"Where do you think you're going?" growled the cook. I flinched, feeling his fingers brush my shoulders.

"Nanny?" I pleaded. The room was empty except for us. I tried to move back, but Nanny blocked my way.

"Liars deserve to be punished," spat Nanny.

Punished? My gut heaved. I reeled back, trying to pull away but bumped into a stool and flung my arms out to break my fall.

❧

"Hey, stop that. Stop lashing out! Wake up," yelled Nanny.

Nanny's head was close to my face. Shrieking, I pushed back. "I didn't take it, I promise."

"Take what? What are you talking about?" Nanny shook my shoulders. "Wake up and listen to me."

I opened my eyes. I was on my charpai, drenched in sweat.

"Are you listening?"

"What's wrong?" I croaked, scrambling up. It had been a dream, a bad dream. I swallowed. My throat hurt.

"It's a mess," whispered Nanny. "Madam's unwell. She quarrelled with Jameel Saab. He went out for a while. When he came back he found her unconscious. She's overdosed, taken dozens of sleeping pills. Saab wants answers." Nanny wrung her hands. "I don't know what to do."

"Why hasn't Jameel Saab taken her to hospital or called for a doctor?" My head throbbed. The dream had been too real, too close to what could happen.

"You don't get to ask questions," snapped Nanny. "Saab has ordered Gloria to take Sehr Madam to the hospital. But I can't find that poker-faced foreigner. I've looked everywhere."

"Have you checked her room?" I stopped at the expression on her face. "Of course you have. Where else have you looked?"

"Everywhere, I've searched the whole house. There's no trace of her. Maybe she's stepped out. You need to go and check before I tell Saab she's not in the house."

"Me?" I reeled backwards.

"Who else? Bushra is on leave, and I've tried calling the guards on the intercom. One line is busy, and the other idiot doesn't pick up. If Gloria's out, she hasn't told Saab."

"But ..." Catching the sharp glint in Nanny's eyes, I fell silent. I didn't have a choice. I had to do as I was told. Bushra had left this afternoon and I was alone.

Pulling my chador over my head, I pushed my feet into my chapplis, followed Nanny down the rickety stairs, through the shadowy corridor, and into the main house. Nanny stopped outside Sehr Madam's room, knocked on the heavy wooden door and slipped inside, leaving the door slightly ajar. I peered through the crack and gasped. A storm had hit the room. The cheetah-printed bedding was thrown off the bed. Curtains, torn down from rods, lay in a heap by the windows. Books littered the wooden floor, torn pages fluttered in the draught from the air conditioner, and shards of jagged glass gleamed under the broken lamp. A dark pool of liquid stained the floor. What had made Sehr Madam wreck the room? Had she hurt herself?

"Stop this nonsense and get Gloria here!" thundered Jameel Saab. I jumped back.

"Follow me," huffed Nanny, shutting the door, and marched off. I trailed after her. "The guards turn into wild dogs at night," she cautioned as we entered the kitchen. "Be careful."

And she was throwing me to them. I drew my chador down to my brows. My legs buckled as I pushed open the side door. Shadows whispered and shifted in the narrow alley. Something alive rustled behind the tall hedges. Did the night eyes watch me? I hurried down the path and turned the corner. What I saw made me jam a fist into my mouth to keep from crying out.

The entwined silhouettes clung and swayed. The dimmed lights did little to hide the fused bodies. The lithe frame with long silky hair, was it Gloria? It was. And who was she with, the guard? I watched them, unable to tear my eyes away. My face was hot, and then my gut flipped. If Gloria ever found out ...

I scurried back, cupped my hands around my mouth and yelled, "Guard, where are you?"

The dogs barked. A crash. Someone swore. I wheeled around and sprinted back down the alley into the kitchen. "She's coming. I have to get to the bathroom." I tried to rush past Nanny.

"Wait," Nanny reached for my arm. "What happened?"

I shook my head, pulled away and raced upstairs. It wasn't cold, but I was trembling as I sank down on the charpai and pulled the sheet over my head.

30

I woke up hot and sticky. The fan had stopped. Pale light filtered in from under the door. Rolling over, I yelped, catching sight of two black boots at the door. Fear clawed my gut. What was she doing here?

"Pack up. Shafique's arranged another maid." Gloria walked inside.

"Another maid?" I croaked. "Why?"

"You're finished. What did you think, that you could fool me? Blackmail me?" hissed Gloria.

"Blackmail you?" I sat up and shook my head. "No, I would never do that."

"Shut up," snapped Gloria, her eyes glinting like daggers. "If you say a word to anyone about last night, you'll be sorry. You get that? If anyone asks, tell them you've been called back, or there was too much work, or whatever." She swerved towards the door.

"No, please," I hurried after her. "I had no choice. Nanny told me to go look for you."

"You saw me?" she asked.

Hesitating for an instant, I nodded, lowered my head, and cupped my hands. "But I didn't tell Nanny anything. I promise. Don't make me leave. I can't leave, not yet." My breath squeezed into a knot. I couldn't leave now.

"That's too bad. You should have had more sense than to listen to that old ghoul. I had begun to think that you would last. Pack your things and get out." Shooting me a hard glare, Gloria strode out.

My eyes blurred, watching her leave.

But suddenlt Gloria was charging back, her eyes fastened on my face. "Wait. What did you just say? You said 'not yet'. What did you mean by you can't go home, 'not yet'?"

I stared back, my breath frozen. Had I said that?

"Tell me!" hissed Gloria.

"Ma'am," I stalled. My mind raced, searching for a spin. She was sharp. She would catch me out. "Shafique," I began.

"Forget him. Tell me the truth. You're hiding something. What is it?"

A tiny lie can push you down a slippery slope. I heard Nani's words in my ears. I couldn't slip down again. I had to risk telling the truth. Taking a deep breath, I related my family's story, starting from the afternoon we had gone to play in the fields to when Amma had spotted Kamran's picture in the newspaper, to how I had plotted to reach Lahore. I finished by telling Gloria about Omer's last visit, and shivered at the blaze in Gloria's eyes. Was she angry? No. It wasn't anger.

"You're a fool to think this man will give her up," growled Gloria. "Your sister belongs to him now. Go back to the village. Forget her."

"No." My gut hardened. "I have to find her. Help me find her."

"Help you?" Gloria narrowed her eyes. "Why would I ever do that? And you're crazy. Do you know what can happen to you if you get caught?"

"I know," I whispered. The dream was still too real. I shivered. I had escaped, but Tara hadn't. Suddenly, I wasn't afraid anymore. The fields had never trapped me, and the burka had never caged me. My thoughts had done that. I had let them. Not anymore.

I had lost my twin, my best friend, my only friend. We had whispered secrets and stories to each other, laughed together, saved each other from Amma's quick temper, and planned to discover the world together. She had asked me to look out for her. I was going to keep my promise. I was going to find her, and find the lost part of me.

"You don't know what you're saying." Gloria shook me by my shoulders. "If they catch you, they'll rape you, put you into the business or kill you. Then what?"

"I can't go back without my twin," I whispered.

Gloria eyed me for a few seconds, shook her head and sighed. "You are a strange girl. Okay, I'm going to think about what you've told me. But if you say a word to anyone about what you saw last night, I'll have you thrown out before you can blink."

31

"I've been looking for you," whispered Nanny. She yanked me to one side. "Tell me what you saw. Right after you dashed off, Gloria sauntered in like a cat that's swallowed a dish of cream and refused to answer any questions."

"Is Sehr Madam all right?" I tried to pull away.

"Shush." Nanny's eyes darted around the room. "A quiet corner is the most dangerous place to talk."

"But is she okay?" I remembered Sehr Madam's delicate frame and pale face. Had Jameel Saab done something to make her want to hurt herself?

"She's better, the poor soul. But it's nothing to do with us." Nanny squeezed my arm. "Now tell me what you saw."

I shrugged. "Nothing. I walked out and called out to the guard."

"And?" Nanny's grip tightened.

"And then I saw Gloria walking across the garden."

"And you didn't see anything else?" probed Nanny. She pushed the spectacles up her nose. "I might be old, but I'm not a fool. Tell me what happened!"

"I've told you."

"No, you haven't. Tell me. I will make working here easier for you."

"Nothing, I saw nothing."

"Nothing? Are you sure?" Nanny's fingers dug into my arms. "That poker-faced foreigner is up to no good, but I need proof to get her out." She pressed her lips to my ears. "It will be better for you if you tell me."

"There's nothing to tell," I mumbled.

"Nothing, huh? Fine, then, you get to work and so will I." Looking around quickly, Nanny stepped back. "Don't come running to me now. I've warned you."

The next afternoon I entered the laundry room to find a heap of freshly laundered clothes soiled with stains, and a pile of ironed clothes ready to be hung into closets, all crumpled. I re-laundered and re-ironed until late at night. The next day it was the same, the heap even bigger. A few days later I found my chapplis slashed, and my clothes cut. The other maids stopped talking to me. When I entered the kitchen they turned away. The cook halved my portions and gave me cold tea without sugar. At night I woke up, soaked in sweat and gasping for breath. It was the same dream every night. The cook and Nanny would be chasing me through the fields when I would stumble, and find myself sprawled over Sehr Madam's dead body. I missed Bushra. I had no one to talk to or confide in. I had overheard the maids saying that she had extended her leave.

A week later, I rushed upstairs to start the ironing. Again, a load of ironed clothes were crumpled and stuffed into a basket. Suddenly wanting to burst into tears, I hauled up the basket, and set it next to the ironing stand.

"Ah, there you are," drawled Gloria. "Phew, it gets hot here." She stood in the doorway.

I nodded, and smoothed Sehr Madam's chiffon dupatta on the ironing board. I dared not switch on the fan. Silently, I began to slide the iron back and forth over the sheer fabric.

"Is everything okay?" Gloria leaned against the doorway.

"Yes, Ma'am." Why was she here? What did she want?

"I have some news for you."

"News?" Suddenly feeling light-headed, I set the iron down.

"Look at your face," mocked Gloria "Did you think I would believe anything you told me? I have many friends, and my friends have friends." She folded her arms and frowned. "I checked your story out." She paused. "Zara, it's risky for you to meet your sister. Go back to your village."

"I can't," I whispered. What had she found out?

"This man your sister is married to, he's dangerous."

"I know." I clenched my fists.

"No, you don't. You think you do, but you know nothing. This man, Kamran, he's a monster."

I shook my head. "Do you know where she is?" I whispered.

"Are you listening? Return to your village. You'll be a fool not to. You can't do anything. Go back."

"Not without Tara."

Gloria exhaled slowly. "Fine, but remember, I've warned you." She set her hands on her hips and narrowed her eyes. "You're right. The marriage ceremony was a fraud. This man has married at least half a dozen girls under this pretence. The rumour is that he's put your sister in his new brothel. The police raided the place some months ago and arrested him, but he used his connections to get out. If you want, I can arrange for you to meet her, but I'll need ..." She brushed her thumb over her fingertips.

"I have the money," I burst out.

Gloria narrowed her eyes. "I know you do. But are you sure you want to do this?" She clasped my shoulders. "Listen to me, it's better if you forget about your twin and return home. That man Kamran is evil. Do you know what he can do to you?"

I nodded. Did I really? There was a hard lump in my throat.

Gloria stared at me for a few moments and then nodded. "Okay, I'll finalise the arrangements then."

"How? You said ..." My voice trailed off.

"I've got friends who've got friends," said Gloria. She squared her shoulders. Her eyes flashed. "You are a fool, but you have spunk and the will to fight for a cause. I like that. In my country too, women fight for a cause. The women in my family, in my city and country, they all fight for a cause."

32

I slipped past the cook's brooding gaze into the alley, and hurried to the guardhouse. Seeing the guard bent over a newspaper, I thumped my fist against the window. The guard lurched back, stared at me, and grabbed the note I held out. Soothing back his thinning henna-dyed hair, he grunted, picked up the receiver, dialled the number, and handed it to me.

"Hello," I stuttered. "It's me, Zara. You remember? Master Saab's student. I want to see Omer, my brother." The words rushed out. Gloria had told me to keep the call short.

"Why? Are you in trouble? I'll send you packing if you are," growled Shafique.

"No, no trouble. I wanted to send my salary back home."

"Foolish girl. I would keep it if I were you," said Shafique and hung up.

ॐ

Two days passed before I heard Sidra, the replacement for Surriya, calling my name. I uncurled my frame from under the mahogany dining table, where I had been trying to loosen the grime lodged in the wooden folds. Nobody in my village would believe that the rich ate on tables as big as boats, with legs shaped like dragons.

"Your brother is waiting outside. You should hurry, he's saying he has to leave." Sidra winked. "Is he your real brother? He's cute."

I sprang up. "Is he still at the guard house?"

"How should I know?" Giving me a blank stare, Sidra walked away. I dropped the cleaning equipment in the laundry room, pulled a chador round my head, and hurried down the hall.

"Hey you, what's your name, and where are all the other maids?" Sehr Madam swayed on her pencil thin heels. She floated in a finely embroidered shalwar kameez in the purest of white. "Here, iron this quickly and bring it to me," she ordered, holding out a bundle.

"Now?" I gaped.

"Yes, now." The thin rose lips pouted, and the thick arched brows furrowed.

"Bibi, my brother, he's waiting outside. Can I see him first? It will …" I stopped. Sehr Madam had dropped the clothes on the floor and turned away. The sound of clicking heels echoed in the passageway. Twenty minutes later, handing over the ironed clothes to Sehr Madam, I hurried to the kitchen. It was empty. Opening the side door, I dashed through the alley and spotted Omer leaning against a pillar on the porch. Aware of the guard's curious stare, I beckoned Omer to follow me to the bench under the tree.

In the next few minutes, I shared everything that had happened over the past few days: how Nanny had sent me out to search for Gloria, what I had seen in the guardhouse, my confrontation with Gloria, and her offer to arrange a meeting. But no, not everything. I wasn't going to tell him the truth about how I was going to get inside the brothel. It wasn't going to stop me.

"This is insane. Amma and Abba will be furious if they find out." Omer scowled.

My breath snapped and fire ripped my throat. He cared about what Amma and Abba thought. Hadn't they done enough damage already?

"I can't believe what happens in this place," continued Omer. "How dare Nanny try to get you involved in this? She should have gone out herself."

I shut my eyes. I had to rein in my anger, harness the fury. Control it and breathe it out. Opening my eyes, I steadied my voice. "This is our only chance to get Tara out," I began, and quickly ran over the plan I had devised with Gloria's help. I had to make him believe me. I had practiced going over it. It didn't sound unbelievable, but it wasn't the entire truth.

"When?" asked Omer.

"Friday night," I answered. Gloria had set the day. Bushra was still on leave, Nanny would be with Babur Saab, and Gloria would make sure the other maids were busy. But the success of the plan depended on meticulous timing. I had to slip past the first guard and reach the main gate. The second guard, a friend of Gloria's, would let me out. Once I was out, I had to reach the main market by 10pm sharp, where Gloria's other friend would be waiting. If I arrived late, her friend would leave without me.

"And where will you go from there?" asked Omer. "You can't bring Tara back to the house, and I can't take her back to the hostel."

"No, not the house." I untied a knot in my chador. "I've been holding onto this card for weeks. It's from Mrs Niaz, a history professor on the bus. She gave me her card, and told me to contact her if I ever needed any help. It has her address."

"Why didn't you show this to me before?" He glanced at the card. "I'm not sure," he muttered. "But what option do we have? Can you trust her?"

I nodded. I remembered the professor's words. She had sounded strong, supportive and willing to help other women.

Omer pulled out a pen and a piece of paper from his pocket.

"Give me that." He tugged the card from my hand, jotted down the details, and looked up. "Hey, why do you have that expression on your face? What's going on? You know you don't have to do this. I'll get inside that place. I just need time." He gripped my wrist.

My throat tightened. "No. We can't wait any longer. I can do this." My voice sounded strange, like it was coming from far away. What was I doing? I had never lied to my brother before.

Omer watched me for a few moments and sighed. "Okay, but tell me again how you'll get in."

Hearing voices, I glanced towards the garden. We didn't have much time. Hoping Omer wouldn't question me too closely, I leaned forward and outlined the plan again. "So what do you think?" I asked.

"It can work, but I'm coming with you." Omer stood up.

"No," I burst out. "I'll be in and out with Tara in minutes." Omer could ruin the plan.

"If you go, I go. That's the deal," insisted Omer. I opened my mouth to protest, but the guard was walking up to us.

"They're calling you inside. Your *brother's* been here a long time," snapped the guard, shooting Omer a warning look.

I nodded. Friday was only two nights away.

33

Heavy clouds. Pale moon. Did the night eyes watch me? I drew the chador over my head and shoulders, loose enough to conceal my black bag. I had less than an hour to reach the main market.

The front door shut with a thud. Voices and laughter floated out. Boots and heels clicked and clacked on the cobbled stone path. I crouched behind a rose bush and peered out. Primped and preened in their suits, Jameel Saab and his friends strolled towards the line of gleaming cars. He was leaving Sehr Madam home again. Was she any better off than Amma? She was tricked and manipulated by everyone around her. And today I had joined everyone.

Fifteen minutes earlier I had been trying to calm a frenzied Sehr Madam. "Bibi, I don't know, I don't know." I had looked away from Sehr Madam's tear stained cheeks. "Someone must have moved the pills without telling you. But don't worry. I'll tell the guard to get some more," I had said, trying to ignore the stinging guilt. A few hours before that, following Gloria's instructions, I had emptied out a supply of silver strips kept in the drawer. *Ptuck.* The sound of the sleeping pills popping out of the foil still echoed in my ears. Leaving a few empty strips on Sehr Madam's medicine tray, I had slipped the stack of empty strips in my black bag. Without fail, Sehr Madam took a pill at 9pm each night. Sometimes two.

Doors opened and slammed shut. I jerked back. Tires screeched, horns tooted and cars zipped through the driveway. It was time to move. I knew that Jameel Saab employed two guards for each shift. One sat in the guardhouse by the gate and the other in the guardhouse next to the garage. Their turns alternated each week. Hoisting my bag on my shoulder, I hurried to the driveway.

The guard sat sprawled on a chair. His uniform stretched over his belly, and some of the gold buttons had popped open. I thumped my fist on the door.

The guard shot up, but seeing me, he slumped back and began to scratch his crotch. "Oye, what is it? What do you want?"

"Sehr Madam wants you to go to the market to get this medicine." I held out the empty strip.

Grabbing the silver strip, the guard held it up under the light and dropped in on the desk. "Where did you get this from?"

"Sehr Madam. She's waiting inside."

"Why didn't she send her maid out, or what about the driver?"

"I don't know." I shrugged. Gloria had told me to play dumb and to pretend I didn't know anything except what Sehr Madam had told me. Eyes down, I watched the guard. Was he testing me? Gloria said he kept a roster on everyone's comings and goings and knew exactly where everybody was. Jameel Saab had left with his friends for his weekly game of cards. One driver was with him, and the other had the night off.

The guard flipped the pages of the register, looked up, and scowled. "I'm not an errand boy." His slammed his fist on the desk. "They'd better understand that." He stared at the medicine strip and then yanked it. "Where's the money?" He grabbed the hundred-rupee note I held out and growled, "Go and tell Sehr Madam I've gone. Then come and stand by the kitchen door. I'll call you when I'm back." He stood up and tucked his shirt into his pants.

"Please," I cupped my hands. "Don't send me in without the medicine. Sehr Madam will be furious. Let me wait here."

"That's not …" began the guard, shaking his head.

"Please," I pleaded. "Sehr Madam said she doesn't want to see my face until I get the medicine."

"Oh, all right. Stay here then, but don't go anywhere. I'll be back soon." Shoving the money and medicine strip into his front pocket, the guard strode towards the gate.

I heard voices, but after a moment it was quiet. I counted slowly and ran towards the guardhouse by the gate. The second guard sat in a corner watching black and white images flicker on the TV. I tapped on the window.

He swung back. I winced. It was Latif, the guard I had caught with Gloria the other night. "I've been expecting you after that fool left." He scowled. "Told Gloria you're no good, but does she listen?" He pressed a button. The door to the right of the main gate sprang open. I stood still.

"Get out," ordered Latif. "What are you playing at?"

"I told the other guard I would wait for him outside," I began.

"I'll cover for you," growled Latif. "But I'm doing this for Gloria, not for you. You're no better than a bitch on the street. Now go, before I change my mind."

I gasped at the sneering look on his face. What had Gloria told him? I ran through the half-open door. I would miss no one except Bushra. The gate clicked shut. I was outside.

34

"Zara!" Omer stepped out from behind a tree.

"You're here!" I hurried across the road.

"Saleem is waiting with the rickshaw," said Omer once we had turned the corner.

"Saleem?" I stumbled and then lengthened my stride to keep pace.

"I couldn't have come out alone. And we can trust him."

"Yes, of course," I said. What was I thinking? But I hadn't heard from him in months. The rickshaw stood on the side of an empty plot. A rapid beat of low Punjabi music vibrated in the air. Spotting us, the driver shut the music.

Saleem jumped out from the front. "You made it," he exclaimed, reaching out. I wavered, wanting to take his hand, but I couldn't. I was gripped by a sudden wave of fury.

"We should go," said Omer, moving towards the rickshaw. I climbed inside. The driver pulled the cord, and the engine burst into a loud rattle. The wind ballooned my clothes. The rickshaw careened through the maze of roads. Clutching on to my bag, I sat up straight. I had to think ahead.

After a few minutes, the rickshaw slowed, and the sputtering died. I leapt out while Omer and Saleem settled the fare. I hitched the strap over my shoulders and looked around. We were at a roundabout. Four narrow roads ran in different directions.

An occasional car or a motorcycle slowed and then sped past the flashing orange signals. A neon blue sign flickered on top of a tall building, but the shutters were down. A few men sprawled on the grassy islands between the roads.

"Did Gloria say where we should wait?" asked Omer.

"No." I looked around.

"I'll try to find out what time it is. Stay here," said Omer, and walked off.

Silence stretched like a tightrope.

"How have you been?" asked Saleem after a pause.

"Okay." I looked down. I had missed him. Friends didn't let go. He could have asked about me, or come to visit me earlier. My chest felt tight.

"I wanted to see you, but I've been busy," he began. I looked up, but he stopped and was looking past my shoulder at Omer, who was coming back. "So?"

"Well, only one of them had a watch and even he wasn't sure if it worked correctly," said Omer. "It's nearly ten. Let's stand where we can be spotted easily." He looked around. "There." Omer pointed to a street light past the grassy strip that ended just short of the intersection. Keeping a watch for oncoming cars, we hurried across the road and grouped under the street lamp. Minutes passed, but none of the vehicles stopped.

Finally, Saleem shifted, and pointed across the road. "Look, there's a rickshaw parked over there. I'll go and get it. We might not have time later." Omer nodded, and I turned back to the road. My breath snagged. What if the car didn't show up? Where would I go?

I jumped back, hearing tires screech. A small car skidded to a stop. The headlights blinked.

"Is that them?" asked Omer. Before I could answer, the door

swung open, and a lithe figure jumped out.

"Let's go." Gloria was striding towards me.

"Ma'am, you? How?" I stammered.

"Of course it's me. I had to make sure there would be no screw-ups." Gloria frowned at Omer. "Who's he?"

"Family."

Gloria shook her head. "We don't have space."

"He'll get a rickshaw," I argued.

"We already have one." Saleem stepped forward.

Gloria turned to him, hesitated, and shrugged. "Fine. You can follow us if you keep a distance. Stop when you see the taillights flash, or the guard will spot you. Got that?"

"Yes," said Omer.

Gloria stared at him. "I promised your sister a meeting, and that's what she'll get. Nothing more."

"That's not ..." I interrupted, but Gloria's stare shut me up.

"If you have other plans, I don't want to know," said Gloria, her eyes still fixed on Omer. "But I'm warning you, once she's inside, she's on her own, and if she gets caught, she's on her own. It's important you get that."

"Caught?" Omer echoed and frowned. "What do you mean?"

"What do you think I mean? She's going in pretending to be a new girl. She knows what she's getting into and if they ..."

"What?" Omer's eyes flashed.

"There was no other way to get in," I whispered.

"You told me you were going into that place to substitute for the cleaning maid who'd fallen sick."

"I didn't have a choice. And you'll be right outside."

"You're not going in there. That's it."

"Is this happening or not?" interrupted Gloria.

Omer shook his head. "No."

"Omer, I have to." I gripped his hand. "Look, I promise I'll be fine."

"No," said Omer.

"Dramas!" muttered Gloria. "I don't have the time for them. Don't expect your money back." She started walking back.

"Let me go," I cried.

"No, I can't risk losing you." Omer stepped back.

I turned to Saleem. "Tell him we've come too far to back down. What if we never get another chance? We can't leave Tara there. I will be out with her in minutes."

Hesitating for a heartbeat, Saleem grasped Omer's arm. "Let her go. She's right; if we don't do this tonight, we might not get another chance. And Tara's your sister too. You can't leave her in that place."

Omer stared at Saleem, shut his eyes, and sighed. He turned to me. "Okay, but only if you promise you will yell or scream if something goes wrong. We'll be right outside, waiting till you come out." He clasped my shoulder as I swung back. "Promise?"

"Promise," I whispered and shuddered. Did I know what I was doing? I rushed to the car, pulled the door open, and gagged at the overpowering stench of tobacco. I felt the brush of silk against my skin. The girl next to me smiled and moved closer to me to make space for Gloria. I shifted further towards the door.

"Hey pretty girl, want to jump up in front?" Pale bold eyes were watching me in the rear-view mirror. I stared back. He wore gold chains and had a ponytail. How did Gloria know these people? What did Saleem mean by saying he had wanted to see me?

"Leave her alone, Salu," ordered Gloria, closing the door on the other side. "She's not your type."

"Oh yeah, Glory," drawled Salu, drumming his fingers on the wheel. "Are you my type then?"

"Shut up, start the car, and try to remember there's a rickshaw trailing us. You get that? Good, let's go." Gloria leaned back against the seat. "This feels like old times," she murmured. Muttering under his breath, Salu started the car, and a soft purring sound filled the closed space. We sped off.

I gaped at the giant buildings, flashing billboards and fountains bubbling with foamy water. We zipped past sprawling parks and brightly lit markets. From inside the car, the city looked like a playground.

We turned into a narrow lane that wove through a marketplace. It was dark. No electricity poles. I looked back and caught sight of the rickshaw rolling into the lane.

"Remember to blink the tail lights," said Gloria, and swore as Salu braked. "We get out here, but you stay in the car."

"Whatever you say, Glory," Salu leaned back and drummed his fingers on the steering wheel.

"We'll walk from here and can talk along the way," said Gloria. "But remember that there are eyes and ears behind every shut door and window." I looked around. Dark and rundown buildings rose up on either side. I looked back. Omer and Saleem stood by the rickshaw, looking over. For one crazy moment I wanted to run back to them. I turned away.

"We're late," whispered the girl, Gita, as we began walking. "It's Friday, so Kamran shouldn't be there. But what if she's not out by the time my client arrives?"

"What time is he booked for?"

"The first one is at eleven," said Gita.

Gloria clasped Gita's shoulder. "You'll have to distract him. You get that?" Gita nodded. Gloria swung to face me. "You'll have about fifteen minutes. That should be enough time if you have any sense. Get your sister and get out."

"But …" started Gita.

"If Kamran is around, don't even take her inside," warned Gloria. "She can pretend to be sick or change her mind. Her brother will be waiting outside. But if Kamran's not there, get her to her sister's room. She's on her own from there. You get that?" When Gita nodded, Gloria turned to me. "The guard, Qadir, usually stays alert, but today Gita has a present for him." Gloria winked.

"What present?" I asked.

"Something to make sure that he doesn't give you any trouble." We stood at the bend. Gloria stopped and gripped my shoulders "I don't know what to think of you. Few would come so far." She paused. "Do you know what you're doing? You can turn back even now." I shook my head. "Go then." She brushed her lips against my forehead and strode away.

I watched her disappear. Did I know what was I doing?

"Follow me," commanded Gita. "We still have to walk a bit."

I followed Gita, mapping the route in my mind. "How many girls are there?" I asked finally. The more I knew about the place, the better.

"Not too many now. Sometimes four, sometimes eight. Kamran allows most of us to come and go but keeps some girls there all the time. Fridays are slow now. Kamran says he's getting more clients, but we all know that business is going down. We used to have a steady clientele of businessmen, generals, judges, bankers, police, politicians, and even bureaucrats. Friday was a busy night. They paid well and treated us well. Then it changed. Other brothels sprang up, closer to the city. You understand?"

"Yes," I answered. But I didn't. How big was this business?

"Then Kamran got arrested, and our clients got scared. The new ones don't pay much, and some have nasty tempers and even beat us. And Kamran is cutting costs. We don't even get meals. Now before I forget, the guard by the gate, he's old, very loyal, but you need to know two things about him. One, he can't resist whiskey and two, he hides the gate key under the floor mat, and thinks no one knows." Gita lowered her voice. "We're close now. Just listen, don't say a word. And for God's sake, take this off." Gita whipped the chador off my head.

At the fork ahead, two broken brick walls joined in a V. A massive container overflowed with garbage. We turned left, walked a few metres, then Gita stopped. A three-storeyed house rose up on the right. A metal gate with spikes barred the entrance, and a small door was cut into the left side.

Gita banged her palm against the door. There was a sound of shuffling feet, and then a curt voice called out, "Who is it?"

35

"It's Gita. Open the gate." Looking at me, Gita pressed her index finger to her mouth warningly.

"Gita? Back already?" A square, pockmarked face popped out. Qadir's hooded gaze skimmed over Gita and then settled on me.

"Let us in, you know there'll be trouble if anyone sees us." Gita stepped forward.

Qadir didn't budge. "Who's this? You know you can't bring anyone else in."

"She's not anyone," retorted Gita. "She's the new maid at Rahat Begum's place. I met her at her grandson's birthday party. Same old story; father needs heart surgery, but they don't even have money for two meals a day. She's the eldest of four sisters."

"Does Kamran Saab know?" demanded Qadir.

"Of course he does," said Gita. "But isn't he here tonight?"

"No. And he didn't tell me anything about a new girl," Qadir folded his arms.

"Well I told him, and oh, here, I almost forgot this, something for you." Gita grinned and pulled out a murky glass bottle with a shiny cap from her tote.

"Aha," Qadir snatched the bottle and smirked. "Why didn't you show me that before? Thank you. Thank you. If you say you've spoken to Kamran Saab, then that's good enough for me. Come. Come. Your castle awaits." He shoved the gate open.

Gita pushed me inside. I stumbled across the small driveway and heard the gate close behind me.

"We need to move quickly," whispered Gita right behind me. At the front door, she paused. "Now," she hushed me, swung the door open and pulled me inside. I blinked. It was dark except for a few flickering lights. A low drumbeat pulsed in the background. We climbed a narrow staircase. I looked down and saw a small alcove with large cushions placed around a faded rug.

"Ah, Gita," a loud voice shrilled. "Back already? Who's that with you?"

I stopped. *That voice.*

"Damn! Look down but keep moving," whispered Gita. She swung her face up. "Auntie, you scared me. Oh, her? I met her at a birthday party. She's another little bird from the village desperate for money. She got lucky when my client demanded two for tonight. Qadir just cleared her. She'll leave after the client leaves, but I have another booking. Need to send more money back home. My husband is refusing to pay for our son's schooling. That bastard."

"Aren't they all!"

"Auntie," cried a voice from above. "Where's my powder? I told you not to touch it."

"Ah, Gurya howls again," snorted Auntie. "Primps and preens the whole time, like it will make any difference to her chimp face. She peered down. "Good work, we need more new girls. Bring her to me once she's done and make sure you put her bonus in my room."

My head spun. The voice. The shrill voice. I had heard it before. Where?

As we reached the first floor, I caught sight of a hefty woman disappearing into a room. Loud shrill voice. Bulging hips. The heat. The smell of death. The cries and wails. I was back at Shaukat

Chacha's funeral. My head reeled. I faltered.

"Hey, what's wrong?" Gita gripped my arm.

"Who was that?" I whispered.

"Who, her?" Gita shot me an odd look. "That was Auntie. She's been here for ages. She was Kamran Saab's ayah, but now I hear he's thinking of throwing her out. She's getting old and lazy and hasn't brought in any new girls for months. Hey, we need to move. What's wrong?" She tugged my arm. "You're not sick, are you?"

"No." I shook my head, trying to clear my thoughts.

Auntie was the hefty woman with bulging hips at Shaukat Chacha's funeral. The one who had wanted to take Zohra to the city. Nasreen Masi had told Amma that she had driven the woman away. Hadn't Amma met her there? No, Amma had been inside. It made no sense. It made complete sense.

"You're lucky Gurya cried when she did," whispered Gita. "Otherwise, Auntie would have wanted to meet you. She would have torn into you like a barracuda."

We reached the second floor landing. The carpeting was threadbare and the lighting dim. "We're here," murmured Gita. "There used to be just two bedrooms, but Kamran had each split into two. More rooms, more business, he said, but as soon as the rooms were ready, he got arrested and the business slumped. Mine is the first room on the right."

"And Tara?"

"She's in the last room." Gita gave me a push. "Hurry, get her and get out of here."

I nodded, and then suddenly remembered. "Gita, my chador. Can I have it back?"

"Huh, what do you need your chador for, you funny girl?" Gita pulled out my chador, and I quickly stuffed it into my bag. "Bye," whispered Gita. The door shut.

I was alone. I leaned against the wall and locked my hands together, to stop them from trembling. My feet were clumps of concrete. I had to move. I reached the last door on the right and pressed my ear against it. No sound. I curved my fingers around the doorknob and turned. It was stuck. I tried again. It didn't budge. I tried harder, but my fingers slipped. How could it be locked? Was Tara even inside? I slammed my body against the door and winced at the stabbing pain. My hairpins. Fumbling, I pulled them out, bent two pins, slid one and the other into the lock and tilted them up. But the doorknob stuck. I drew the pins out, wiped them dry, and stuck them in again. Remembering Bushra's instructions, I ran one over the other and then bent the other. A click. Twisting the lock, I shoved the door open.

36

It was dark. The ceiling fan creaked. I dropped the bag and stepped inside. The room was empty. I squinted, trying to see into the shadows.

Choking back a shout, I lunged towards the mattress. My hands shook as I flung back the sheet. It was Tara. My other half. My twin. Finally!

"Tara, wake up. It's me. Wake up," I whispered, gently shaking her. Why was I crying?

Tara moaned. I shook her again, but there was no response. I felt her pulse. Steady. I pinched her cheek. Nothing. "Wake up, it's me," I whispered. There was no answer. Was she drugged? I swerved around. My gaze skimmed over the room. It was empty except for a ceramic lamp on a wooden shelf. I hurried to the curtains, opened the latch, and pushed at the glass windows. A breeze wafted between the thick bars. A jigsaw of uneven rooftops stretched as far as I could see. There was no way out from here. I crouched, hauled Tara into a sitting position, and shook her again. "Tara, it's me, wake up." Seeing Tara's lids flicker, I lost my balance and sprawled on top of her. She lay limp and unmoving. A dead weight. I had to get help.

Pushing back, I stopped to stare at the floor. Puzzled, I brushed my fingers over the silver sheen on the carpeting. The empty strips from Sehr Madam's pills! They had fallen out of my bag. Bending to gather them, I suddenly stopped. My heart slammed against my chest and raced.

I had just figured how to get us out of this place.

I scooped the foil strips and stuffed them back into the bag. Done. I pulled Tara up against my chest and froze as the doorknob turned and the door creaked. A beam of light slanted inside. I held my breath and then let go. It was going to be okay. Limp with relief, I lugged Tara towards the door.

"Zara, I'm so sorry ..." began Gita.

37

Eyes pinched tight, I lay numb and motionless, pinned under the stranger. Screams died inside my parched throat. Thick hard fingers groped and prodded between my thighs. What was he doing?

I cried out. Pain knifed and shot up to my belly, again and again. It ripped down into my legs, to the soles of my feet. Ripping. Tearing. I gasped, trying to breathe. I wasn't here. I counted. Seconds. Minutes. It had to stop. This couldn't be happening. Not to me. With a grunt, the weight rolled off.

I heard the rustle of the starched shirt, the pants being zipped up. The door creaked open and shut. I lay unmoving. It was over.

No. It would never be over.

In a terrifying blur, Gita had dragged me into the other room. I'd stared in disbelief when a young, clean-shaven man, looking like he belonged behind an office desk, had emerged from the shadows. Gita had slipped out. I had shrieked then, but the man had clamped his long fingers over my mouth. I stared up now. Moths danced a frenzied dance around the naked lights. I would be okay if I didn't blink. But wait. Tara. I had to get to her.

I tried to move, but my legs jammed. Emptying my mind, I bent to pull up my shalwar and froze. Dark streaks. I felt my thighs, and my fingers came up red. Blood. More blood. Shivering, I crouched on the floor, but then jerked up as my hands felt the notes: wads of hundred-rupee notes. For me? For my blood? My stomach cramped. Bile surged up. I had to get out. Grabbing the cash, I rushed out and to the next room.

Tara was still there.

Staggering, I dropped to her side, curved my body around hers, and held tight. I shut my eyes. I was drained and spent. My head lolled. I drifted, sinking.

Thub-dub. I opened my eyes. Thub-dub. Faint, steady heartbeats. Tara's and mine. From birth. My pulse flickered. A surge roared through me. We weren't dead. We had to get out before they killed us.

I shot up, hauled Tara out to the landing, and ran back to the room. I grabbed the bag of sleeping pills and the ceramic lamp and hurried back to the landing. My heart raced as I scattered a handful of the empty silver strips around Tara's hands. Standing by the railing, I heaved the lamp above my head and let go.

A crash. Silence for a second. Then screams splintered the air.

38

Cries soared, doors banged, and footsteps echoed. A wailing swelled in the air. I sprinted back to the room and peered out.

"What happened?" boomed Auntie.

"It's God's wrath," cried a shrill voice. "We've been punished." Shrieks muffled her voice.

"Shut up, shut up," roared Auntie. The noise subsided. "Any men still inside?"

"No, none," called a girl. "But Kiran's foot is bleeding. There's blood all over the floor."

"Enough. Everyone return to your rooms. Did you hear me? I said, now!"

"But Auntie look, Kiran's foot!"

"It's just a scratch," growled Auntie. "Kiran, stop being a baby. Seema, take this wretch to the kitchen and bandage her up. More clients will be here soon, so hurry. She can rest in her room if she likes, but no one else. And mop up this mess. I'm going up. God's wrath, my foot!"

I saw Gita's head pop out of the doorway. She began to walk towards the landing. Another door opened, and a tall girl in a red chemise slipped out. Gita had reached the landing. For a second she stood staring down and then reeled back, and shrieked.

"Shut up!" shouted Auntie. "Howling like bitches in heat, what's wrong with you all tonight? I said that I'm coming."

Wrapping my chador low over my forehead, and up to my nose, I hurried out. It was time. I had to make the plan work.

"What's this?" Auntie's voice cracked as she heaved herself up the stairs. "Oh God, Oh dear God."

Seeing Auntie's heavy-lidded eyes and fleshy face up close, I cringed. How could Amma and Abba have trusted her?

"She's unconscious," murmured Gita. "But breathing, thank God." She cradled Tara's head on her thighs.

A group of girls crowded at the top of the stairs.

"I told you it's God's wrath."

"What happened to her?"

"Overdose?"

"Good riddance. She always thought she was better than us."

Auntie swung towards them and snarled. "Get down. You hear?" She squatted down and clutched the silver foil. "Where did she get these pills from, and so many? Only Kamran Beta is allowed to give her medication. I've never seen him with this one. And how did she manage to walk out of a locked room, throw the lamp down and then faint?"

Gita shrugged. "I don't know. I've been in my room since I got here."

Auntie's eyes narrowed. "She's acting. Slap her!"

"That's right," muttered a girl at the landing.

Auntie swivelled round, "Didn't I tell you whores to go down?"

"But …" protested a girl.

"One word, just one more word, and you'll be sorry," screamed Auntie, and the girls fled down. "Slap her!" ordered Auntie.

"Auntie, no," protested Gita.

"Now!" hissed Auntie, her lips drawn back. Gita pulled her hand back and smacked Tara's face. I clenched my fists. What did they want to do, kill her?

"Again, harder." Sweat glistened on Auntie's face.

"Auntie, she's not acting," protested Gita. "Believe me, she's unconscious and barely breathing. What if we hurt her?"

Auntie shut her eyes and rocked back. "Oh God, If something happens to this wretch, he'll never forgive me. Oh God, help me."

"Call Kamran Saab," suggested the girl in the red slip.

"Are you mad?" growled Auntie. "He must never find out. I'm tempted to throw her in the garbage dump. She's been nothing but a nuisance since he brought her here."

"You can't," protested Gita. "She'll be discovered in the morning. And we don't need another police raid."

"Gita's right," said the girl in the red slip. "Better you take her to a private doctor. But tell them you found her on the street so they can't trace her to …" Her voice trailed off.

"Yes, there's a clinic in the main market," urged Gita. "I've been there. It's open all night. The doctor is good and doesn't ask too many questions."

Auntie spat on Tara and got to her feet. "She deserves to die."

"I would go with you but I have another client coming," said Gita.

"Yes, me too," said the girl in the red slip.

"I can go," I croaked. I stepped forward.

Auntie's eyes bulged. "You?" She swung towards Gita. "Who's she?"

"I told you, I met her at …" began Gita.

"Ah yes, the new girl," cut in Auntie. "You brought her, right? How did you meet her?"

"At a birthday party. She wanted the extra cash. She's done, but don't take her. She needs to get back home." Gita frowned at me.

"Then who should I take?" demanded Auntie "You're all busy. She's covered up too, unlike you whores. Oh wait, did you get the bonus on her? She was a new one, right?"

"Yes." Gita flushed. "I've put it in your room."

"Good," said Auntie. She grunted and narrowed her eyes at Gita and the girl in the red slip. "Nobody tells Kamran Saab anything! Is that clear? Now get lost, both of you." She watched the girls walk back and turned to me, "Let's go. I need to get my bag and glasses first. Can't see a damn thing in the dark. Didn't you hear? I said pick the wretch up."

My legs trembled, trying to haul Tara up. "Hurry," ordered Auntie and yanked Tara up from under the other shoulder. "Throwing down a lamp like that. Where does she think the money for a new one will come from?" Hauling Tara between us, we began to trudge down the stairs.

By the time we reached the last few steps, Auntie was wheezing. Her breath came in short spurts. "Wait here," she rasped as we reached the ground floor.

A few minutes later, she reappeared with a small bag. "Can't find my glasses. These wretches must have hidden them," she muttered, lumbering ahead and pushing the door open. Taking the hint, I dragged Tara out, lowered her across the stairs, and straightened up.

Qadir sprawled on his chair with his head flung back, snoring heavily.

"Look at him," growled Auntie. "If Kamran Saab caught him, that would be the end of him." She squatted on the steps and began to fan herself. "What are you standing around for? Leave your bag here and go get a rickshaw. You know the way, right?" I nodded, afraid to speak. Turning to go, I hesitated. I didn't want to leave Tara alone with her. "Are you going or …"

"How do I get out? The gate's locked." My voice shook. I had to pull myself together.

Auntie looked at me oddly. "The key should be under the floor mat. Check there."

Metal gleamed against the dark floor. My fingers fumbled. The lock clicked, and I sprang to hide the key back under the mat. With a last look at Tara, I pushed the door open and shot out through the narrow opening.

39

I hurried down the road towards the rubbish heap. A mangy dog bounded away with a kitten locked in his jaw. My gut heaved. What had I done? I shook my head. I hadn't done anything.

"Zara?" Omer's voice rang out. I saw him rushing up, with Saleem close behind him. I took a deep breath. I had to shut down my spinning mind. I had to stop the howling inside my head. I had to be someone else. For Tara's sake, I had to pretend I was the same as before.

Within minutes we huddled on the deserted roadside. In a few jumbled sentences, I related the events, from when I'd found Tara to how I'd planned the escape, skipping the part from when Gita had opened the door to when the man had left. I looked up to see Omer staring at me. My voice had sounded wobbly even to me. My heartbeat slammed in my ears. Did he suspect my story?

"I can't believe you got her out," exclaimed Omer. "I don't know how you did it. But right now, you need to get Tara out of here. Are you still planning to go to the professor's place?

"Yes, but I'll need a rickshaw." I swallowed the lump in my throat. They believed me. I should have been relieved. But I felt sick.

"I'll get you one." Omer jumped up. I watched him leave.

"You okay?" asked Saleem.

I nodded without looking up.

"You have to know I wanted to come to see you before but …" began Saleem. I swung my head up. Our eyes met. I couldn't listen to this. Not now. I began to tremble, and my eyes stung.

"Saleem, you coming?" called Omer. Throwing me a curious look, Saleem went after Omer.

I watched them approach the rickshaw driver. Speaking in a low tone, Omer drew out a wad of notes and gestured towards me. The driver shrugged and shook his head. Omer and Saleem exchanged a quick look. Saleem pulled out another handful. The driver grabbed it and grinned. He headed towards the rickshaw and Omer and Saleem followed.

"He's ready," said Omer. My lips moved, but nothing came out. I jumped into the rickshaw sensing Saleem's eyes on me. Would I ever see him again? It didn't matter now.

I leaned back as the rickshaw driver pulled the gear, the motor sputtered to life, and we sped back towards the house. We turned left at the fork. I pointed to the gate and signalled to the rickshaw driver to stop. "Shut off the engine," I told him.

Charged like a live wire, I bounded out. The gate was slightly ajar, the way I had left it. Auntie squatted on the steps, breathing heavily. Tara sprawled over the bottom step. Qadir snored.

"Auntie, the rickshaw's here," I called from the gate. I waited until she opened her eyes. "The rickshaw's here," I repeated.

"So? What do you want me to do? Take this wretch out and put her inside the rickshaw!" snapped Auntie.

I nodded. Eyes down, I hurried over, clasped my arms across Tara's chest, and lugged her across the driveway. Suddenly Auntie sat up and her legs stuck out like two stumps. "You tell me when you have her in the rickshaw, understood?"

"Yes Auntie." My heart raced. In less than a minute I had hauled Tara inside the rickshaw. I leaned forward. "Now," I whispered.

The driver pulled the lever, and the engine rumbled.

"What's going on? What's the noise?" roared Auntie. I lurched back as the rickshaw shot forward. "Stop! Wait! Stop! Wake up, you fool, wake up!" she shrieked. I swerved and shivered. Auntie resembled a wild hippopotamus charging towards us. And then Qadir was out too, swearing and running after us. We turned the corner, the driver cranked up the gear, and the rickshaw sped ahead. Qadir was left behind. I clung to the side railing with one hand and Tara with the other. The grey road blurred into hot tears.

40

When I woke up the room was dark. Jungle dark. Tara slept. It had started drizzling when the rickshaw had rattled to a stop. I had stuck my head out and choked on the overpowering stench of garbage. We were on a mud track. On the left, a sewage canal glistening with sludge disappeared into the dark night. A row of crooked buildings loomed on the right.

"This is it," said the rickshaw driver. "Get going." A dim tube light dangled over the door. I had checked the number on the card against the building number painted in black on the rusty metal, before banging on the door.

If Mrs Niaz had been startled, she hadn't shown it. She had helped me to carry Tara inside and listened to me, without saying a word. When I had finished, she had told me it was late and we could sleep in the lounge.

Was it morning now? I tugged the curtain, and flinched at the bright glare. Letting it drop, I looked around. A single mattress and a small sofa took up most of the space. I nudged open the narrow door; it led to a toilet. There was another door, but it was locked.

I pulled at Tara's arms. "Wake up." Tara moaned and turned away. I rolled her over and prodded harder. There was no reaction. I shook her shoulders. "Tara, wake up, it's me." She moaned slightly.

"Come on, wake up!" I whispered, seeing her eyelids flutter, and cried out as she opened her eyes. In a heartbeat I wrapped my arms around her.

"No." Tara shrank back."No."

"Hey, it's all right," I said, trying to pull her hands away from her face. "It's me."

"How? What are you doing here? Where are we?" Tara looked around wildly.

"You're safe. We're at a friend's place."

"No!" Tara moaned and shook her head.

I curved my hand around her shoulders. "What no?" I murmured, tightening my grip. It was my twin, her face, and her smell. I kneaded her shoulders gently. "Tara, look at me."

"Go away. Leave me alone," cried Tara.

Stumped, I drew back. "I'm not going anywhere. You're safe now. With me. We're going home."

Closing her eyes, Tara shuddered. I stared at her, confused. Had I made her cry? I loosened my hold and Tara pushed back. "I can't go home," she whispered.

"What do you mean, you can't go home?"

"You know why. I've disgraced our family."

I froze. Had Amma and Abba said anything to her? "What did you say?"

Tara shut her eyes. "There's no place for me back home. You should go. Stay away from me. I've ruined our family name. Dishonoured our family."

"Honour can't be taken by force," I shot back. Flames struck my breath. "The men who raped you have no honour. The people who punished and betrayed you have no honour." Did I say the words for Tara or for myself? My throat stung.

Tara shook her head. "If anyone finds out about me, our family will be ruined. Amma said no one would understand. They would make up stories. Shun us."

"They should shun us. For pushing you away, and marrying you to a monster, when you needed our love and support."

"They didn't know!" protested Tara. "Amma and Abba thought they were marrying me to a good man."

"But, it was a mistake, our mistake. Why should you be punished?"

"Because I'm guilty," murmured Tara. "I should have stayed at home, as Amma said. I shouldn't have run out alone. I shouldn't have left the house."

I gasped. "Are you mad? What are you saying? That it was your fault? That it was okay for them to rape you because you left the house?" I trembled with fury. What had they done to her? Nothing made rape okay. Nothing. What had they said to her?

"No, no, you know what I mean."

"I don't. And I don't care what anyone's told you, Tara. You did nothing wrong. I let you down. We all let you down." I gripped her arm.

"What could you have done?" whispered Tara. My heart raced at the flash of gold in her eyes, but the next instant it was gone. "I'm tired," she mumbled and moving away, she lay down, turning her body away from me.

I leaned back against the wall and shut my eyes. How could I take Tara back home? But I had promised Mrs Niaz that we would leave soon.

She had woken me up before she left for school. Over a quick breakfast of tea and chapatti, she had asked me to relate my story again. When I had finished, she had begun to talk, her voice flat and eyes dull, like someone had squeezed the life out of her. She sounded different. What had happened?

Her papers had come. She was leaving to join her husband in

Saudi Arabia. This country was not safe. You could trust no one. You could talk to no one. The rulers wore uniforms and switched hats; striped top hats to please the West, round white prayer hats to appease the Middle East, and peak caps to pacify the Far East. They had shredded the constitution and were conjuring up new laws every day. They had already sold the women. Children would be next; hundreds of religious schools for young boys were being set up across the country.

It was also a dangerous time. The men in power could judge you and accuse you of blasphemous crimes. She had been accused of talking too much and was being forced to leave this hostel. She was leaving the country, and I should leave as well, the sooner the better. I would be safer in my village. I was a clever girl, but it wasn't the time for clever girls to be out. I should return home. There was no other way.

I had stared at her in disbelief. The professor had changed. She had given up. Why? On the bus, she had talked about being tough and strong. What had happened to her talk about fighting back?

41

"Did your brother call?" Gloria cross-examined. I nodded. Omer had called after Mrs Niaz had left. "What did he say?"

I hesitated. Mrs Niaz had warned me not to open the door for anyone, but hearing Gloria's voice outside the door, I knew I had no choice. For a moment, I had wondered how Gloria had traced me here, but then Gloria knew everything. "He'll visit tomorrow, and we'll leave the day after, since it's a holiday in school," I answered.

Gloria nodded. "The sooner you all leave, the better. There will be trouble if the word gets out that there are two single girls here." Gloria paused. "I've taken an appointment for you at the clinic tonight. It took some connections."

I stared back. In Jameel Saab's house, I had overheard the maids whisper excitedly about a new operation in town. It took just a few minutes and a few stitches to close the tear. It was a cure for single girls with dark secrets. It made them as good as new for marriage.

"Get it done. You don't have a choice. And it won't take long, a few stitches." Gloria shook my arm when I remained silent.

"What should I tell Mrs Niaz?"

"Tell her you're going to collect your remaining wages." Gloria slung her shiny black bag over her shoulder. "You should be grateful there's no risk of a child. Gita said the man used protection."

My gut heaved. "Gita, is she okay?" I muttered, wanting to change the subject.

"She slipped out in the chaos that broke out after you left. Doesn't plan to return. Auntie's been thrown out." I was quiet. Had Gita called the man in on purpose? Was Gloria helping me out of guilt?

"What are you thinking?" asked Gloria.

"The doctor, is he good?"

"He's referred by a friend. He doesn't make a mess." Gloria shrugged. "So?"

"I'll do it." Gloria was right. I didn't have a choice. I had to protect myself.

"Clever girl," said Gloria.

42

"Age?" demanded the hook-nosed woman. She tapped her pen on the grey desk, under the dim fluorescent light in the waiting room.

"Don't answer, just hand the money over," said Gloria.

I slid the wad of crumpled notes across the metal surface. The woman frowned, flipped through the bundle twice and dropped it into a steel drawer.

"Age?" she repeated, finally looking up. I shook my head. The woman clucked disapprovingly and tapped her pen again. "Address?" I was silent. She sighed. "Go inside, take your pants off, and lie down. The doctor will be there soon."

In minutes, I was lying on a narrow steel bed. I stared up at the moon-faced light. A balding man in a long white coat loomed over me, and a sharp smell filled the room. He spoke, but his voice came from far away. A ringing sound echoed in my ears. I was back home, racing out. Suddenly, the fields tipped towards the horizon and I stumbled, I tried to run but kept falling and sliding down into the giant stalks that closed around me. I opened my eyes. The balding man had raised his hand; I caught a glint of a needle.

What was I trying to do? Lie? Hide the truth? Why? Was I going to let the fields trap me again?

I leapt up, shoved his arm away, and ran out, ignoring the shouts behind me.

ↀ

The knocking sound wasn't going away. I opened my eyes and winced. My head throbbed and my thighs were sore. Gloria had dropped me back at the hostel, repeating that I was a fool, that I would regret my decision, and she never wanted to see me again. The professor had left for school even though it was a holiday, saying she had to attend a teacher training and she would be back before evening. How long had I slept?

The raps came again, louder now, but before I could answer, Tara leapt towards the corner. "It's Omer. He said he would visit," I whispered. Why was I whispering? "I have to let him in," I continued. "Is that okay?" Tara didn't reply and hunched in the corner like hunted prey.

"What took you so long?" demanded Omer, as I unbolted the door. He pushed past me. "Tara!" he cried out but halted, seeing her bury her head in her arms. "Tara!" he repeated, and frowned when she huddled against the wall. I stood up and beckoned towards the door. He followed me to the door. We passed a veiled woman dragging a young girl with long braids.

There was no one on the mud track except for a few men returning from work, and a stray mutt nosing through trash. I winced, and eased down onto the narrow stone steps. The bitter, antiseptic odour of the clinic still filled my head, and the ground spun.

"Zara," Omer's voice seemed to come from a distance. He sat beside me. "Are you okay? What's wrong?"

"I'm fine." My breath shook. Why did I feel like crying?

"I never thought," started Omer and paused. "Why doesn't Tara want to see me?"

"She needs time." Was I trying to convince him or myself? I quickly filled him up on how Tara had reacted.

"The sooner we get back, the better," declared Omer. "We don't have to wait till tomorrow. We can leave tonight. I've checked the bus schedule."

"We can't go back to our village."

"Why?"

"Everyone will make up tales. Abba will be angry. He doesn't want Tara back."

"He still loves her," protested Omer.

"Does he? He told us to forget about her." I met Omer's gaze.

Omer sighed. "Well, if not home, then where?"

"What about Khalid Chacha's?" I rushed ahead. "I know you think Chacha is to blame, but he helped us."

"Helped us? How?" Omer frowned.

"He convinced Abba to let me go to Lahore. And he rescued Saima Appi from her terrifying marriage."

"And his friend got Tara into this mess in the first place. How can you forget that?" asked Omer.

I shook my head. "No. We can't blame Khalid Chacha for a suggestion that Riaz Chacha made. It was Abba's decision to send Tara away and marry her to that man."

"Did they leave him with any choice?" burst out Omer. He took a deep breath. "Okay, maybe you're right. It might be better if Abba finds out from Khalid Chacha. I'll go along with what you think is best. What do you think everyone will say?"

"I don't know. They'll make up stories. We can't stop them."

"I can stay longer if you need me to," started Omer.

"No, you have school. We'll be fine." I tried to sound convincing. The fight wasn't over. I had won a few rounds, but not the match.

Book Four

HOME

43

The indigo sky was fading as I dozed off. When I woke up, the bus had stopped at a station and the conductor was swearing at the loaders, telling them to get moving. The sun was up in the sky. A gold balloon, a sea of brilliant blue. The lush green fields raced to the horizon. Nothing had changed. Everything had changed. Nothing could be the same. I felt a nest of worms slither in my gut. I was going to be sick.

"You're up," remarked Omer, tapping my shoulder. He had been lucky enough to get a seat right behind the women's section.

"Yes," I took a deep breath and twisted my body towards him. The bus was nearly empty now except for two old men, fast asleep.

Omer glanced at Tara and frowned. "She didn't say a word last night and didn't look at me even when I tried talking to her. I thought she would want to talk, or say something at least. I don't understand."

"We have to be patient. We don't know what she's been through," I said, feeling as if a fist squeezed my heart. *I did know.*

Omer nodded and took a deep breath. "I can't believe you got her out."

"We all did."

"No," corrected Omer, "You did it alone. But I never asked." His eyes met mine. I saw the curiosity in them.

"Asked what?" A blade of heat lashed my face. I had been

waiting for this. A low drumming sound filled my ears. I forced myself not to turn my face away.

"Inside the brothel? Did anything happen? You were there for some time, and when you got out, you looked strange, all pale. I didn't ask then …"

I swallowed, and tasted grit. I had to say it. "If something happened, would it matter, would it change anything?" I held my breath. His answer mattered. A lot.

Omer stared at me for a few seconds and then shook his head. "No, we're together, that's what counts. Nothing else matters." He squeezed my hand and let go.

I turned to look out of the window. The bus hurtled down the thin blade of a road. It was the beginning of another day, the two hundred and seventy-fifth day.

44

The wind raged, hurling whorls of sand everywhere. I jumped down from the bus and helped Tara out. Omer went to hail a tonga. The tonga walla chatted nonstop through the ride. The day before his wife had locked him out and told him not to return until he'd earned enough money to feed their five children. Not a single customer had approached him the whole night. Near dawn when he had decided to sell the tonga he had inherited from his father, to try his luck at the brick kiln, Omer had come along. That was fate. It was in his blood to drive tongas.

An hour later the tonga turned onto a dirt track. I inhaled the scent of fresh earth. Roosters crowed, birds chirped, tin pots and pans jangled as women prepared breakfast. I was home. These were my sounds. I had carried them with me.

The tonga stopped outside Chacha's door and we jumped off. Omer waved the tonga-walla goodbye. As we stood outside the door, Tara slumped against the wall. "I can't," she choked.

"It'll be all right," I assured her.

"Trust us," reassured Omer, but Tara shook her head. I thumped my fist on the door and hearing a noise I nodded to Omer.

We waited, but nothing happened. Omer stepped up and banged harder. A shuffling noise came closer this time.

"Who is it?" called a voice.

"Saima Appi?" I answered. "It's me, Zara, please open the door."

"Zara?" exclaimed Saima Appi. "How? Wait, just opening." The latch dropped with a soft thud, and the door swung open. Saima Appi gasped. Her eyes flew from Tara to me, to Omer, and back to Tara again. "Tara?" she murmured. "How, what's going on? When did you ... How?"

"Everything's fine," I said. "Can we come in?"

"Sorry, sorry. Come in," Saima Appi stepped back, "I had just started preparing breakfast when I heard the noise. I thought I had imagined it, but then it started again. I never thought..." Not finishing her sentence, she shut the door.

Once we were sitting on the two charpais set across from each other, Omer asked Saima Appi about Khalid Chacha.

"He's still sleeping. Your Chachi and Nazia aren't home either," answered Saima Appi. "But tell me, what's going on?"

"I'm tired," interrupted Tara.

"Can she rest in your room?" I asked.

"Yes of course. Come, Tara." Saima Appi got up.

"No," Tara shook her head.

"Let me." I got up and pulled Tara up with me. We followed Saima Appi to her room. I gazed around. We had chatted and laughed in this room less than a year ago. It seemed so long ago. Suddenly, I longed to puff at the hookah again.

"Don't leave!" Tara gripped my hand.

"I won't. I got you out. I won't ever leave you," I said, sitting by her side. Tara sighed, and lay down on the charpai, facing the wall. I watched her for a few minutes, and when she closed her eyes, I tiptoed out into the courtyard.

"What's going on, tell me," prompted Saima Appi, sitting on the charpai. I nodded and beckoned towards Omer.

We had agreed that Omer would tell the story, a mix of truth and lies. No one would dare question his word; they would believe him. Omer had warned that if Abba even caught a whiff of the fact that I had entered a brothel, he would disown me. The villagers would also punish me. I believed him.

By the time Omer had finished relating the events of how he had lied his way inside the brothel to rescue Tara, Saima Appi was nodding her head. "Before my marriage, I would have said you were making this up, but not now." She paused, "Tara, is she …?"

"She's still sleepy," answered Omer. "They drugged her, but with what or how much, I don't know. I found her unconscious, but she woke up the next morning."

"The pills take time to wear off," said Saima Appi. "My in-laws mixed them in my food. I was confused all the time. Tara's lucky to have you both." She was quiet for a few seconds, and then gasped. "But you must be hungry! I'm a fool for not asking you earlier. What would you like?"

"We're starving," said Omer instantly. "Chai, if possible?"

"I can do better than that," said Saima Appi. "How about parathas with cream and gur?" Omer beamed.

"I'll help," I offered, following Saima Appi to the kitchen.

"When does Khalid Chacha get up?" I asked as we started to put the meal together. "Soon," answered Appi, handing me the saucepan and tea leaves. "But, you're in luck that your Chachi is not here. She would have thrown a fit, declared Tara to be a bad omen."

I nodded, remembering Chachi's moods. I filled the saucepan with water, set it on the stove, and added a generous helping of tea leaves, milk, and sugar. "And how are you?"

"I'm better than I was," said Saima Appi, starting to knead the dough. "But it wasn't easy. After Abba decided the marriage was over, your Chachi seethed for days. When that didn't work, she shut herself up for three days and refused to speak or eat. She wore black and declared that only my dead body should have left my husband's house. Abba had to promise he would find me another husband before she agreed to come out."

"She's mad," I declared. "But where has she gone?"

"She's visiting my grandparents, along with my brothers. And since there was a wedding in their village, she took Nazia along. Some distant relatives wanted to see her for their son."

I was quiet, remembering Nazia telling me that she liked some boy. "She's only thirteen," I murmured.

"Yes, but your Chachi's on a rampage. She doesn't listen to anyone these days. I try to stay out of her way."

"What about Chacha?" I asked. "Can't he do something?"

"She blames him for destroying my marriage, so he doesn't say much any more." Saima Appi swirled the dough in the air and deftly dropped it on the hot tawa greased with ghee.

"Your in-laws were crazy," I burst out. "They would have killed you eventually."

"Maybe," murmured Saima Appi and sighed. "I was my mother's angel before I got married. I could do no wrong, but since my divorce, I can't do anything right. Like I was only worth something while I was married." She flipped the paratha over. "Here, bring the basket over."

I looked at Saima Appi. "You must be wondering why we came here."

"You want your Khalid Chacha to tell your father that Tara's back, right?" Without waiting for an answer Saima Appi continued, "I know my father, he'll do it, but you will have to be strong."

The food was ready. I inhaled the scent of fried dough. Loading everything onto two platters, I followed Appi into the courtyard. Omer lay on the charpai, his eyes closed.

"Is he asleep?" asked Appi.

"Not a chance." Omer opened his eyes and grinned. "Only a fool would sleep, with the aroma of parathas in the air." He sat up, and in silence we devoured hot parathas with cream and gur.

A creaking sound from the room made us jump.

"That must be Abba. Don't worry. Finish your tea. I'll go talk to him," said Saima Appi. "And no, I won't tell him anything," she added, seeing Omer's questioning look. "I'll just let him know you're here. The talking and explaining you do yourself."

"I'll clear up," I said, as I stacked up the dishes and headed towards the kitchen.

I had started rinsing when the door opened, and Chacha's voice boomed through the courtyard. "Omer Beta, what a surprise! Come here," said Chacha. His voice sounded welcoming, but I couldn't be certain. Omer started talking in a low voice, and I wavered, uncertain if I should join them or let Omer finish the story. I decided to finish rinsing. After a while, with nothing more to do, I walked out. Khalid Chacha sat with Omer on the charpai. "Salam, Chacha," I mumbled.

"Zara Beti," Khalid Chacha reached out to pat my head. "I can't believe you are both here with Tara. It's a miracle that she's back." He glanced from me to Omer.

"Yes," I murmured.

"But is she all right?" Chacha frowned.

Omer looked away, leaving me to answer. "We don't know. She sleeps a lot. We think he might have drugged her," I began.

"That bastard!" exploded Chacha. "Should I call the doctor? He lives close to us."

"I don't know. What will we tell him?" I asked. Khalid Chacha opened his mouth to speak, then sat back and nodded.

"Zara, come quickly. Tara's awake." Saima Appi's head bobbed at the door and disappeared.

45

Seeing Khalid Chacha rise, I sprang up. "Maybe I should go alone."

Khalid Chacha paused, his feet half-thrust into his shoes, then he nodded and sat down. Inside the room, Tara huddled against the wall with knees drawn together. Seeing me in the doorway, she scrambled up and whispered, "I need to use the bathroom." Ignoring my outstretched arm, she followed me to the tin stall behind the room. When she came out, she had plaited her hair. Her face was pale except for the dark smudges under her eyes.

"Khalid Chacha wants to meet you," I started.

"No!" whispered Tara. She pulled her legs up and wrapped her arms around her knees. About to argue, I stopped, seeing Saima Appi walk in with more parathas and three cups of steaming tea.

"Thanks, Appi," I murmured.

"Thank you," echoed Tara. We drank our tea in silence. "I'm not the same. I can't ever be the same," Tara blurted out. She pushed her half-eaten paratha aside and looked up, her eyes flashing sparks.

"You don't have to be the same." I edged closer, but Tara shrank back. "We still love you and want you back," I whispered.

"Do Amma and Abba?" Tara's eyes searched mine.

"Yes." I said, but it came out a split second too late. Tara had turned away.

"I want to lie down," she murmured. I nodded. Was it the

drugs? Holding the cup between my palms, I sipped my tea, hoping it would ease the throbbing ache in my head.

It was late afternoon when I sat down to cook a pot of yellow lentils.

"We'll have to tell Amma and Abba about Tara," began Omer, walking inside. He squatted next to me.

I drew the wooden spoon through the lentils to temper the boil. Why did we still seek their approval? "Yes," I muttered, "But there's no hurry, is there?"

"Chacha is leaving now. He'll reach our village by early evening," said Omer.

"Now?" My hand stopped moving.

"Yes. He's saying he can't keep Tara here without telling Abba. And Chachi returns tomorrow morning. We'll stick to the same story, all right?"

I nodded, and watched the bubbling blend swell and simmer. There was no space for the truth in my village. I had to tape and pack my thoughts and feelings tightly until there was no space to think and feel.

I shut my eyes. There was no place to escape. Did I want to go back? I didn't know. But I knew I didn't want to be caged. I longed to discover the world. Why did my life tie me up, bind me, and hold me back? Why couldn't it set me free to do what I wanted, whenever I wanted?

46

I heard the tonga wheels rumble outside. When the door rattled, everyone moved at once. I pushed aside the platter of grains, Saima Appi hurried to open the door, and Tara sidled closer to me.

Entering through the doorway, Amma called out for Kulsoom Chachi. She gasped on catching sight of us. "Tara," she cried out. Before Abba could react, she had leapt towards us. A spasm ripped my gut. What was she going to do?

"It's you. My daughter. How? You have to forgive me. I didn't know. Forgive me. Can you forgive me?" I sagged, watchng Amma's hands move lovingly over Tara's face, neck and arms. Tara's eyes stayed shut and her body remained rigid.

"Khalid Bhai," began Abba, his voice hard. "You told us that Kulsoom Behen was unwell and that it was an emergency."

"I'm sorry Bhai," began Khalid Chacha. "I needed to bring you here, but didn't want to worry you." Khalid Chacha reached out but Abba moved away. When Khalid Chacha tried to grasp Abba's shoulder, Abba dodged, and Khalid Chacha sighed. "I thought it would be better to talk once we got here." Ignoring Chacha's outstretched hand, Abba fixed his hawk eyes on Tara, who was squirming in Amma's arms.

I exchanged a quick look with Saima Appi. "Amma, let's go inside. Tara's tired."

"Yes, come," insisted Saima Appi, pulling at Amma's hand.

"You need to rest as well." Without protest, Amma followed Saima Appi inside the room.

"Abba's not happy, is he?" whispered Tara, leaning close to me.

I shook my head. "He's just shocked. It's going to be fine."

"It's not," interrupted Tara and pulled away.

Leaving Tara with Saima Appi and Amma, I faltered on the edge of the courtyard. Abba and Khalid Chacha sat on opposite ends of the charpai. Omer stood in the shadows; but seeing me, he stepped forward.

"What's been going on?" Abba's voice boomed.

"It's better if Omer tells you," murmured Khalid Chacha.

"Omer? What's he got to do with it? And why isn't he in school?" growled Abba. His scowl deepened as Omer began to speak. Skipping over the details, Omer related again how he had lied his way inside the brothel to get Tara out while I had waited outside. It was the same slush of truth and lies we had told Khalid Chacha earlier.

"You have no idea what you've done." Abba's eyes blazed.

"What? I don't understand." Omer looked confused.

"What's not to understand? Tara's married to that man. She's his wife, and …" Abba's face darkened.

Khalid Chacha leapt up. "What are you saying? Didn't you hear Omer? The marriage was a farce! Do you even have their Nikah Namah?"

"No, but …" started Abba.

"Then we have to accept there was no marriage. It was a sham. Never even registered," said Khalid Chacha. He looked grim.

"I married her to Kamran in front of my eyes. There was a Moulvi there who filled the papers. That's enough proof for me."

"He put her in the brothel, Abba!" protested Omer.

"You say that, and yet you found her in a room alone and sleeping. Do you have proof? Did you see her with any man?"

Abba glared at Omer.

Khalid Chacha swore. "This is absurd. Don't deceive yourself. Her husband was a dangerous man. A monster. She was living in hell and …" he paused, seeing me step out of the shadows.

"Hell or no hell, she's his wife, and he can do as he pleases with her. It has nothing to do with us," declared Abba.

Khalid Chacha frowned. "I can't believe what you're saying. Our faith doesn't condone this."

Not answering Khalid Chacha, Abba glowered at Omer, "And you risked yours and your sister's lives? You gave no thought to what could happen to Zara while she waited outside. And you pulled her away from a perfectly good job where she was earning money for her dowry."

"We couldn't have left Tara there. Not once we knew!" retorted Omer.

"That's no answer," said Abba. "Tell me Bhai," He wheeled towards Khalid Chacha. "How can I take Tara back? What do I do with her?" He paced back and forth, then stopped abruptly. "What will everyone say? And her husband, Kamran, gave us so many gifts. This watch." He waved his wrist and the gold metal jangled. "And the radio, and the tea set. What if he comes after us? And if the villagers find out, we will be ruined. Isn't this what you warned me against?"

"Yes, but at that time we thought Tara was going to work as a maid. Later you said you had married her to someone you knew, a decent man. No one thought she …" Khalid Chacha paused, struck by a thought, and his eyes narrowed. "You didn't suspect Kamran at that time, did you?"

"What? No, no," said Abba, his face flushing. "You can't think that." He stopped as Amma had walked out and now stood by the charpai, swaying.

"Mariam!" started Abba. "Are you all right?"

"Yes, I'm okay, we're fine." She took a deep breath and turned to Chacha. "Thank you for helping Zara and Omer when they came to you."

"You don't have to thank me," said Khalid Chacha.

"And you two." Amma swung her eyes from Omer to me. "Thank you. You've returned my life to me."

"Mariam," declared Abba. "Nothing's decided as yet. We have to discuss this."

"No." Amma shook her head. "No more discussions and no more listening to others. We listen to our hearts now. We take Tara home."

"What?" growled Abba.

"We take Tara back home!" repeated Amma.

"We don't do anything until I say so." Abba's voice was hard.

"You can say what you like," said Amma. "But I won't go back unless Tara comes back with us."

I gasped. What had come over Amma? She had never disagreed with Abba.

"Have you lost your mind? You will do as I tell you." Clenching his fists, Abba moved forward, but Omer stepped between them.

"Bhai, no," admonished Khalid Chacha, lowering Abba's fists.

"Lost it? No, I think I've finally found it," murmured Amma and turned to walk away.

47

"I've been thinking," said Amma, opening her sewing basket. "It's not right that the girls still share a room with us. They need their space."

Dropping the clothes I had finished rinsing, I crouched to rinse them again.

"You know we don't have enough rooms," answered Abba. He set his tea mug down. He hadn't said a word since our return yesterday afternoon.

"We will, if we clear the sitting room and give it to the girls." Amma zipped a needle in and out of the cloth.

"You're bursting with answers today. Tell me then, where will our guests sit, outside with your stray cats?" snapped Abba.

"If they have to, then yes," Amma bit the thread, tied a knot, and looked up. But Abba had already stalked off.

The following morning Abba emptied the family room, stacked the furniture in one corner of the courtyard, and packed all the plastic mats, plates and cups in a crate. He hauled in sacks of mud and wheat and piled them to one side. Was he going to build a room for us? Why? What hold did Amma suddenly have over him, I wondered. Tara and I lugged our charpai into the empty room and arranged our few possessions in the cardboard box I had found under my parents' charpai. Remembering our silver birth bracelets, I pushed the thought away. It wasn't yet time.

Over the next few days, at fleeting moments, I missed the grand house, the brilliant crystal lights that lit up the evenings, the clean water gushing out of gold taps, and the cool air conditioning and fans. But nothing else. In my village, I walked barefoot on the earth, under the open skies, and breathed in fresh air. I slept as the sky darkened and woke up to see it shimmer pale pink. I thrilled in the rush of wind, the muggy heat and even the sweat on my skin. This was home. This was my place in the world. I was part of a world that was bigger than me.

Busy with one chore or another during the day, I feared the night, filled with dark dreams, with menacing beasts. I would wake up with a jolt, remembering the heavy body smothering my breath and tearing into me. But seeing Tara asleep next to me, I would lie down again, drenched in sweat. Doubts clenched and clawed me from inside. Why had I not run out? Why hadn't I fought back harder? Why had I even gone inside the brothel?

Abba disappeared each morning and returned after dinner. No one asked where he ate. Amma hovered around Tara like she was a broken doll. Tara became that broken doll. When I tried to talk to her, she looked at me blankly. And even Amma didn't say much and looked through me most of the time. At times I wondered if she had forgotten I was there. Or was I jealous? How could I be jealous of my twin?

A few days later, I squatted down to sweep the heap of leaves and branches left by a storm while Tara and Amma sorted clothes inside. When the door rattled, Amma called for me to open it. I lifted the latch and was pushed aside by Bari Masi, our neighbour, who shuffled in, carrying a large straw basket. "Salam, Bari Masi," I muttered. What was she doing here?

"Where's your mother? Call her quickly and bring me a glass of water and a large platter." Bari Masi's gaze lingered on the heap of mud and wheat waste. "Why is the furniture out? What are you building?"

Pretending I hadn't heard, I hurried inside. "Bari Masi's here," I began. "Oh Tara, you look pretty in that shirt. No, don't hide." But Tara had already ducked behind Amma.

Amma frowned. "What does she want from us? She's chased Nasreen and her daughters off and now is acting pious enough to drive anyone crazy."

"She wants to see you and she'll walk right inside if you don't go out soon," I warned.

"Come and meet her, Tara," urged Amma. "She's always had a soft spot for you."

"I have a headache," murmured Tara. I caught the strain in Amma's eyes. Tara's headaches started as soon as anyone walked in through the door.

"Amma?" I began.

"I'm coming. You go and make tea."

"Okay," I turned to Tara. "Rest up, but make sure your headache's gone by the time Bari Masi leaves. I need your help with the chores. You're becoming a real majj."

"Zara!" chided Amma. But satisfied by the hint of a smile on Tara's face, I hurried out and began to brew the tea. The sooner Bari Masi finished and left, the better. Walking up with the tea, I saw that Bari Masi had lined up some bottles, a total of six, on the platter.

"Pour three drops from each bottle into a cup of water and after reciting prayers, sprinkle the water over Tara, or better still, make her drink it. Remember, once a day at least. Do it right, and all your sorrows will vanish in a few days," explained Bari Masi.

"But Bari Masi," began Amma.

"And shame on you for not coming to me. If Zubaida hadn't

mentioned it, I would have never found out," scolded Bari Masi. "As the village elder, it's my responsibility to guide you. Do as I tell you, and your son-in-law will come begging on his knees."

"Hope not." The words were out. I reddened.

Amma glared.

Bari Masi's face twisted. She threw me a quick look, then turned back to Amma. "What did she say?"

"Nothing," said Amma, shooting me a warning look. "She said she hopes the drops will work."

Bari Masi scowled. "Of course they will work. What does she know? I've been brewing my potions since before she was born. If you do as I say, Tara will be back with her husband in no time."

"Yes," cut in Amma. "But I must tell you. It's good to have Tara back."

"Oh rubbish," cut in Bari Masi. "You know as well as I do that once a girl is married, only her dead body should leave her husband's house."

"That's not what our religion says. Even women have rights." protested Amma.

"Rights?" echoed Bari Masi. She picked up the cup of tea and poured it into the saucer. "You're coming up with some strange ideas. Our traditions and customs give meaning to our life. We must preserve and protect them. Surely you're not saying our fathers and forefathers were wrong?"

"No, but …" started Amma.

"No buts. Whatever happens, it's a wife's responsibility to make the marriage work. Imagine if all married daughters started returning to their parents' homes?"

"They should return if they're not happy," declared Amma.

"I see." Giving Amma a cold stare, Bari Masi set down the untouched saucer. "I thought your husband had done a better job of guiding you. I should go now. Let's see, there are six bottles, and each is for four rupees, so that's …" Bari Masi flicked her thumb over her fingers. "That's twenty-four rupees. If it's a bad time, I can extend credit." She glanced slyly at the heap of furniture.

"Phitteh muh," I murmured. She had come to sell her potions. Seeing Amma beckon, I hurried inside and brought out the pouch.

Bari Masi pounced on the notes Amma held out.

"You don't mind if I count too, do you?" she said, flipping through the notes. "Good, good." Tying the money into one end of her chador, she picked up her basket. The chador dropped to the side, and I noticed other knots. How many other women had she bullied into buying her potions, I wondered.

Bari Masi stopped at the door. "Come to me immediately if you have other family problems, you know, like sibling rivalry, or …" Her words trailed off as she glanced at me.

"I think we are fine," interrupted Amma.

Bari Masi sniffed. "Is that so? We'll see after I speak to your husband." Without looking back, she walked out.

Amma shut the door and turned to me. "Not a word to Tara, you understand?"

"I won't, I promise. But Abba?"

"Don't worry about him. Khalid Chacha sent a message that he is coming to visit us. He has promised to support me."

"And what about these, Amma?" I asked, pointing to the murky bottles.

"Oh throw them out. I don't trust Bari Masi and her concoctions for a second," said Amma. "I only fear what she will tell others."

48

The next morning, when Abba opened the door to leave for the fields, a swarm of women with curious eyes, draped in dark chadors, swooped inside. Bari Masi had done her work. Crying out, Tara rushed inside. The women crowded on to the charpais. Some sniffed and gazed at Amma with pitying looks, but others pounced.

"Sent back, how awful."

"A mother's worst nightmare."

"How do you sleep?"

"You've been cursed."

"Go to your saints. Seek forgiveness."

"Nothing wrong with your girl, I hope."

"I always thought she was too pale."

"But what happened?"

Following Amma's instructions, I laid out mats and served cups of tea. The questions flew out faster and faster, like fleas hopping on rotting flesh. Amma's feeble answers failed to appease the women's appetite, and they began to speculate. Had Tara fought with her husband? Had she been rude to her in-laws? When was she going back? Had a demon possessed her? Had someone cast an evil eye on her? Why hadn't she taken Tara to the shrine? There had to be an antidote to the black magic.

The women tossed out nuggets of advice, dug out tales, shared tried and tested recipes for brews and potions, and urged Amma to seek the protection of her Pir. They also downed cup after cup of hot tea along with hot savoury rice.

After a few hours, Amma slunk off to the room to be with Tara. Left alone, I nodded blankly, dodged questions, and when the women demanded more tea, I retreated to the cooking pit. The stock of dung dwindled, and the fire petered out. After the third cup of tea the women struggled to their feet, and declaring that it was up to a girl to make a marriage work, they left. Shutting the door, I sank down on the charpai. I hadn't come back for this. There was nothing left for me here, not my lessons, not even Tara.

❧

Leaning against the door the next afternoon, I shut my eyes. My skin burned, but I couldn't stop shivering. It couldn't be true. But Zubaida Masi couldn't be lying. Filling me with horror, she had flitted to the next house to do the same to them.

A loud crackling noise resounded. "What's that?" Tara came rushing out.

"It's just …" I began, but a blaring noise drowned out my words. I waited until the sound faded. "It's Moulvi Saab on the new loudspeakers. Our landlord has donated speakers to our mosque."

"Oh," said Tara, turning away.

"His timing couldn't be better. Amma said our landlord is setting up a committee for religious affairs," I said, trailing behind Tara to the cooking pit.

"Uh, do you want some chai?" asked Tara, pointing to the saucepan.

"No, I'm fine." My eyes flew to Tara as the noise boomed again. The words crackled, and the sputter died out. Watching Tara sprinkle the tea leaves into the water, I held back. I couldn't tell her, not just yet. The speakers blared again. "If anyone knows anything, it's your responsibility to come forward." Moulvi Saab's voice crackled.

"Knows anything about what?" Tara glanced at me. "What's he talking about?"

I shook my head, unable to speak.

"We will hunt out the criminals!" Moulvi Saab's voice rang out.

"What criminals?" Tara leapt up, her face drained of colour. "What is it? Is it Kamran? Has he found out I'm here?"

"No, no!" I gripped Tara's arm. "Kamran has no idea where you are."

"Then?"

"It's, it's …" I began and then hesitated. I had no right to keep anything from my twin. But was she strong enough? She had to be. I didn't have a choice. Dropping down by Tara's side, I related what Zubaida Masi had shared. Bhola Chacha's nieces and nephews had come to visit him yesterday. The children had run out to play, but a while later, Ayesha, the youngest girl, couldn't be found. Search parties had set out in the evening, but returned without any trace of Ayesha. Police had been called from the neighbouring town to comb the forest this morning.

"Did they find her?" began Tara.

"Yes, they discovered her body near the river this morning. Her mother has gone mad with grief, and her father is set on finding the criminals. They're announcing a reward for anyone who can help."

Tara shut her eyes. "Was she …?"

"Raped and strangled."

"How old?" whispered Tara.

"Eight."

"A baby!" choked Tara. Tears ran down her face.

I set the pan down. The tea could wait. "Come with me," I insisted and, ignoring Tara's protests, I pulled her inside the room. Once we were sitting on the charpais, knees drawn together, I reached for my twin's hand. "The police will find the criminals. You're safe now."

"No," choked Tara, "I'll never be safe. It's too late."

"It's not. You are safe." I tightened my grip. "But you have to talk. Get it out. Tell me what happened that afternoon."

"No," Fire exploded in Tara's eyes.

"Yes," I insisted. "Every day that afternoon drills a hole in my head. I hate myself for letting you run alone."

"No," cried Tara. "Don't say that, don't ever say that. It was my idea. It was my fault. I'll tell you what happened. Then you'll understand why I can't live here with you."

I flinched. Was that why Tara stayed away from me? "You don't have to …" I began.

But with a fierce expression, Tara jerked back. "No, you wanted to know, so let me tell you." She took a deep breath and began to speak. "I took off through the fields. I wanted to run faster than you, and reach the water tank before you. Hearing the sound of feet behind me, I spun round, thinking Omer had caught up. But it wasn't him. It was two men with black chadors draped over their faces."

"Our landlord's men?" I whispered. Who were they, these men covered up in black scarves? Why hadn't the police caught them yet?

"I don't know," Tara dragged in a breath. "One of them laughed. I froze and tried to scream, but nothing came out. The other shouted something, but I couldn't understand." Tara's voice dropped to a whisper. "I tried to run, but they caught me. One flung a chador over my head, and everything went black. I lashed out, but he covered my mouth with his hand and threw me to the ground. They didn't talk, but their breathing … I remember their breathing. Before I knew what was happening, they tore my kameez and pulled my shalwar down. I didn't understand what they were trying to do. I thought they wanted to steal something; I didn't realise. Suddenly they stood up. I thought they were going to let me go, and tried to get up, but they thrust me down again. I must have hit my head on something because I blacked out. That didn't stop them. Everything happened fast, but as if at a distance. One got on top of me and shoved down. I cried at the pain, sharp inside me, and stopped moving. After him, the other man got on top. They left me there. I could breathe, but I wanted to die, to disappear." Tara shuddered.

"When I woke up, Amma was there, cleaning me with a washcloth. I started crying. I asked for you. Where were you? Amma told me to sleep. She said everything would be all right and I needed to rest. I didn't want to rest, I wanted to talk, I wanted to talk to you, but she didn't want me to talk. She said I had to rest and forget everything. How could I forget?"

I gripped Tara's hand. "They wouldn't let us see you. We tried, but Amma and Abba forbade us."

"I needed to talk. I couldn't understand why Amma pretended nothing had happened and kept telling me to forget. Then Abba said we had to leave." Tears ran down Tara's cheeks.

My breath hurt. "There was a meeting. Moulvi Saab, Abba, and Khalid Chacha wanted the men caught and punished, but then Riaz Chacha convinced Abba to send you away, saying it would be best for you, and for the family. He warned Abba of what would happen if the villagers found out." I paused, remembering. "They took you to Lahore the next morning."

"I remember the journey and meeting this woman who called herself Auntie," whispered Tara. "She reminded me of someone, but I couldn't remember. I was terrified of her, but I couldn't have disappointed Amma. There was this strange ceremony in a small room. I was afraid of Kamran and his beady eyes. I cried and begged Amma not to leave me, but she told me that it was for the best. I had to forget the past, make my home there, and begin a new life. And then they were gone."

"What happened? Was he? Did he?" I started.

"He raped me, again and again. It made no difference to him whether I resisted or cried. He was quicker if I didn't, so I stopped. He laughed and said the marriage ceremony was a sham. He could do anything he liked with me." Tara's voice was flat. "Then there were other men. He said he had to recover the money he had spent on me. I tried to escape once, but he caught me. After that, he began to drug me. I was always drowsy and couldn't think or plan. I didn't know if it was day or night. I wanted to kill him, but I was helpless."

"You're so brave, braver than anyone I know, " I said.

"Wait. How did you know where I was?" interrupted Tara, pushing my hand away. She sat up. "I saw you in the room. I tried to say something but couldn't. I was too drowsy. When I woke up next, you were there! I couldn't believe it. How did you get me out?"

Silently, I stared at Tara, feeling cold and clammy. What was I going to tell her? I had never lied to her. Taking a deep breath, I began to narrate the muck of lies we had told everyone, but stopped mid-sentence. Tara was shaking her head.

"No, it was you. I dreamt of you, and saw you, and not Omer. I am sure about that. And they would never have allowed Omer near me while I was drugged. You're lying, why?"

I gripped the jute weave, trying to fight the grainy darkness.

"Zara!" repeated Tara.

"You're right," I whispered. "I was inside the brothel, not Omer, and I got you out."

"How?" burst out Tara. "I know that place, the way it works. Qadir would never let you inside, and Auntie would never let you out, unless ..."

My breath felt squeezed. "I got you out. The rest doesn't matter. Does it?"

Tara clenched my fingers. "It matters if they got you. Tell me they didn't. Please, no. Not because of me?" Her voice cracked. She blanched.

"No, not because of you." I shook my head to clear the murky fog. Why was I punishing myself? For what? What had I done?

"You were! Because of me you've lost everything."

"The only thing I've lost is my virginity and the paisa worth of honour attached to it," I spat out.

"What?" gasped Tara.

"And is that all there is to me?"

"Huh?"

"My honour, the izzat I bring to my family. Is that all there is to me?" I exhaled hard. "I went inside to save you, but that man raped me, so it's his shame, his honour and his izzat that's lost, not mine. And yes it hurt, but it's over."

"It's never over," said Tara.

My voice hardened. "It's over because there's more to me. I can't accept that my honour and izzat is defined by one act, which I didn't even have control over. And neither should you. Men encase our honour in a glass showcase, and then shatter it with rocks. They put us under burkas and then strip us. What kind of justice is that? They suck honour from us like marrow from the bone to strengthen their power, their name. Why don't they look for honour within themselves?" I paused and looked at Tara. "What happened to you was wrong. But there was no law, no system, not even one person, nothing to help us. So I did what I had to, to get you back. Do you understand?"

Tara stared. "Yes," she whispered and reached out.

Her fingers brushed my damp cheeks. I clasped her hand, hoping I had my twin back. I leaned over the charpai to unzip the black bag. Reaching inside, I dropped the silver birth bracelet into her palm. It was time.

49

I clung to the fading dream. Master Saab pointed to the blackboard, but I couldn't hear him. Babur Saab stood in front of me now, blocking my view. What was he doing in my school? I jumped up, wide awake. Outside, cotton clouds filled the pale blue sky. I could hear Amma moving about.

In less than an hour, Tara and I were busy with chores. Kulsoom Chachi was expected later in the day. It was the first time she was going to visit since Tara's return. Done with mourning Saima Appi's divorce, Chachi was on a mission to finalise Nazia's marriage. Amma had set a milad in honour of Chachi's visit, Tara's health and happiness, and Omer's success. Omer had sent word through Master Saab that he and Saleem were doing well and would stay in the hostel to work during the holidays. I wasn't sure if Amma believed in milads, but I knew she felt indebted to Khalid Chacha, and said the milad might lessen the increasing pressure from the villagers to send Tara back to her husband.

The afternoon simmered like an egg yolk in a frying pan. Sweat dripped down my neck and back. Trying to stop thinking about my dream, I swept the floor, laid out mats, washed the dishes, and cooked savoury rice with chickpeas.

Late morning Majjo Phuppi came bursting in with news from the city. There were more protests in the city, and rumours about a failed assassination. But no one paid attention, and the preparations continued. Later that morning the door shook and rattled. A horde of women entered, laughing and chatting. They crowded together on one side of the mats, and after a few minutes began to chant religious hymns. The soothing voices rang out and soared with fervour. Nazia and I sat outside to listen, but Tara had retreated to her room at the first knock. A while later, the door shook, and another pack of women trooped inside and chose to sit on the other side. Snippets of gossip spiralled in between the hymns.

"I swear my tongue will dissolve into ashes if I lie, but I heard this from my neighbour," declared a square-faced woman. Looking around, she sniffed and went on. "Last week a woman wide as a buffalo came looking for Nasreen at Bari Masi's door. She called herself Auntie and insisted she was Nasreen's relative from Lahore and needed to meet her urgently."

I strained to listen. Had the infamous Auntie been here?

"Bari Masi flew into a rage," continued the woman. "She wanted nothing to do with anyone who knew her daughter-in-law. She screamed that if her daughter-in-law had been a good wife her son would have never joined the protests in the city and would still be alive. And threatening to kill her if she ever saw her in the village again, Bari Masi chased her out of our village with a hatchet."

"How did I miss it?" moaned Sabiha Masi, but a moment later her eyes gleamed. "But listen to me. I have bigger news. I swear my nose will fall off if I lie, but I heard this from my cousin, who heard it from his uncle." She paused, and the women leaned forward eagerly. "Our rulers are pimping our country to the highest bidder."

"Sabiha, language!" chided Qudsia Masi.

"What language? We're not five-year-olds, are we?" said Majjo Phuppi. "Give the details, woman."

"Money is pouring in from powerful countries; too much

and too quickly. We've been sending our boys to fight the war in Afghanistan. Many say it's not even our war. And hundreds of thousands of men, women, and children are crossing the border into our country. Where will they go? Where will they live? The rulers can't provide for us, they can't better our lives, and they're letting foreigners enter our land. This madness will cripple us."

"What are we fighting for?" asked a woman.

"For money, and more money. Can the pockets of our rulers ever be full?" Sabiha Masi rolled her eyes.

"Never," said Mujjo Phuppi, "So much wealth, where does it go? We see so little of it. We have no hospitals or schools, no drains, no gas or electricity. The factories dump waste into our rivers and we, being the asses we are, continue to drink the water and bathe in it."

"True, true," another woman piped up.

"I hear Master Saab has received funding for a school for boys and girls in our village," started Zubaida Masi. Startled, I leaned closer to listen. Amma hadn't mentioned anything about a school. Tiny wings fluttered in my belly.

"One school, what can one school do?" spat a thin-faced woman.

"She's right. The whole village stinks. It's like a cesspool in the monsoons. Over a dozen of our children died of malaria. And still no sign of a doctor or dispensary," added another woman.

"You talk about problems," Zubaida Masi sniffed, "Then start with the rape and murder of that poor Ayesha. There's enough evidence to convict the landlord's men, but will it ever happen? No. Even the police are scared. The landlord's men roam the fields like wild dogs."

"It's because of the new laws," added Sabiha Masi. The murmurs swelled. I shifted even closer to hear the women. The singing had reached a crescendo.

"Laws?" hissed Mujjo Phuppi, leaning forward. "You call them laws?" She pulled out a roll of newspaper.

"What's that?" asked Sabiha Masi.

A rhythmic chant of prayers filled the air. Majjo Phuppi smoothed the page and pointed to the top right side. "It's madness," she began. "My brother read out the news to me."

"Tell us now, what news?" urged Zubaida Masi.

Majjo Phuppi shook her fists. "A sixteen-year-old blind girl has been sentenced to fifty lashes and a prison sentence. Her crime? That she was raped by a businessman and his son while her mother, their maid, was at the market. Upon discovering her daughter was pregnant, the poor mother took the case to court. But the judge let the businessman and his son go free, saying there was no evidence against them, yet convicted the girl, saying she must have been with someone to get pregnant."

"No, no!" protested the women.

"Can't be," protested Zubaida Masi. "This can't be the law. Our mothers and grandmothers fought to create this country and gave up their lives for it. Why are they doing this to us?"

Majjo Phuppi looked around. "We can fight back. There's a protest in the city. Women are getting together, forming an organization to challenge this ruling. I'm going, join me. We need to unite and organise a group in our village."

More murmurs. Many women shook their heads. "Leave the city-folk to solve their problems," said Sabiha Masi finally. "Don't we have enough of our own, and who wants to risk the landlord's wrath?"

"Who would look after our children?" added another woman.

"Take them along. We need to work together!" urged Majjo Phuppi.

"Who would do the housework?" asked a young, sharp-faced woman.

"Leave it for a day," pleaded Majjo Phuppi. "Your homes won't fall apart. Or ask your mothers-in-law or sisters-in-law to help out. This is important. Our rulers must see us united. We must show them we will not accept this."

"Forget it," said Sabiha Masi. "Have the city folk ever stood up for us or come to our help?"

"They get everything, all the benefits, the gas, electricity, water," grunted another woman. Mujjo Phuppi frowned, but then sighed and tucked the newspaper back under her arm.

"Well, with such laws, it's safer that we cover ourselves and keep our girls inside," warned an elderly woman.

"With young daughters in the house, do we have a choice?" added another woman.

"If our laws can't protect our daughters, then *we* have to protect them," declared Zubaida Masi.

The women sniffed, frowned and nodded. I stared at their chador-covered heads, their hard eyes and tight lips. I looked around, willing even one of them to protest, willing even one woman to say something, but they were silent. A wildfire blazed inside my chest. Why were they giving up? Our grandmothers had struggled beside our grandfathers without any thought of honour or dishonour. They had fought alongside the men for our country's birth and its freedom. Had we forgotten? I glanced at them again. No. They weren't going to protest.

Anger reared up inside me like a beast spewing fire. *This silence.* Was this their answer to the madness? It destroyed any hope for justice. How many girls had been raped before Tara or me? How many women were being raped at this moment, how many in the next minute, the next hour, the next day and next year, across villages, towns, and cities, across other countries and continents? How many girls and women? How many daughters, sisters, aunts, mothers, and even grandmothers raped over land, water, war, money, revenge, or just because they were there? How many more would it take to stop? Would it ever end? Not if everyone kept silent.

At a nod from Amma, Sakina Masi raised her voice to lead the soulful prayers. Once the prayers were over, the women sniffed and murmured into their cupped hands. The sight of dishes heaped with rice, mango pickle, and kheer made the women get up and start eating. I watched them shovel food into their mouths.

Their silence strangled them. Why were they silent? Because of the laws? No, it was about shame and dishonour. Rape shamed and dishonoured. No one spoke about it. My mother's friends, the women I had known since my childhood, were willing to keep their daughters inside and cage them for fear of the shame of dishonour, but not willing to challenge those who smeared them with shame and dishonour. They didn't deserve to have daughters.

They were cowards. We were cowards. Why didn't we shame and dishonour the men who raped girls? Why did we not speak up against them? Why didn't other men speak up against them? It made no sense. In a dacoity, the law didn't accuse the victim of leaving the door open, or leaving the cupboard unlocked. But with rape, the victim was accused and charged for being raped. Like it was her fault for being there.

It took hours to clean up after everyone had left. The floor and mats littered with grains of rice had to be swept and rolled up. We washed the plates, glasses, and spoons that we had to return to the neighbours. Amma and Kulsoom Chachi went inside to rest.

The sun was sinking into the horizon when Tara and I sat down to rest. I groaned at the loud knock on the door. "I don't have the strength," I mumbled.

"Let me get it," said Tara. I glanced up in surprise. Ever since our return, Tara had never volunteered to open the door. When someone knocked, her eyes would fly to our room to gauge how much time she had to run inside. I stood up after her, and then slowly sat down again.

As she reached the door, I called out, "Don't forget to ask who it is."

"Salam," called the voice from outside. "Zara Beti? It's me, Master Saab. Can I come inside?"

"Yes, yes, I'm just coming," I shot up. Why had Master Saab come over? Everything was all right with Omer, wasn't it? "Hurry up and call Amma," I whispered to Tara. Giving me a puzzled look, Tara nodded. "Salam-a-laikum," I said, pulling the door back.

"Walaikum-a-Salam, Beti. I heard you were back from the city," started Master Saab. His eyes gleamed. "How have you been?"

"I'm well. Please come inside, Master Saab," I replied. "Amma will be right out. Would you like some tea?"

"Thank you. I could do with a cup," he responded.

Leading him to the charpai, I headed to the cooking pit that we had just cleaned. I lit the fire again, boiled the tea leaves and added a generous helping of milk and sugar. Waiting for the tea to simmer, I went inside.

"Come and meet Master Saab," I urged Tara, who sat on the charpai with her back against the wall, humming softly. "He helped me find work in Lahore."

"No, I want to finish these," said Tara. She tipped the box filled with gold foil wrappers I had collected after eating the chocolates in Sehr Madam's cupboard. She had started shaping them into small animals and had built a collection of goats, chickens, and buffaloes. Unable to persuade Tara to join us, I returned with the chai. Amma had joined Master Saab and sat on a charpai opposite him.

"Thank you. Yes, you've heard correctly, I've been selected to set it up," Master Saab was saying.

"What an honour! But how did it happen?" asked Amma.

Curious, I perched on Amma's charpai.

Master Saab didn't reply immediately. He picked up the cup, poured the chai in the saucer, let it cool, and then poured it back into the cup. He repeated this movement a couple of times before gulping down the chai in one go and sighed. "I needed that. What can I say? Pure luck maybe, or maybe God answered our prayers. An old colleague of mine was transferred to the education department in the federal government. I had spoken to him about our village some months back and told him how well our boys had done in the exams and admissions. He was impressed, and called to tell me to say he had recommended our village for a primary school project for both boys and girls." He paused. "They've also agreed to set up a dispensary in the school. I insisted on it. So many children, how could we not have one? They finally agreed." He glanced at me.

"What an achievement!" said Amma. "When does it open?" I stared at Amma. Since when had she started supporting girls' education? And why was Master Saab looking at me like he wanted me to say something?

"It's already been a month since the approval," said Master Saab. "I was busy preparing budgets and providing them with information. They signed the papers today and sent the first instalment. We have the go ahead. But there's a lot to be done, and I need all the help I can get." Master Saab shot me another look and nodded.

I froze. That look. It shouted I could scale mountains and cross the seas. What did it mean?

"I'm sure there's a lot to do," agreed Amma. She sighed. "But how exciting. I never thought so before, but it's important for girls to study."

"It is. It is. And I am so happy you think so too. We need all the help we can get," declared Master Saab.

"Amma, let us help Master Saab. We can work at the dispensary, or even at the school." The words were out. My pulse raced. Blood rushed to my face. *Dreams were like fireflies. We had to grasp them. Catch them. Otherwise, they would fly away. And it would be dark again.*

"Let you help, how?" echoed Amma turning to me. "How? You haven't …"

"What a good idea. I could do with their help with the dispensary," interrupted Master Saab. "There's too much on my shoulders already and …" He paused, seeing Amma frown.

"I don't know," muttered Amma, looking at me. "She hasn't even started her secondary. How will they help?"

Master Saab cleared his throat. "It's your decision. I know these girls haven't received any formal education, but they're clever and hardworking. And I do need someone to manage the dispensary. It won't be easy though. They will have to go through four months of basic dispensary training. Maybe Zara can finish her secondary while she's there and has the time."

"I don't know," repeated Amma. "It's not only up to me, you know." She shook her head. "And what will everyone say? That we've put our girls to work."

"People will say what they have to!" I burst out. "They're like woodpeckers, chipping away at others until they're left hollow. If we're not doing anything wrong, why do we have to answer to them?"

"Shush!" admonished Amma and turned to Master Saab. "Do you really need them to help you? And will you have the time to help Zara clear her secondary?"

"There's so much to do, Behen, that their help would be invaluable. And I'll pay them a salary, of course," said Master Saab. "Once the school is set up we can see how Zara can continue her studies."

"Their father …" began Amma and paused.

"You must talk to him," said Master Saab. "His approval is important. But I should go now. It's time for prayers." He rose and then added, "Let me know soon, but I beg you not to miss this opportunity. Zara, you can see me out." He looked at me questioningly. Amma nodded but didn't answer.

I followed Master Saab to the door. My head spun like a top. At the door, Master Saab turned to me. "For you," he said. Surprised, I grasped the white envelopes and looked down. One was from Omer, but the other? Saleem? It had to be Saleem. What had he written? My pulse raced. I looked up, but Master Saab had slipped out. I slid the envelopes inside my shirt and placed my palms on my burning cheeks. Why had he written? And what? And why now, when I had decided that everything I felt for him had only been in my head?

"Zara!" called Amma.

I bolted the door, then walked back. "Amma, please let us," I began.

"Shush," hissed Amma.

I shivered at the hard, beetle look in her eyes. My heart shrank into a lump of grit. Had she put on an act for Master Saab? Maybe nothing had changed. Was she going to stop me again? Take away what I wanted?

Amma sighed and locked her fingers. "I'll tell you something. I've been forced to see what I didn't want to. I've been brought back to the point I started from, to the choices I thought I would never have to make again. Why, if anyone had told me that I would even think about letting my daughters work two years ago, I would have laughed and said that I would chop my hair off before letting that happen. I wanted you both to be married and settled in your own homes. But now …"

"But now?" I echoed.

"But now I don't know." Amma shook her head. "I don't know what's best for you both. You have to decide that."

"What about Abba?"

"He will follow what your Khalid Chacha advises. Khalid Chacha cleared your father's debt, so he has no choice but to listen to him. But tell me, do you really want to study, to work? You say you do, but are you ready? I can still try to get you both married."

A surge swelled inside of me. I soared higher and higher. I was up in the sky. Flying beyond my village, beyond the fields. I stared back at Amma. Was I ready? I had been ready for years. I had been knocked down, lost a few rounds, but won more. I was up, and in the ring again. And this time the fight wasn't just about me. It was bigger than me. It was about hundreds and thousands of other girls wanting to study, and wanting justice. We had to stand up and shout out to be heard. Majjo Phuppi was right. It was the only way to get education and justice. Was it too late? No. I was only sixteen or seventeen. There was more to learn, and more rounds to win.

Author's Note

In 1998, after graduating from business school, I launched an enterprise development program in five villages. During the fifteen years (1998-2012) that I worked with girls and women of rural Pakistan, I met and talked with hundreds of daughters, mothers, wives, and grandmothers. They were my clients. I had to put together an economic development program that worked for them, a program that made the markets work for them. Today, Kaarvan Crafts Foundation works in over 1000 villages and with over 20,000 women entrepreneurs in low-income communities.

Beyond the Fields is inspired by the time I spent with the rural women of Pakistan. It is a testament to my admiration and respect for their determination, strength, and resilience in moments of despair – with so little they manage to achieve so much.

The protagonists in *Beyond the Fields* challenge the roles that have been defined for them, determined instead to persevere and achieve their dreams. The characters are fictional, but the voices are real. They speak of violence, poverty, strength and perseverance. I hope they speak to you as powerfully as they continue to speak to me.

Acknowledgements

Thank you Ammi for believing in me and pushing me when I was about to give up. This novel would not have possible without your love and prayers.

I am deeply grateful to the fantastic team at Marshall Cavendish International (Asia) for their support and commitment. Thank you Anita Teo, She-reen Wong and Mindy Pang.

Thank you Tara Dhar Hasnain for your zeal and meticulous editing. I appreciate the dedication and skill with which you worked on the manuscript from our first meeting to the last edit.

Aran Shetterly, your feedback and encouragement has been invaluable in bringing this novel to life.

Fran Lebowitz, thank you for your insightful comments and keen eye. Thank you Mehvash Amin, for your wise comments and critique.

Thank you Eman Khan, Zawi Hoodbhoy, and Manal Mohsin. Your feedback and comments shaped the beginning of the novel and made it what it is today.

I am immensely grateful to Danish Khan, Sumeera, and the Kaarvan team for helping me fine-tune the details and for getting back to me so promptly.

Thank you to all my family and friends. Naveen, Tariq, and Nomi – I am so grateful to you for your support and encouragement.

Thank you, Singapore, for giving me the space to write this novel. And I'm thankful to The Singapore Writers Group for providing a supportive and nurturing environment that got me started on this project.

Thank you, Lahore American School, for teaching me how to dream and to pursue my dreams.

Thank you, Mount Holyoke College, for sparking a passion for development and giving me the strength to believe in what I could accomplish.

Thank you, LUMS (Lahore University of Management Sciences) - some said that we didn't quite fit, but you taught me an invaluable set of skills, for which I will always be grateful.

There are probably some unacknowledged influences and phrases; I apologise in advance for such omissions.

About the Author

Aysha grew up in Pakistan. Graduating as valedictorian of her class, she won a scholarship to Mount Holyoke College, where she studied International Relations. Her time in college sparked a passion for economic development, and upon her return to Pakistan, she saw that the poor needed access to economic resources and networks before they could voice their demands for social justice. In 1998, armed with an MBA, she founded a pioneering not for profit economic development organisation, Kaarvan Crafts Foundation, focused on poverty alleviation through the provision of business development and market-focused trainings for girls and women. In 2013 she relocated to Singapore.

She is on the Board of Kaarvan Crafts Foundation, an Ashoka Fellow, and member of the Singapore Writers Group.

Find her on Facebook: Aysha Baqir